BOUNDED BY THE BOND

STEVIE D. PARKER

LITERARY DREAMS PUBLISHING, LLC

Dedicated to Aeris

CHAPTER 1

The faint sound of beeping wakes me. Trying to open my eyes, I suddenly feel as if each eyelid weighs ten pounds. Struggling to push them open, I feel dizzy and nauseous as the room seems to spin. I hear my breath against the plastic mask covering my face, and it appears to be in sync with my heartbeat. I'm panic-stricken as I overhear a police officer on the phone in the near distance, "Mrs. Johnson, this is officer Russo of the NYPD. We have your daughter..." he is immediately cut off by the intercom blaring, "Doctor Chin, Ext 102." I manage to open my eyes just enough to see the IV in my arm. I'm in a hospital. I know that much, and I am moving fast. As I try to focus on my surroundings, I can barely move my head. A nurse is at the foot of my stretcher, pulling me with urgency. She is head to toe in blue scrubs, a paper mask, and plastic goggles, but for a quick second, we make eye contact, and her eyes scream fear.

"Relax." I barely hear the nurse behind me, who must be pushing the stretcher, say, just above a whisper.

Another nurse rushes to open the door to a room as a

team pushes a different stretcher in. Mine follows behind. I should be in pain; however, I suspect whatever they have running through the IV must be exceptionally strong, which is most likely adding to my state of sedation. They place the first stretcher under the window and park mine parallel to it. I manage to tilt my head to the left as the patient next to me, in a similar state, tilts hers to the right. The last thing I see is her emerald green eyes staring back at me with sympathy, before everything fades to black.

I stared out the window, taking in the view. It seemed like a commercial for an island getaway; a DJ was playing music, and fit, tan, good-looking people were sunbathing and frolicking in the pool. If you were an outsider looking in, you'd think it was some sort of exclusive resort for the rich and famous. Well, it kind of was. I mean, that's what we were, rich and famous and it was *exclusive*. A private island off the coast, completely off the radar. They had me flown in on a private jet. "Calista?" I heard again, this time with annoyance in his voice. My attention shifted from the pool to his office. A much different view. A sizable L-shaped mahogany desk took up most of the room, with diplomas and Ph.D.'s hanging in fancy frames on the walls. Pictures of his family filled his desk, and a leather sofa with matching seats sat across from him.

I looked him up and down. He had a very "doctor" look to him. He was tall and lean, slightly graying, with dark-rimmed glasses, dressed in khakis and a polo shirt.

"What do you remember about the accident?" he asked again; I'd say pretty calmly, considering it was probably the third time he had asked.

"Not much," I finally answered, and returned my attention to the window.

He folded his hands in his lap. "Okay, what were you doing before the accident?"

I looked back over at him and let out a sigh. "Dr. Michaels, you got the toxicology report. With all due respect, you know exactly what I was doing before the accident. I already had my day in court, so why are we having this conversation?"

He grinned and clenched his jaw. "With all due respect? Look out that window. You should be in jail, you could have killed someone. As a matter of fact, you almost did. Instead, you are in a fancy rehab facility for spoiled, entitled, rich assholes and 'court ordered' to talk to someone about 'why' you do drugs, and you can't even do that much? Are you kidding me right now?" He was being very dramatic with his hand gestures, using a lot of air quotations to emphasize his words.

I was taken aback by his tone but impressed at the same time. No one spoke to me like that. But he was right, and I should have been in jail. I sat back in the chair and crossed my legs. "I was in San Diego for an autograph signing. I went out with my friend Colleen that night. We met some guys, and I got a little carried away with the partying and got behind the wheel. I don't remember the accident at all. That's the truth."

He flipped through some notes on his pad. "Tell me about your mother." Great, his next subject. My heart sank, and I stared at him, dumbfounded.

"What does my mother have to do with this?" I asked. There was one piece of the story I left out; did he see through me? Did he somehow know? I mean, I am an actress after all; you'd think I would be able to successfully tell a story while leaving one small piece of information out.

"Maybe nothing," he said. "But when someone abuses drugs and has a history like yours, we try to get to the deeper issues, the root of the problem…." Awesome, he was saying I was crazy.

"I don't want to talk about my mother," I growled angrily.

"I see this is upsetting you. I'm not trying to upset you, Calista. I am simply trying to understand…."

"Understand what exactly? You think I did a bunch of cocaine and drove a car at twenty-seven years old because my mother was a selfish bitch and killed herself when I was five? That's kinda reaching, don't you think?"

"That's interesting," he simply said.

"What's interesting?"

He straightened himself out and leaned in towards me, putting the end of his pen in his mouth.

"That you think she was selfish and not sick."

"Who have you been talking to, my sister? If she was so 'sick,' she could have gotten help. Shit, I have to see a therapist, right? No, instead, she left a five-year-old and a seven-year-old to be shuffled around from foster home to foster homes our entire lives. Sorry Doc, I don't care how sick you claim she was. But as much as I hate her, I can't blame the accident on her- that was all me. Are we done here?"

He put his pen down and rested his chin in his hands. "Calista, I didn't mean to upset you."

"Upset? I'm not upset. I'm tired, and I want to go lie down."

He nodded his head. "Okay, go lie down."

CHAPTER 2

A girl in her early twenties met me outside the doctor's office. She was taller than me, Spanish, with blue eyes and an olive complexion. She was wearing the same light blue uniform the rest of the staff had, bearing the name Ocean Haven on it. Ocean Haven—they make rehab sound so fancy.

"Hi, my name is Julie," she said, extending her hand to shake mine. I abruptly took her hand in mine and flashed a fake smile. "Let me take you to your room." I followed her through the corridor; the sight was truly breathtaking. On one side of the development was a beachside view with all-white cabins, and on the other, a resort with everything from a pool to an outdoor spa, golf course, tennis courts, and outside dining. She led me up in the elevator until we got off at the fifth floor. She seemed to know everyone by name as she walked past them. Once we got to the room, she opened the door and held it for me to lead the way as she handed me the key.

"If you need anything, do not hesitate to call the front desk, and ask for Joe. He runs the grounds. All your belongings have been brought up already. There is a carton of Marlboro's in the left-hand drawer of the night table; we just ask that you smoke outside. Except for drugs or alcohol, anything you need can be obtained by calling Joe."

I gave a sarcastic smile. "You even know my cigarette brand; that's just scary."

"We try to be accommodating; we want you to feel at home," she answered as she closed the door behind her.

I sat down on the bed, laid back and rested my head in my hand as I spun the key she had handed me around in my right hand. I was mechanically moving it between my fingers. I couldn't get the therapist out of my head. How dare he bring my mother up? That was none of his business. My mother's mental issues were none of his concern. Yeah, she had issues. He doesn't need to know that. Maybe it wasn't fair that I hated her for it, but that was my problem to deal with. He wasn't there, and he didn't have the memories I had. He didn't know about her visions, that she had seen things that didn't exist. Why didn't he know? Because there was no record of it. She refused to get help. Instead, she killed herself and left my sister and me to fend for ourselves. I was getting madder and madder, bringing myself back to that day, remembering the police coming to the door. I remembered the bullshit note she had left me, "find it in your heart to forgive me." "Forgive you? Forgive you? I freaking hate you!" I screamed out loud. Shit! I barely remember doing it, but I do recall my left fist lodged through the wall. I was grimacing in pain as warm, wet blood trickled down my arm.

I pulled my hand out of the broken drywall and went into the bathroom to grab a towel. Tightly wrapping my fist in it, I called the front desk to inquire about the infirmary. My first day was off to a great start. I put the key in my pocket and headed downstairs.

I kept my head down most of the walk and tried not to be noticed as I made my way to get help.

Alex, the nurse, stayed quiet most of the time as he cleaned up my hand. He stood about six-foot-two, extremely tan, with blonde hair and light eyes, and had an athlete's body. He looked like a real-life Ken doll. I sat on the stretcher, my legs dangling while staring over at the white counter covered in gauze bandages, Band-Aids, and applicators.

"Long day, huh?" I asked, trying to make small talk. He barely even looked at me as he iced me up. My hands started shaking, and my breathing became heavy. I looked up at the clock. It was only six p.m. I started rocking back and forth, and my palms became clammy. My body felt like it was aching, not from the pain of my injured hand, but the lack of drugs and alcohol in my system. I squeezed my eyes tightly shut as I felt my heart race with anxiety, and I got the sudden urge to vomit.

"Hey," I said, a little above a whisper, to get his attention. He looked up and finally made eye contact. "I'll give you whatever you want for a Xanax."

"Good news. You don't need stitches," he said, turning around to grab a bandage. My cheeks grew warm as I guessed I was probably turning red.

"Do you know who I am?" I asked as he came back with the dressing.

"Yes, you're Calista Reed. The Golden Train was fantastic- you should get an Oscar."

"Did you hear what I offered you?" I asked, angry now that I felt he was mocking me.

"Yes, I did, but I don't have drugs, so I can't help you. But your hand should heal nicely," he said as he finished wrapping me up. He looked up at me and smiled. "And I wasn't kidding; I do think you should get an Oscar for your performance."

"Yeah, thanks a lot. I'll remember to mention you in my acceptance speech if I do," I sneered sarcastically and headed out.

Annoyed, I started heading back to my room. The sun was setting, daytime was becoming night, and the bright full moon lit up the concrete pavement. The trembling in my hands started to get worse. My sweating progressed, and my body felt as if it was getting weaker by the minute. Finally, I stopped to light a cigarette and could barely keep my hand still long enough. From the corner of my eye, I saw a guy headed in my direction. He was tall, at least six-foot-five, wearing a black hoodie and gray joggers, with jet black hair, blue eyes, and a very neatly groomed beard. He walked confidently, like he knew he was sexy, but he wasn't some-body I recognized from the Hollywood scene.

"Hey, Southpaw," he called out as he approached me, speaking with a deep, slurred voice, as if doing some sort of impersonation. I exhaled my cigarette and looked up at him, unamused.

"Southpaw?" he said again, in the same tone. Then he started humming the Rocky theme song while hopping back and forth from one leg to another like he was jogging up steps while swinging his fists in the air. "You're from Holly-wood," he continued, motioning with his hands and being very dramatic. "You don't know who Rocky Balboa is? Left-handed boxer from Philly…."

I started looking around to ensure no one was watching us, as he was acting ridiculously. "Yes, I know who Rocky Balboa is," I said, waving my pointer finger up and down the length of his body. "Can you make this stop? You're acting like a freak." His jogging came to a halt, and he shot me a smile. A perfectly gorgeous smile. Great teeth and a dimple that appeared out of nowhere. I didn't know who he was, but he should be in Hollywood based on his appearance. He pointed at my bandaged hand.

"You put your fist through a wall to get painkillers?" he asked.

I looked down at my hand and shook my head. "No, but that's kind of a genius idea. Instead, I went straight to bribery," I said, laughing in embarrassment.

"Ah, yeah, Alex gets more things offered to him than any man I've ever witnessed. I gotta tell you, since I have been here, never, not once, has any chick offered me anything for drugs."

"Can you get drugs?" I asked with a glimmer of hope.

He shook his head. "No, no drugs can ever make it to this island. Nothing, not even ibuprofen. Tell me you want celery juice; maybe I can make it happen. Drugs or alcohol, however, definitely not."

"So why would someone offer you anything?" I asked, now confused by his statement.

"Well, if they knew that, they wouldn't. But they don't, which makes me wonder. Does it look like I can't get drugs, or I don't take bribes? Now, I'm in rehab, so clearly, I could get drugs in my day, so….. "

I was taken aback for a minute. I took a pull of my cigarette and studied him from head to toe.

I pictured what he would look like under that hoodie if I were to take it off him. I imagined he'd be toned, probably with a six-pack; he looked like he spent a reasonable amount of time in the gym. He had big hands, and I imagined what they would feel like wrapped around my waist and what he would taste like if I were kissing him. I bit my lip slightly at the image, and it got me a bit aroused. As if he were reading my mind, he inched closer and leaned in to whisper in my ear. His cologne had a musky sensual scent, and I could feel his beard slightly touch my neck. Suddenly, I felt like he had me in some sort of trance. "You're thinking about it now, aren't you? Wondering what I would taste like?"

My eyes locked intensely on his as I backed away. "Is this some sort of mind trick?" I asked.

"No," he simply said as he slowly sucked in his bottom lip. "But you know what you're not thinking about? Drugs. Wouldn't you rather be thinking about what I taste like kissing you than what you feel like getting high?" He had a point. I looked down at my hands, and they weren't shaking anymore. He had somehow calmed me.

"So, your hand. What happened?" he asked, changing the subject.

"I got angry," I stated matter-of-factly.

"Oh, I love me a girl with some anger management issues. It's always the tiny ones, also. What are you, four-foot-eleven?"

"Five-foot-one."

"Turn around," he prompted, turning his pointing finger in a circular motion.

"What? I am most certainly not turning around for you," I said, shooing him away.

"C'mon, one spin," he teased, giving me a playful pout. I pushed my hair behind my ears and put my cigarette out.

"Fine," I finally said, and reluctantly did one spin around. When I came back around to face him, he was gazing at me with a genuine smile on his face.

"Five-foot-one, and what, a hundred and fifteen pounds soaking wet? 36 C cup, blonde hair, green eyes—you're like a gorgeous, angry little elf."

"An elf?" I asked hastily.

He touched his lip with his finger and scrunched up his nose. "Well, I was going to say troll, but that sounded even less attractive than an elf, which was the exact opposite of what I was going for. How about a fairy? Fairies are sexy. Tinkerbell's hot. I'd definitely do Tinkerbell."

Slowly I ran my eyes down his entire body. "Something tells me you'd destroy Tinkerbell," I smirked.

He leaned in towards me. "Are you trying to turn me on?"

"Why do I think it wouldn't take much to turn you on?"

He straightened himself back up and winked. "Confident and feisty—I think I may be in love with you."

I let out a laugh. "Careful, I can assure you; I am not the type of girl you want to fall in love with. I'm Calista. My friends call me Cali."

"I know who you are. I'm Josh, and my friends just call me an asshole," he introduced himself.

"Why don't I know who you are? Don't you have to be someone to be here?" I asked.

"I am someone. I am someone whose money is just as green as yours. I'm just not famous yet. I'm working on it, though."

"What are you going to do to be famous?" I questioned.

"I'm gonna be a Gen Z'er," he answered so seriously.

"What? How old are you?"

"Thirty-two."

"I don't think it works that way," I laughed. This guy was truly hilarious. He reached into his pocket, pulled out a vape, held it up to display for me, and took a step back.

"Watch this," he said. "I've been watching YouTube videos and practicing." He took a deep inhale of the vape and held it in for a few seconds, then released the vapor into the air, making it form into circles that appeared to be dancing. "I'm working on it, but once I master it, I'm going to TikTok the crap out of this shit and watch—I am going to go viral!"

"And that's your claim to fame? You're going to blow fake smoke for a living?" I asked.

"Yes. Not everyone has the talent you do, and you are

very talented. I am a big fan of yours. The Golden Train was awesome."

"Thanks, you know I almost didn't take that role," I revealed.

"Really?" he asked, surprised.

"Yeah, really. But that's a story for a different time. I'm very exhausted. It's been an...." I looked down at my hand. The pain was setting in, and the realization that I couldn't even get ibuprofen in this place made me realize exactly what type of hell I was in for. "It's been an interesting day, to say the least. I need to sleep this off."

He started cracking his knuckles and nodding his head in acknowledgment. "Yeah, cool. So, you maybe want to exchange phone numbers? Unfortunately, I can't get you drugs, but if you ever want to dabble in celery juice, go for a run, talk, hang out, or whatever...."

"Are you nervous? You're rambling?" I asked, teasing him.

He smiled and bit his bottom lip. "I mean, you do put your fists through walls; you are a bit intimidating," he said.

I unlocked my phone and handed it to him. "Text your-self," I commanded. He typed something and handed me back the phone. I took the phone and slid it into my back pocket.

"Nice meeting you, Josh."

I made my way to the elevator and pressed five. I just needed to get into my bed and go to sleep. The day needed to end already. When I got off, I realized I hadn't noted what my room number was. I dug in my other pocket for the key and held it to the light to see the number etched into the metal. I stood in disbelief, staring at the number, bringing me back to the night of the accident. The part I didn't tell the doctor. The hallucination I had seen right before I ran out of the hotel that night had scared me so much that it made me get into the car as intoxicated as I was. My room number: 542.

I slowly opened my door and scanned the room for signs of anything unusual. Nothing seemed out of place or weird. I opened the suitcase I assumed Joe had placed in front of my dresser, took out a nightgown, changed into it, and laid down on my bed. I was too exhausted even to wash my face. When I plugged my phone in, I saw a text from Josh. He had stored his name as: "Your Lifeline." I couldn't help but smile as I read his text:

If you feel the urge to punch something, text me.

CHAPTER 3

*V*ertigo hit me the second I awoke. Almost immediately falling back into bed, I grabbed my stomach as I felt my body uncontrollably drop into a fetal position. My hand throbbed from being thrown into the wall the day before, and my veins craved drugs. My head pounded like it never had, and my forehead dampened with droplets of sweat. My eyes filled with tears as I tried my hardest not to let them drop. I hated myself for allowing this to happen. For permitting myself to be in this position. For losing all control of my life and everything around me. I wasn't even able to make it to the bathroom. Finally, I steadied myself on the bed, leaned my head over the side, and vomited on the floor.

My breathing intensified, and the smell of my puke made me even more queasy. I felt the tears pouring down my face; I couldn't resist them anymore. There was nothing I could do; there was no one who could help. I was completely and utterly alone. Desperate, I whispered out loud, "Please help me."

I almost jumped out of my skin when there was a knock

on my door. "Be right there," I called out as I struggled to make my way to the bathroom to rinse my mouth with Listerine. The zest of the mint-flavored liquid hitting my taste buds made me want to throw up again. Splashing cold water on my face, I carefully tried to fix my hair from looking too disheveled. As casually as I could, I opened the door to see Josh standing there, dressed the same as he was the day before, except his joggers were black this time, his hoodie was red, and he had a backpack on. His mouth hung open, and his eyes scanned me up and down. Then, with his eyebrows raised, he said, "Now, normally, I'd comment on the atrocious smell coming from this room, but considering you greeted me in lingerie, I'll let it go."

I was still shocked by the sudden knock on the door; I had totally forgotten I was in my nightgown. "Shit," I said as I grabbed him by the arm and dragged him into the room, shutting the door.

"Seriously though, what the hell is that smell?" he asked as I went through my suitcase, looking for an outfit.

"If you must know, I threw up over the side of the bed," I replied, pointing to the area I vomited.

"Ew, nasty," he choked out, leaning over the bed, trying to get a better look.

"So, why are you looking for it?" I asked, annoyed. "And what are you even doing here?"

"Better question. Who'd you think was at the door when you answered it wearing that?" he asked, waving his finger up and down my body.

"I wasn't sure."

"You weren't sure? So, you always answer the door dressed like this?"

I grabbed a pair of jeans and slid them past my thighs. "What exactly do you want?"

"I was going to go for a hike, and well, I thought

that…" he paused for a minute as if he were thinking of what to say. "I thought maybe you could use some company."

"So, you came to hang out?" I asked.

"No, definitely not here. It stinks. How does such a teeny, little person create such a horrendous odor? I don't know what you ate, but it's vile."

I rolled my eyes. "You're charming."

He smiled at me, his dimple appearing. "Would you like to come for a hike with me?"

"I don't know; I am really not into your kind," I answered coldly.

"And what 'kind' is that?" he asked.

"People." He let out a laugh.

"Oh, come on, it will be good for you to leave this room. If you don't like it, you can just come back."

I thought about it for a minute. I really had nothing better to do, and he was right, the room truly smelled awful. Finally, I nodded. "Sure, let me change into something more comfortable."

"Hey, if you wanna hike in lingerie, I am cool with that," he chuckled.

"It's not lingerie; it's a nightgown," I argued.

"If you don't call that lingerie, I'd love to see what you *do* call lingerie," he said, biting his lip.

I brushed my teeth quickly, changed into joggers and a tank top, and threw my hair in a ponytail.

"Damn, you look good in literally anything," Josh commented as I came out of the bathroom, grabbed a sweat-shirt and my room key before leaving.

"Thanks," I said as we headed out.

"I called Joe for you and told him about your incident."

I put my head down in shame. "So embarrassing," I murmured.

"Cali, it's day one in rehab. I'm sure the dude cleans vomit all the time. It's normal."

I turned around to look at him. "Is it?"

He put his hands in his pockets and walked a little faster. "Yes. It's physical withdrawals. And it will get worse. You'll vomit, you'll shake, you'll sweat. You'll pray for death. It's good to do physical things; try to keep your mind and body as active as possible, although it will be hard. Work out, hike, meditate. You're an addict. Addicts substitute one addiction for another." He knew it. He knew I was having a rough time.

"Is that why you asked me to go for a hike with you?"

"I hike every day," he answered.

"That wasn't my question," I said.

He stopped and looked directly into my eyes. "Yes, that is why I asked you to come with me." As we walked through the development, I examined my surroundings. Everyone seemed acclimated and in their cliques. It was like they had their own society. A group of young girls sat at an outside table, eating frozen yogurt, and a few older teenage boys were on skateboards doing tricks. Josh puffed his vape, which made me light a cigarette.

"I have to say, this place is pretty accommodating. I got a lifetime supply of cigarettes." I laughed.

"You got cigarettes?" he questioned, disbelief in his tone.

"Yeah, why you didn't?" I asked sarcastically.

"No, nothing!" he jokingly whined.

My attention was drawn to an older man, in some sort of yoga stance, doing what seemed to be a meditation practice. I motioned my head in his direction.

"Who's the weird meditating dude?" I asked.

Josh shifted his eyes up to look at the man and shrugged.

"Oh, that's the weird mediating dude," he laughed. "No one really talks to him. He is always by himself. He never really says anything to anyone."

"Where are your friends?" I asked as we reached the end of the development. He looked ahead at the trail and then back at me.

"Are you ready?" he asked as he opened the gate.

"Yes, I am ready."

I followed him down the path. Dirt and twigs broke beneath my feet. I wasn't in as good of shape as he was, stumbling along rocks along the way. Walking uphill proved to be a challenge, and I found myself growing frustrated. My chest was heavy, and I was sweating. Panting, I finally barked, "Slow down!"

He stopped for a second and turned to look at me, taken aback by my sudden outburst.

"What's wrong?"

Clearly, I am not in as good of shape as you are," I said nastily.

"You can do it," he assured me.

"No, I really can't!" I rasped out, my voice cracking as I fought back the tears.

With shaking hands, I leaned up against a tree for support and put my head down to keep from looking at him. I was mortified. Why did I tell this complete stranger I would go into the middle of the woods with him in the first place after throwing my guts up on day one in rehab with an injured wrist? What the hell was wrong with me? I was definitely losing my mind; turning more and more into my mother every day, and it was scaring the shit out of me.

"It's only a little further to the top," he said quietly, extending his hand to take mine. "Come on; I'll help you. It's beautiful; you'll love it…."

"Don't tell me what I'll love!", I quipped, snapping my hand away from his. "You don't know me! You don't know what I'll love! You wanna know what I'd love? To be the hell off this island! To be in my gorgeous apartment in the Upper

East side, or even my one in Malibu will suffice, not this crazy excuse for a rehab."

Frustrated, I squatted down, leaned against the tree, pulled my knees against my chest, and began crying. No, not crying. Bawling. Ugly, disgusting sobbing. Beads of rain started tumbling from the sky. I pulled my hood over my head. The water didn't seem to bother him, as his hair got wet, and liquid dripped down his face. He squatted down to get eye level with me.

"Cali, look up at me for one second, and then I'll walk away, I promise."

I looked up at him, crying so hard I could barely breathe. He continued speaking in the same relaxed tone. He ran his fingers through his wet hair to push it away from his forehead, reached into his backpack, took out a thermos, and handed it to me.

"Here, drink some water. I'm not going to say I know what you're going through because that is the last thing you want to hear. I hated when people told me that. But I'm also not going to leave you here because you have no idea where you are. I'm going to be by that tree, right over there." He pointed to the left at a tree about a hundred yards from where I was. "When you're ready to do whatever you want to do, and I mean *whatever* you want to do because I'm down for literally anything, that's where I'll be."

I sipped the water and watched him in amazement as he got up, walked over to the tree, and stood there, so patiently, completely soaked. He was so calm and collected, so opposite from me. There was something so incredibly sexy about him, aside from his obvious good looks and demeanor, but how he could soothe me almost instantaneously without even touching me, just by talking to me. I couldn't help but wonder if he had that type of control over me with his words, what kind of power he'd have over me with his touch.

I was suddenly captivated by the notion of his hands on my body, his fingers touching my skin, his lips on mine, his facial hair scraping my neck as he whispered in my ear. He was like a drug. Addicts substitute one addiction for another. At that moment, it occurred to me. Josh was going to be my addiction. I stopped crying and inhaled deeply. The rain stopped. I composed myself and slid my hood back off.

I stood up and slowly made my way over to him.

"You okay?" He asked.

I nodded. "I think so."

"You want to keep going?" He tentatively questioned.

"Yes, let's keep going."

CHAPTER 4

*J*osh was right. The view was breathtaking when we made it to the top. The sun set into the ocean, leaving a purple hue. It appeared as if the clouds trailed off with no end. It was surreal, like some mystical universe that seemed unlike any place on Earth I had ever been. The scent of grass after a fresh rainfall instantly eased me as I took my sweatshirt off, and Josh took a blanket out of his backpack and set it down on the grass. As I sat, I watched him lift his hoodie over his head, making his t-shirt lift a bit over his stomach. I smirked slightly while he exposed just a sliver of his incredibly toned six-pack before he pulled his t-shirt back in place and fixed his now messy hair. He started shuffling through the bag as I studied his body, his muscles retracting and a hint of a tattoo that appeared to be flames peeked out from his shirt on his left bicep.

He took out a wrapped sandwich and handed it to me.

"You like turkey?"

"Sure," I said as I took the sandwich from him. He put the thermos of water between us, opened a granola bar, and leaned on his elbow as he took a bite and looked over his shoulder. "I told you it's beautiful," he said, taking in the view.

I swallowed the bite of my sandwich. "That's an understatement. It's stunning. Is that all you're eating?"

"I only had one sandwich. I wasn't expecting company," he replied, taking another bite of his granola bar. Suddenly, I felt like a complete jerk for not even thinking I had just taken his only sandwich.

"Oh no, here, take half," I said, springing up to my knees as I tried to break the sandwich.

"It's fine; really, eat it," he insisted, laughing as if I were the most amusing thing that had happened to him in a while.

"We can share it, really," I demanded. I finally broke the sandwich in half and held it out to him, but he clenched his lips together. "What are you doing?"

"Revolting," he mumbled through his closed lips. "You can't force me to eat."

I shook my head. "Oh, you're going to be a massive pain in my ass."

He shot me a mischievous smile and laid down on the blanket, his hands behind his head. "Oh, you have no idea how true that statement is," he said.

When I finished my sandwich, I followed his lead and laid down next to him, staring up at the clouds. We spoke about Haven. He filled me in on all the details, what it was like being there, the ins and outs, how to survive, what to expect, and how to cope. He had been there for three months and had three months left. He hadn't spoken to many people until I came along and kept to himself. He hiked a lot. He had learned to do Reiki, a form of mediation, and told me he would teach me how to do it when I expressed interest. He was the son of a billionaire CEO and was handed his own company at twenty-one. He got to choose what company he wanted, making him the CEO of a modeling agency in New York. I tried not to roll my eyes, so typical. Despite how predictable he was on the outside, there was something unusual about him. For starters, the way he made me feel. I was so comfortable around him. He had a way of making me feel like I could tell him anything and everything. He could calm me down in a second, even though I didn't know him. We spent all day out there; the sun was setting as we both lay there gazing up at the stars that appeared as the darkness was setting in.

I told him all about the night that landed me there. The night the therapist had asked me about. I was in San Diego for an autograph signing. My friend Colleen and I were partying hard that night. We had a VIP table at the hottest nightclub in the area. We met a few guys, went back to my room, and let's just say, things got a bit crazy. The next day, my agent Debbie tried to get me up, but I was so hungover that I could barely move and refused to go. The only thing she could do to entice me to go was to throw a bag of cocaine at me. I shouldn't have driven. It was stupid. If I could take back that night, I would in a heartbeat. I didn't see the car coming; all I could remember was that it was pouring, and then a loud crash and black.

As I relaxed, I confided that I didn't like the therapist they assigned me, and that he was trying to blame my mother. My mother had committed suicide when I was five years old, and my biggest fear was inheriting her mental illness. I couldn't understand how a therapist could try to blame a DUI on that.

"What was the part you didn't tell him?" he turned his head toward me and asked.

I tilted my head and looked into his blue eyes. How did everyone know there was something I wasn't telling them? Shit, for an actress, I was doing a pretty shitty job at hiding one damn detail. I took a deep breath and exhaled. Whatever

—who cares if this guy thinks I'm crazy. What's he going to do, tell his therapist on me? I needed to get it off my chest, to someone, *anyone*.

"I had a massage the day before, right before I went out," I began. "The girl giving me the massage told me all this crazy shit."

He leaned in towards me. "What kind of crazy shit?"

"That I had a curse on me. She said I was a witch, and that I had all these powers, except I was bound. I was a healer and some other weird stuff." He was staring at me intensely, listening to me tell the story. "After Debbie gave me the coke that day, I watched something being traced in the mirror when I got out of the shower. Like a ghost or something, I don't know what it was, but I watched it, Josh, clear as day. The message '542 days' was written in the fog."

His mouth dropped, and he stared at me, speechless for a second. I was expecting him to say I must have been hallucinating from the drugs, but that was not what he said. Instead, he asked, "542 days? What does that even mean?"

"I have no idea, but I freaked out, ran out of the hotel, and got behind the wheel, high." We sat silently for a few minutes as he processed what I had just told him.

"What kind of mental illness did your mom have?" he asked with empathy.

"I don't know. Dementia? Schizophrenia? Hard to say; she refused to talk to a therapist or get a mental evaluation. She saw things.". Then it hit me. He didn't believe me. He was implying I was hallucinating. Of course he would. What the hell was I thinking, telling some random guy something as bizarre as that. I quickly stood up and grabbed my sweatshirt and zipped it up.

"I want to go," I said crossly.

He jumped to his feet and came over to me with a look of

concern. "Why? What happened? Did I say something wrong?"

I started rocking back and forth, and my eyes burned; I could feel my anger rising. Tiny droplets of water started falling from the sky as Josh bent down to put his hoodie back over his head. He pulled his hood over his hair and reached his hand out to mine. I tried to pull back, but he wouldn't let me. Instead, he took his other hand and placed it on top. I felt the warmth of his hands flow through my veins as if his touch were a sedative. He inched closer to me, his hands still cupping mine, his eyes penetrating me.

"Cali, what's wrong?"

"You don't believe me. You think I'm crazy," I said, my lips quivering. Yet, surprisingly I was calming down as if he had me under some kind of spell.

"I don't think you're crazy, I promise you. What kind of things did your mom see?" he asked.

"She thought she was a witch," I elaborated.

"She thought? Or she was?"

I stared at him blankly. Thought or was? What the hell kind of question was that? Did he believe in Witchcraft? I couldn't get into it with him. Not then. I was hesitant enough after telling him about her visions; I wasn't comfortable sharing that she performed rituals and cast spells, not yet anyway. But I was interested in hearing what his thoughts on Witchcraft were.

"Do you think I could possibly have a curse on me?" I asked, now incredibly curious what his answer would be. He led me by the hand back to the blanket. Letting go, he sat back down. He took his hoodie back off as I looked up and noticed the rain had stopped again. He jerked his neck towards the ground for me to sit back down as I rested next to him.

"Yes, I think a lot of unexplainable things are possible.

Curses, ghosts, gifts. Look, I think I have something on me, also. I don't know if it's a curse or a punishment, but I know for certain I am paying the price for something I've done in a past life," he said.

"How do you know that?" I asked.

"I can't explain it. But I've always known. A feeling I have had ever since I was a kid, a weight I've always carried. Visions I've always had in dreams. You must think *I'm* insane," he scoffed as he shifted his eyes to the ground in embarrassment. Evidently, he wasn't used to having this type of conversation with anyone.

"So, I take it you believe in reincarnation?" I asked.

"Oh, for sure," he said without hesitation. "You ever have that déjà vu feeling, like you've been here before? I think most likely you have, just in a different life. Dreams or events that come back to haunt you. The law of karma—you get what you put out into the universe, good or bad. That's what I believe anyway."

In realizing Josh had such a spiritual side to him, the occurrences of the past two days started racing through my mind. The way he was able to calm me down instantaneously. When I met him that first day, he knew I was picturing what he tasted like kissing me. He spontaneously knocked on the door as soon as I asked for help, or how he even knew my room number, for that matter. He had said "revolting" through closed lips. I never informed him that I hadn't told the therapist I was leaving a part of the story out. It occurred to me that his mouth never actually moved when he was asking me any of these questions. It was like we were communicating telepathically. Without opening my mouth, I looked directly into his eyes. *Are you reading my mind?*

"Yes."

"What number am I thinking of?" I silently asked.

He smiled as his eyes seemed to twinkle with sudden

excitement. He lifted his hand to his forehead and extended three fingers in the air. I sprung up and looked at him in awe.

"That's incredible!" I exclaimed. "Could you always do this?"

He sat up excitedly.

"Yes, but I never met anyone else who could. I knew you were special, Cali."

CHAPTER 5

The following day, after unpacking and settling in my room, I took a long shower. As I washed my hair, I felt a wave of relief run through me as the warm water trickled down my body. Memories from the day before flashed through my head. Being up on that mountain with Josh, out in the open, everything was so peaceful, surrounded by nature and feeling so comfortable around him. I had thought from the moment I met him something was different about him; he wasn't like other men I had come across, and I couldn't quite put my finger on exactly what it was. Knowing that we could communicate telepathically was frightening and exciting at the same time. I got out of the shower and rummaged through my drawer for something cute to wear to meet him for breakfast.

Settling on a pair of ripped jeans and a light blue tank top, I sat in front of the mirror and began to put on my makeup. Why was I trying to look good for him? No idea. Shit, could he read my mind? Would he think I was intentionally trying to look good for him? I closed my eyes and tried to block out my thoughts. Frustrated, I put on lip gloss, grabbed my purse, and ran to the café to meet him.

When I arrived at the place, he was already seated with a coffee in front of him. Wearing jeans and a white t-shirt, he smiled at me as I sat down, then looked back at his menu.

"Look at you in jeans; all dressed up," I commented.

"It's a special occasion. Not everyone gets to eat breakfast with Calista Reed," he said. The waitress came over to take our orders. Josh looked at me to order.

"Oh, um, I'll just have the fruit cup. And a green tea, please," I said, handing the menu back to the waitress. She jotted my order down on her pad and then looked at Josh.

"I'll have two eggs over easy with corned beef hash and home fries," he said, handing the menu back. "Oh, and a toasted bagel with butter, please." She took the menu and walked away as I stared at him in shock at all the food he had just ordered.

"What?" he asked defensively. "You starved me last night!"

I crumbled my napkin into a ball and threw it at him. He leaned his elbows on the table to get closer to me.

"So, I've been thinking of the 542 days thing. It reminds me of that movie, *The Knowing.* Did you see it?"

"No."

"Imagine it's like the end of the world type shit?"

I rolled my eyes and let out an exaggerated sigh.

"Josh, can you be serious for a second?"

"I am being serious. What part are you thinking I am not being sincere about? It was clearly a message. We realized last night we can communicate telepathically; what part do you think I'm not taking seriously?"

The waitress came over and placed the food in front of us. He picked up his fork and filled it with potatoes.

"You want some?" he asked as he shoveled it in his mouth. I shook my head as I picked at my fruit.

"Do you believe everything happens for a reason?" he asked between bites.

"Yes."

"Okay. So, you and I have had these abilities our entire lives; that's a given, correct?"

"Most likely. I mean, you have been aware of your abilities long before I have," I answered.

"And your mother also had capabilities from what I'm hearing, so it's the assumption you were born with gifts. Then, I just happened to meet you a month after you were delivered a message. I think it is fair to expect *something* is going to happen in 542; well, now, like 512 days, and you and I were meant to meet each other, no?"

"Yes, I suppose that sounds accurate," I agreed. I rested my forehead in my hand. "You really think the world is ending?"

He put his fork down and looked at me. "I really hope not because I have to be honest, I don't think we're the best candidates to handle anything of that magnitude. Abilities or not."

"What the hell am I going to say to my therapist today when my mother comes up?" I asked, now in a panic.

"Well, definitely none of this. No witches, mind-reading, 542 days, leave all that shit out." He took a sip of his coffee and clenched his teeth. "You're an actress. Can't you just cry on demand?"

"Of course I can cry on demand. That is like acting 101!" I sniffed, insulted.

"So, cry and come up with a nice, heartfelt story. Shrinks love that shit. They get, like, bonus points if they make you cry; they feel like they did their job if they brought out emotions," he said.

"Did your therapist ever make you cry?" I asked.

"No, but I'm not an actor," he answered.

"Oh, right, you're a model entertainer," I answered.

He looked down at his watch. "Don't you have an appointment to get to?"

I glanced at my phone. I had five minutes to get to my appointment. "Shit, I do. You're gonna show me the meditation after, right?"

"Yes," he said, nodding. "Now, go play along with your therapist so we can get back to business."

～

"How are you feeling today, Calista?"

"I'm much better today, Dr. Michaels," I answered. Okay, just listen to what Josh said and play along, so I can get back to him.

"I am sorry I upset you the other day," he said.

"You didn't upset me. I was just drained. I'm much better today."

"Can we talk about your mom?"

"Fine, if we must, let's talk about my mom. Her name was Olivia. She was twenty-nine years old when she killed herself. I was five, and my sister was seven. She swallowed an entire bottle of something, not really sure what she took. We found out when the cops came to tell us and left a lot out, I suppose, for what they felt was to our benefit. Protecting us, I guess. We were shuffled around from foster home to foster home after. Anything else you care to know?"

"And your Dad?"

I shrugged my shoulders. "Don't know. He left us when I was still a toddler; I have no memories of him."

"Not one?" He sounded surprised by my last answer.

"Nope, not a single one. I mean, I was like two."

"Do you know why he left?"

I could feel myself getting annoyed at his ridiculous questions. "No, I don't know why. I can't imagine he sat me down and told me his reasoning," I snapped. *Calm down, Cali, I silently coached myself. Pretend it's a movie role.*

There was an awkward silence as he studied my facial expression. I tried my hardest to channel Josh to ask if this is where I should start crying, but it turns out telepathic communication is not like using a two-way walkie-talkie, and I still had a lot to learn. It looked like I was on my own. He jotted down some notes.

"Do you remember the last time you saw her? Your mother?" he asked.

"The night before she died."

"What do you remember about that night?" he asked.

"I had a dream. I asked to sleep with her."

"A bad dream?" he asked.

"No, just a dream," I simply said.

"Do you recall the dream?" he asked.

I closed my eyes. It had been a long time since I had been back to that night. Twenty-two years, to be exact. Yet, I remembered the dream as if I had just had it, like it permanently implanted in my brain. The memory played out before me.

I was walking up concrete steps leading to a cabin, an old one that could have been a hundred years old; the door held closed with one rusted hinge. I went into the cabin, knowing full well it wasn't the first time, nor the last time I would ever be in that exact cabin. There were two meditation mats in the center of the room and one window in the middle of the wood panel walls with just a dab of sunlight peeking through.

On one of the mats, a teenage boy sat with his legs crossed, and a candle in the center. I can picture his face as if I knew him. He was thin with clipped dirty blonde hair and grayish-blue eyes. He had a matureness to him as if he had been around for lifetimes, yet a sadness behind his stare. He gave off a protective vibe, and I felt very comfortable around him. I instinctively sat next to him and gazed into the candle with him, resting my little head on his shoulder.

I woke up, went into my mother's room, and stood over her bed as she slept, which forced her to awaken a bit. "Honey, are you okay?" she asked.

"Can I sleep with you, Mommy?"

"Of course," she had said, lifting her blanket to let me in. I curled into her body as she pulled the blankets over us and pulled my head into her chest.

"Did the boy come back tonight?" she had asked, and I nodded into her chest. I sensed pain in her chest as she held my head to her heart and clutched my hair in her fingers like my touch was giving her instant relief. I could feel her pain run through my veins like it was my own. I could almost feel the pain again at that moment. "Did he ask you to do anything?" she asked me.

"No, Mommy," I had answered.

Suddenly my memory was interrupted by Josh's voice. "Start crying, Cali!" Opening my eyes, I let the tears stream down my cheeks.

CHAPTER 6

*J*osh met me back in my room, back in his usual hiking attire, as I scrambled to get changed in the bathroom. He stood by the bathroom door, raising his voice so I could hear him. "Okay, so who's the kid?"

I pulled a t-shirt over my head and pushed my hair behind my ears, taking one quick look at myself before pulling the bathroom door open. "I forgot to tell you part of the story," I said, heading to the refrigerator, taking out two bottles of water, and handing him one. I opened mine and took a sip as he held his in his hand, his eyes not leaving mine until I completed my sentence. "The day that Debbie tried to get me up for the signing. The night before, after the guys left, I had the same dream with the same boy. The same cabin. I've had this dream numerous times in my childhood, but as far as I remember, that was the first time he had spoken."

"What did he say?" he asked.

"I asked who he was; he said I was the same as him, a

'flame.' That we were all 'flames,' for lack of a better term, a soul brought into the world."

He opened his bottle and took a sip.

"He said I was here to serve a greater purpose, that we all are. I asked what my purpose was, and he said he couldn't tell me; I had to figure that out on my own. He said things were going to happen very fast, and I shouldn't be afraid."

"Is that all?" he asked.

I thought for a minute. "No, I asked him his name. He said his name was William."

His eyebrows raised, and his mouth hung open.

"That's a pretty important piece of information to leave out! Was that before the 542 was drawn on the mirror?"

"Yes, the night before," I said.

"So, maybe he wrote it," he said.

"I don't know, maybe," I said.

"So, he's been coming to you your entire life?" he asked.

"No, only when I was a kid. I don't remember exact instances, Josh. I did a lot of drugs, hence the rehab facility I am in!" I said, waving my hand in the air to gesture around the room. "But I know for a fact when he did come, my mother was very disconcerted by it, although she never told me why I felt it from her. He never gave me a bad feeling. I always felt very comfortable and protected around him, and he never aged. He always looked around the same age, maybe sixteen or seventeen."

He scratched his head. "Okay, a new piece to the puzzle, William. I think you really need to start documenting all these things so we can keep track. Let's go, we need to teach you how to meditate."

We made our way through the development, back through the trail, and up the mountain. I stood for a moment, lost in the view. A vision of my mother came back to me, playing with her in a similar field. I was running around with my sister as my mother was collecting daisies. *"Morgan, come here, look at this!"* she had yelled over to me. I remember running over to her, and she held this little frog in her hand. I smiled at the memory; I had almost forgotten I enjoyed collecting frogs.

"Why did your mother call you Morgan?" Josh asked, bringing me back to reality.

"Okay, just because you read my mind doesn't mean you should!" I said, turning my back to him.

"Sorry, force of habit," he mumbled.

I looked up at him and closed my eyes. I envisioned laying him down on the grass and slowly running my hands up his chest. Lightly lying on top of him, I imagined myself sensually kissing him.

"What the hell are you doing?" I heard Josh ask, his voice now cracking a bit.

Keeping my eyes closed, I envisioned slowly sinking my tongue in his mouth, as I extended my hands up through his hair. I opened my eyes suddenly, and Josh was staring at me wide-eyed.

"What was that?" he asked.

"Stay out of my head, Josh," I said, smirking.

"Ah, so now you're a mental tease. Real cool, Cali, real cool."

"Will you stay out of my head?" I asked in a threatening tone, inching closer to him.

"Yes, I promise. Unless you need me, deal?" he asked.

"Yes, deal. And Morgan is my real name. Calista is what I changed it to when I came to Hollywood," I said, answering his original question.

"Good choice. I like Cali," he said. "And now that we've thrown sexual tension in the mix, let's do some Reiki and calm it down a notch."

He laid down a blanket, sat legs crossed, and had me do

the same.

"I'll teach you some basic information before we get into specific techniques. Reiki is a form of energy healing where I simply use my body as a channel to transfer energy from the universe into your body. We trust that the Reiki energy knows which of your chakras needs healing and then repairs it on its own."

"So, you're not actually putting energy into me?" I asked.

"No, my body is just a channel," he reiterated.

"Have you ever done this to anyone?" I asked.

"No, only myself, which I'll also show you how to do. There are five main principles associated with Reiki that you should keep in mind and try to remind yourself every day, even if you just say it to yourself in your head."

"What are they?"

"You can say it however you want, but the easiest is to start with 'just for today,' then say the following: Just for today, I will not worry. Just for today, I will not be angry. Just for today, I will do my work honestly. Just for today, I will be thankful for the many blessings that I have, and just for today, I will be kind to all living things."

I repeated the principles.

"Very good," he said, nodding in approval. "Now, you have seven main chakras associated with different areas of your body. First on top of your head is the Crown chakra. This is your state of higher consciousness. Enlightenment, inspiration, this is the chakra you want to fully immerse your mind in during mediation. Right here is your Third eye," he said, bringing his pointer finger above the middle of his eyebrows. "That's intuition. Psychic abilities, likely your mother's third eye was open if she had visions; I know mine is." He ran his finger down his Adam's apple. "Throat Chakra, this controls speech, needs, will, communication."

Running his hand down, he covered his heart. "Heart

chakra—unconditional love, compassion, self-esteem, and forgiveness."

"That's it, that's the problem," I interrupted. "I can't love. Maybe that's the curse."

"Of course, you can love; you just haven't found the right guy yet," he simply answered.

I shook my head. "No, Josh, I *can't* love. I know that as much as I breathe. Same as you know you are paying for something you did in a past life, I know I will *never* be able to love anyone. Maybe I am being punished too, I don't know, but I do know that I do not have that emotion."

"I don't believe that. That isn't the curse, you can love, and you will," he stated firmly. "And we're gonna get that curse off you anyway," he smiled as if to say, don't worry, I am going to help you. He slid his hand down to his naval. "Solar plexus: desire, inner strength, self-control, anger. In my opinion, you may also need a little help in that area," he said, laughing.

Playfully, I slapped him. "That's not funny."

He motioned towards his groin, "Sacral: sexuality, intimacy, desire. I don't know if you need help here, but willing to lend a hand if you do," he winked. That made me laugh.

He touched the back of his spine. "Root Chakra: survival, fear. Now, lie back."

He guided me back, my head resting between his legs as he looked at me from above. "Place your tongue on the roof of your mouth and inhale. Count to seven, then with your tongue still there, exhale and count to three," he instructed. I listened to his directions and repeated the breathing method. "I want you to continue to breathe like that and close your eyes. I am going to play some calming music, and I need you to just listen to the music. Envision a room of darkness with only a candle burning in the room, and I want you to focus only on that flame. Concentrate on nothing but that flame.

Think of absolutely nothing, Cali; the main idea is to get your brain into the level of subconsciousness. You cannot think of anything; you need to clear your mind. It's going to be hard to do, but you need to try. Get it?"

"Yes," I said. He took out his phone and started playing calming music as I closed my eyes and concentrated on the flame in my mind.

"One of the first things they teach you in Reiki is to build a space in your mind. Build a place that is only yours, kind of like a safe place, where you would want to end up when you reach that state of spiritual awareness. A place that is tranquil and serene and only yours," he said softly. I closed my eyes and envisioned a beautiful lake surrounded by grass. The lake led into a flowing waterfall, streaming rapidly. It was a place I had never remembered being in physically, but felt so familiar.

"You got it? Your spot?" he asked.

I nodded. "Yes."

"Okay, good. Now, I can do this one of two ways: without physically touching you, or I can touch you. Which would you prefer?"

"Touch me," I said, almost in a whisper.

"You're not going to do something stupid, like imagine us making out or something, with me being on you like this, right?" he said in the most serious manner I have ever heard come out of him.

"You're not going to do something stupid like read my mind while I'm trying to get to a level of subconsciousness, are you, Josh?" I asked, opening my eyes to look into his.

He smiled. "No, I promise I won't."

He shifted his position and rested on his knees. "Try not to get turned on when I touch you, okay," he said jokingly.

"I'll try my hardest not to," I quipped sarcastically. I closed my eyes again and pictured a flame as the meditation music rang through my ears, and Josh's hands touched me, trying my hardest to get to the waterfall.

I could feel my bare feet scraping on the gravel as I was dragged across the ground, my wrists burning from trying to break out of the rope that bound them together. Pulled by a man twice my size, my throat felt like razors from screaming. He threw me to my knees before another man. I refused to look up at him. "Stand," he growled in anger.

I looked around to take in my surroundings. I was in some sort of white, sheer dress, my long, curly blonde hair dangling down. My knees were bleeding and bruised, most likely from being thrown around. A crowd of people had gathered around watching; we were on a podium, on display for the village to see.

"I said stand," he snarled again. I looked up and caught a glimpse of him. He was a large man, well-dressed for the time, which I would estimate from history classes, placed us somewhere around the seventeenth century, with bright blue eyes and a fury behind them that showed no mercy. He gave me a cocky grin. "Fine, so be it. You won't stand? Perhaps he'll make you stand." He gestured behind me to call someone over. I looked to my side to watch a man hauled in before me, his arms also tied behind his back, bloody and beaten, with a hood covering his face.

I bolted up, my heart racing, gasping for air. Josh immediately came around to face me, handing me a bottle of water. "Are you okay?" he asked.

"What happened? Where was my waterfall?" I asked.

"You tell me. You seemed to be out. I did the healing on you. You didn't even flinch. By the time I finished with your last chakra, you had bolted up like you had seen a ghost. Was it the kid? William? Did you see him?"

"No, but I do think I went into a state of subconsciousness. I think, maybe, this is going to sound insane…."

He leaned closer. "Really? You think *anything* you say at this point will sound crazy?"

"I think I saw a vision of a past life."

CHAPTER 7

For the next three months, Josh and I became inseparable. He was right about substituting one addiction for another, and it proved to serve us both well; we had a routine down. Our goal was to train ourselves to be in the best physical, mental, and spiritual shape possible. Our day started with meditation, then went into an hour workout at the gym, breakfast at the café, followed by a hike and studying—a lot of studying. The withdrawals eventually subsided, and all we focused on was figuring out who and what we were and, more importantly, our ultimate purpose, why the universe suddenly brought us into each other's life. I hadn't had another vision of a past life or William, for that matter, but we were learning a lot about the art of meditation and the history of Witchcraft, something that I had been afraid to explore further my entire life. So much so that I hadn't even spoken to my sister for almost ten years over it. I hated her and my mother for being so into it and blamed them for my terrible upbringing.

Reiki and Witchcraft had some interesting similarities. In the same way Reiki uses the Earth's energy, Witchcraft was alike in that aspect. Most rituals are performed in honor of the universe. Using the five elements: fire, water, earth, air, and spirit. Having faith and trust in the universe, as William told me in my dream, every living thing is here to serve a greater purpose. I had always associated Witchcraft with magick and not good magick. I don't know why I just assumed it was always used to manifest physical objects, like money. Or things like love. It turns out, love spells backfire. That was in almost every article we read—do not perform love spells. One of the most important things is showing gratitude to the universe. Different moon phases affect energy levels that penetrate the earth, which can intensify any spell. A spell is only as good as the intent behind it. Therefore, if the person does not have good intentions, it does not matter what they say or do. The spell will reflect the preferences set forth.

As the human mind grows, it gets plagued by society's ideological beliefs. So, it is only natural to get corrupted by these thoughts and emotions, such as greed, anger, and jealousy. These sentiments can alter any spell, ultimately making it backfire; even if that is not what the original purpose was, it is what the subconscious objective did. Confusing, I know. But Josh and I found it fascinating at the same time. It was like being in school all over again, and we texted each other at all hours of the night when we found new information about anything on the subject.

Suddenly, there we were, three months later. Probably in the best shape of our lives, learning how to handle our newfound abilities and enjoying studying with each other as I examined him up and down. He looked fantastic in his navy-blue joggers and a gray t-shirt, standing by the door of his room with just one suitcase next to him.

"All your stuff fits in that one suitcase?" I asked, pointing at the luggage.

"Yes, Ms. Hollywood, not everyone is as bougie as you," he answered.

Wrapping my arms defensively around my chest, I looked down. "I can't believe you're leaving me."

He inched in closer, until I could feel his breath on my cheek. "I'm not leaving you; I am leaving Haven. It's only three months until you're out, too. You're gonna go to your place in New York, right? We're going to see each other all the time. Plus, I'm going to bug the shit out of you on Face-Time and practice my vaping techniques. I still have to get my TikTok routine down if I am going to be famous."

"I know," I pouted. "But it's not the same."

He pulled me into him and hugged me. I wrapped my arms around him as I buried my head into his hard chest. I could feel his heartbeat against my ear as I silently prayed for him to kiss me. He pulled away from me a little. *Kiss me, Josh. Kiss me, Josh.*

"So, I'll call you later?" he asked.

Damn you, Cali, why'd you make him promise not to read your mind?

I nodded. "Yep, call me later." He turned to leave.

"Josh…" I said as I made my way back towards him. *Just kiss him.* He turned back around.

"Yeah?"

Don't lead him on. You can't fall in love. "Don't forget about me."

He smiled. "How could I ever forget about you, Cali?"

That night, I lay in bed, staring out the window at the stars, feeling empty. He was my only friend in Haven since day one; it was the first time since I had been there that I felt so utterly alone. Closing my eyes, I started my meditation breathing. Maybe if I could put myself into a state of subconsciousness, I could at least dream about him? It was worth a try.

When my eyes opened, I was on our mountain. All my senses were intact; it felt so real. I could smell the crispness of the grass and feel the sharp breeze. I ran my fingers along the coarse bark of a tree. My feelings were all on point. Cautiously, I made my way towards our spot, and there he was, standing where he always was, with our blanket beneath him. He was wearing the same blue joggers and gray t-shirt from earlier that day when I had seen him. He smiled as I approached, gazing at me as if he were genuinely happy to see me.

"It worked," I said excitedly.

He tilted his head and raised his eyebrows. "What worked?"

"I missed you. Before I went to sleep, I thought maybe if I put my mind into a meditative state, I could see you in my dreams, and here you are!"

"You missed me?" He bit his bottom lip. "That's cute. But I hate to break the news to you, sweetheart. You're in my dream."

My smile faded for a minute. "What? No, honey, sorry, you're in *my* dream."

He came in so close that I could feel his breath on my face. "I'm loving the pet names, I think we should use them in real life, but seriously, you're in my dream."

"Really?" I huffed, annoyed now. "If I were in your dream, would I do this?" I lifted my shirt above my head and took it off, now standing in only a black lace bra.

Josh took a step back to take in the view fully and said, "Yes, actually, you've done that quite a bit in my dreams." He lifted his hands up and, holding them an inch apart, started moving them around in a circular motion as if we were molding a ball. "Check this out." He took his right hand and made a gesture as if he were throwing a baseball at the tree, and suddenly the tree erupted into a gulf of orange and yellow flames. "My dream," he reiterated.

Looking into his eyes, I licked my lips and extended my arm in the air. Expanding my fingers towards the clouds, I twisted them and pulled them down, releasing a massive downpour. Colossal raindrops fell from the sky, immediately turning his flaming tree into a cloud of smoke and soaking the both of us. It drenched his jet-black hair, now hanging in front of his blue eyes, his t-shirt so doused it was translucent. His protruding chest was prominent, and his nipples were erect. He grabbed me by the shoulder and pulled me into him.

Without warning, he pressed his lips against mine, and his tongue was in my mouth. I aggressively ran my fingers through his hair as he lifted me and wrapped my legs around his waist. I could feel how turned on he was as he rocked my body back and forth against him. My mouth traveled down his neck as he whispered, "Have you ever dreamt about me?"

"Yes," I muttered. "Show me what you dream about."

He slowly dropped to one knee while still holding me, then the other, and placed me down on the blanket, lying me on my back. With the rain still pouring down on us, he fiercely kissed me.

His lips never left mine. The harder I clenched his hair between my fingers, the more passionate his kiss became. After only moments I opened my eyes, and suddenly, he was fading.

"What's happening?" I asked in a panic, holding on to him tightly.

His breathing became heavier. "You're waking up, don't wake up; hold on to me. Keep your eyes closed. Don't wake up, Cali!"

Suddenly, I felt like I was plummeting, as if I were being dropped from the sky. My eyes opened, and I was in my room. Alone and dry.

There was no way that could have just happened. That had to have been a dream. Suddenly, my phone started ringing. I looked down, and Josh was Face Timing me. I tried to compose myself and casually picked up the phone. He was lying in his bed with no shirt on and a bit out of breath.

"Anything weird just happen with you?" he asked.

CHAPTER 8

So that really happened. Well, whatever "really happened" actually meant, all I knew was what occurred the night before to me did to him as well. I hadn't gotten much sleep. I stayed up all night and researched the possibilities of what that could have been, which wasn't easy. I mean, it's not like you can type into google "kissing in a joint dream you both remember." Well, you can, but a bunch of porn popped up, which certainly was not what I was looking for. So, I went a different route, now looking for the connection between Josh and me. Clearly, we had a unique relationship, unlike one I had ever experienced with anyone before. That is when I discovered the concept of Twin Flames.

When souls are created, or "born," for lack of a better term, they are split in two, creating your Twin Flame. A memory stirred. This must have been what William was talking about when he told me that we were all flames. Twin Flames are similar to a soul mate; however, one can have many male and female soulmates, having nothing at all to do with sex or other myths that society has grown to believe associated with the term. People are drawn to others that we know we've met before, that déjà vu feeling everyone experiences at some point in their life. They are souls that are present in our lives, reoccurring in all our lifetimes because they are there to serve a purpose. Teach a lesson or *become* the lesson. Even in toxic relationships, a lot of times, that person is a soul mate. You will always find each other, and every time around, there will always be a lesson to learn from them.

A Twin Flame is entirely different. Although you will always meet, there are distinct differences and multiple stages every twin flame goes through. Eight to be exact: yearning, meeting, falling in love, the ideal relationship, turmoil, separation, surrender, and reunion. Whatever was blocking me from loving, whether or not it was indeed a curse, was most likely preventing me from the yearning and falling in love part, but obviously, we've met. So, if he were my Twin Flame, we'd have five more steps to go through, including separation. Unless this was the separation part? No, it couldn't be. We hadn't experienced the ideal relationship or turmoil yet. The turmoil part scared me even more. So now turmoil was coming too? Is that what was going to happen in 542 days?

Fascinated, I continued reading about Twin Flames. There were specific numbers correlated with Twin Flames as well. Numbers that frequently appear were not a coincidence. 1111, 1212, 2222. All Twin Flame numbers. The more I read about Twin Flames, the more sense it made, putting my mind at ease with Josh and our weird connection. But at the same time, the more stressed out I became because I felt there was so much I didn't know, and we were only just beginning. My eyes hurt, so I set the phone down on my night table and lay back down to close them for a minute. No sooner than my head hit the pillow, the phone started ringing. Josh was Face Timing me.

"You look tired," he commented, smiling at me with a boyish grin like he was still a little embarrassed from the night before.

"I didn't get much sleep, you?" I asked.

"No, which is weird. Normally I'd sleep like a baby after a night like that," he said. We smiled like two school kids crushing on each other. "I've been doing some research, and I found something very interesting," he said.

Just as the words "Twin Flames" came out of my mouth, at the same time, he said, "Astral Projection." We both paused, then together said: "What?"

"You first," he said, shaking his head and laughing.

"No, you go," I said, feeling like a complete idiot because I told him he's basically the guy I was supposed to fall in love with, and I had absolutely no idea where he was going with astral projection.

"Okay, so there were two different things I found," he began. "There's lucid dreaming, which I've done many times, and I know from our conversations you have as well. That's when you know you're dreaming and can control the dream. You can make things happen and wake yourself up, so at first, that is what I thought we were doing. How I was able to set the tree on fire, or you were able to make it rain, but then I stumbled across astral projection." He paused for a minute. He looked past me to see my surroundings. "Oh good, you're lying down because this one is kinda out there. Astral projection is the belief that your spirit can leave your body while your physical body is sleeping and go into an astral plane."

"Like an out-of-body experience?" I asked.

He nodded. "That's exactly what it is. Now that's the direction I'm leaning towards. That is what I think we did. We somehow put our bodies concurrently into this state and met in a different realm. You know that feeling like you're falling people get when they're sleeping? Did that happen to you that night?"

I thought about it for a minute. "Yes, it did, right before I woke up. I felt like I was falling from the sky while trying to stay in the dream."

"Me too. It says that is what happens when your spirit returns to your physical body. We must have been subconsciously yearning for each other, and that mountain was common ground, so that's how we ended up there. Didn't you say you put yourself into a meditative state before sleep? Maybe I also did accidentally." *Yearning.* I looked at him in silence, absorbing all the information he had just told me. "What do you think?" he asked.

"I think you're right," I said. "I think it makes sense. But I think there's something else. I think there's a specific reason why you and I were able to do this since you mention the word yearning. Not that I'm saying I was yearning for you or anything…"

"Except you did say you missed me, and if I remember correctly, you did take off your shirt. Willingly, in fact, in what you thought was *your* dream, not mine, correct?" he teased.

"Anyway," I continued. "I read about this thing called Twin Flames."

I filled him in on my past hours of studying on Twin Flames as he sat and silently listened. When I finished, I waited for a response, but he stayed quiet. I studied his facial expression to try to get some sort of indication of what was going through his mind, but he was good at keeping a poker face. I knew what he was thinking, though. He was nervous that he would fall in love with me, and I couldn't love him back. He wouldn't be wrong; it was a valid concern.

"Say something," I finally said.

"I don't know what to say," he admitted.

"Say anything," I said in an almost desperate tone.

He opened his mouth to speak, but nothing came out. He closed his eyes, took a deep breath, and opened his mind. He couldn't articulate the words, and he wanted me to see for myself. I closed my eyes to read him and see for myself what he was thinking and feeling. It was the separation stage he was worried about.

When I finished, he closed his mind again and opened his eyes. "That would suck," he finally said. "After all this time, we found each other and learned all this cool shit we can do, and then we get separated?"

He wasn't wrong. "Well, at least there is a reunion to look forward to," I said, trying to lighten the mood.

"So, what are your plans for today?" he asked, changing the subject. I looked at the time. It was already nine a.m.

"I'm going to take a quick shower, order room service, and sleep all day. Someone kept me up all night in another plane," I said. "You?"

"That sounds like a good plan. I think I'll do the same. I think we found the trick to the safest sex possible!"

I hung up with him and got in the shower. William wasn't kidding. Everything was happening so fast that I needed a second to slow down. Now I couldn't get the fear out of my head that this separation would occur in 542 days. I had grown so used to being around Josh; he had become my best friend. I could barely manage at Haven without him, and it was only one day. How long was this separation going to be? I drove myself crazy with these thoughts until I finally fell asleep.

Mud spattered my legs as I held his hand, trying to keep up with his speed. He was practically dragging me, running in front of me, holding my hand, and pulling me. If this pace continued, I felt like my knees would buckle beneath me at any moment, or my chest would cave in from running so fast. I turned around to get a glimpse behind me. Rain poured down behind us, and there must have been a hundred men chasing us, all bearing weapons. "Don't look back," he yelled. "Hold on to me."

Pulling me harder, we made it to a cave and made me crawl in first as he scrambled in behind me.

"He has a damn army!" he exclaimed.

It was dark, cold, and damp, and I covered my face to close my nose from the horrid odor of dead rodents. There wasn't much room to do anything but sit against the wall, with my knees against my chest. My sheer white dress was torn and dirty, my knees bruised and bloody. "Stay here," he said as he quickly went outside and collected large rocks and brought them back. Once he had enough, he started barricading the opening, so we were locked inside.

He sat up against the wall next to me; his bloodied knees pulled up to his chest as he put his arms around my shoulder and pulled me into him. It was so dark that I couldn't see what he looked like, but his touch was comforting. I buried my head in his chest as he kissed my forehead. "How long can you hold the rain?" he whispered.

"As long as I can stay awake," I answered.

"I will keep you awake. It is raining too hard for them to make it up the hill. They won't be able to get up here until it stops. Perhaps they'll tire."

I ran my hand up his chest to his face. I could feel his facial hair, shaped in a goatee. I knew we were in danger, and I didn't know how long we had or who he was, but I did know one thing for sure. For the time being, I felt safe with him.

My eyes bolted open as I sprung up from bed without knowing where I was for a second. Realizing I was in my room, my heart accelerated. That definitely wasn't a lucid dream or an astral projection; that was another past-life memory. And it wasn't the same man who was telling me to stand either, but likely the one with the hood. I looked up at the clock—5:42 p.m. Of course, it was. I took out my phone to document the occurrence.

CHAPTER 9

For the next few months, I found myself in a constant state of depression. Without Josh, I truly had no one. I felt like a loser eating in the café alone, with no one to work out with, and no one to talk to. Except for Dr. Michaels, and most of the time, I just felt like I was being judged and interrogated by him, so I kept to myself. Finally, I decided to go for a hike one morning after my breakfast. The weather was beautiful, and it was a perfect day to go for an outing.

As I climbed the path, a sense of nostalgia swept over me. Thinking of all the times Josh and I had been there together. I went to our spot and placed the blanket on the ground. I got on it and laid back, taking in the entire scene. A light breeze made the trees sway, the chirping of birds singing through my ears; it was amazingly peaceful. I stayed there for a few hours, lost in my thoughts. Memories of my mother trickled back. She was very into nature, always picking flowers or taking us to some park or outside activity. I remembered how she would get mesmerized by butterflies. She used to say they were loved ones who had gone, coming to visit. She used to tell us that death was merely your soul leaving your body and that your spirit would always be present, as you would become one with the universe. She believed in signs that certain things had a greater spiritual meaning. Anything from the butterflies to birds, even chipmunks, all had messages to tell, a significant reason for their presence. Suddenly I felt myself getting angry with her again, so I redirected my thoughts back to Josh.

We were right here on this mountain on the night of the astral projection as he held me up in the rain. I remembered the night in San Diego, right before everything had happened. My friend Colleen and I had gone for massages and then out to a hot club in the area. I thought back to our conversation right before we picked up some guys and brought them back to our hotel. The chat we had before my whole life ultimately changed. She had been so excited I was able to get us into such an elite club just by dropping my name, and we had scored a VIP table in the back.

"Man, I wish I had your job," she said smiling, *taking a sip of her drink.*

"Which part? The money or the fame?" I asked, *knowing full well she was being facetious.*

She shook her head as she layered one of her crackers with hummus. "Both," she joked. "But seriously, I think it's just awesome that you can get lost on a daily basis in a different world that you create for yourself."

I took a sip of my drink. "I don't create any of that. The writers built the world. I just portray the character they've made."

"You make it your own. I don't think any author could have made a character come to life as you have done on film. You think The Golden Train would have done so well if you didn't play Krista?" she asked.

I smiled. "Thanks, that I will take credit for. I did kick ass as Krista, didn't I? I'd much rather have your job, though. Deal with animals all day instead of humans? Sign me up! At least they don't talk back."

"There is a beautiful ignorance to animals," she agreed. "An innocence and unconditional love; almost like babies before they are corrupted by society."

"Imagine a world in which people aren't tainted by such things," I had said in a dramatic tone for a philosophical effect.

I shook my head at the memory. I wondered how she was doing as her words echoed through my brain. Being a veterinarian, she loved animals. *An innocence and unconditional love.* Nothing I possessed. The truth was that the money, the fame, and the ability to get lost in a character got old quickly. All I felt at the moment was completely and utterly alone. I took a deep breath and started to pack my things. My memories seemed to torture me. I needed to go back to my room. I packed up my knapsack and headed back towards Haven.

As I walked, I suddenly heard a snap as my foot buckled, and I plunged to the ground. I held my ankle as I screamed out in pain and cursed the branch I tripped over. I tried to get up, but the agony was so excruciating when I stood that I tumbled back down. I applied pressure to my ankle as I grabbed my cell phone to call for help. No signal. Great. I started yelling, praying someone would hear me, but no such luck. I closed my eyes tightly and tried to contact Josh. He said he would be able to read my mind if I needed help. *Josh, I need you. Where are you?* I silently pleaded for an answer. Nothing. I tried to remain calm; I was anything but. I was terrified no one would find me, and I would die all alone on that stupid mountain. I started crying hysterically. Anger-filled tears poured down my face; I hated everyone and everything at that moment. I hated my mother for leaving me, I hated Josh for not being able to hear me, and I hated myself for even coming here.

The rain started pouring down, drenching me and

turning the dirt below me into mud. I covered my head with my hood and, and with much difficulty crawled under a tree for shelter. The winds started blowing fiercely, pulling me back to a time in my childhood when my sister had wanted to contact my mother. We were only seven and ten at the time, and she wanted so desperately to get in touch with her. She had never gotten over her death, constantly depressed and trying anything she could to talk to her. I recalled being in a field where our mother would take us often, as she sat with a Ouija board and tried her hardest to contact her. At the time, I had thought it was a dumb idea and accused her of making the piece move on its own as it drew out words. Then, the wind started blowing uncontrollably, and it scared me to death. I had started crying, begging her to stop. The deeper she got into asking the questions, the stronger the wind became, and rain poured down. That's exactly what was happening as I pressed against the tree, the wind becoming more potent and the rain falling harder. Filthy now, covered in mud, I lay my head against the tree and begged for someone to help.

I woke up the following day, freezing and soaked, to two police officers standing over me. Haven had reported me missing and sent out a search team. They called for an ambulance, laid me on a stretcher, and brought me to the infirmary. After Alex had wrapped up my ankle, I lay in my room, reading about twenty messages Josh had texted me. I was so angry with him that I refused to answer him back. He was supposed to always help me, and he wasn't there for me when I needed him the most. A few days later, there was a knock on my door. Joe handed me flowers that had been delivered- beautiful red roses in a crystal vase. I took them from him and read the card: *I haven't heard from you, hope you're okay. -Josh.* I threw the vase on the floor, watching the glass shatter and the water pour out. Then, I picked up my phone and FaceTimed him.

"Hey," he said enthusiastically.

"Don't 'hey' me, in case you haven't realized by my lack of response to you, I don't want to talk to you." I turned the phone to the floor so he could see the flowers, scattered in a mess. "And I certainly don't need your flowers." He stayed silent, looking at me like he didn't know what to say. "Are you stupid? I can't fall in love with anyone, so I'm not exactly sure what the point of these flowers is. Do you know who I am? I don't need your flowers. Even if I liked flowers, which I don't, I could get them for myself!"

"I didn't get them for you for any other reason than I thought maybe you were having a rough time, and I wanted to make you smile," he explained.

"Well, your attempt to make me smile didn't work," I said nastily.

"Are you mad at me?" he asked, realizing my nasty tone.

"Yes, I am. I got hurt the other day."

His facial expression changed from confused to concerned. "Hurt? How? Are you okay?"

"I'm fine; I sprained my ankle. I tried to contact you. You said you'd be able to read my mind if I needed you, but you were nowhere to be found. So much for being there for me."

"Cali, it doesn't work like that. I am sorry I couldn't hear you; I don't know what to say about that other than if I knew something was wrong, I would have absolutely helped you…."

"You left me," I cut him off. His mouth dropped as his eyes shifted down.

"I didn't leave *you*; I left Haven," he said softly. "I was done with my time. I had no control over that either. Trust me, being back in real life isn't exactly joyful. I would much rather be there with you." I couldn't even listen to him talk, so I hung up on him.

≈

As I sat in Dr. Michaels' office, I hadn't spoken to Josh for almost a month. I couldn't tell him I was mad at Josh for not being able to read my mind when I was stranded, but he could sense my resentment when he asked if I had spoken to him. I tried to change the subject.

"Do you think maybe you have abandonment concerns? You feel as if your mother and your father both left you, now Josh," he asked. I rolled my eyes.

"No," I simply answered. Then, detecting I was getting bitter, he changed the subject.

"So, your agent called, tell me about that," he said, trying to cheer me up.

"Nothing much to tell. She got me a gig, a movie; I start when I get back. It's in New York, so I will be going to my apartment there."

He looked down at his pad. "You only have a month left. Are you excited to get back to your life?" Josh's words came back to me, how he had said he wasn't happy being back in his regular routine. I smiled and nodded, but the truth was, I was nervous about going back to New York and returning to the movie scene. I was terrified I would fall right back into my old habits.

When I returned to my room that night, I couldn't sleep. I felt bad over what I said to Josh that day. He was right, and he didn't do anything wrong. It wasn't his fault he couldn't hear me. Maybe Dr. Michaels was onto something when he said I had abandonment issues. Deep down, I really missed Josh, and once again, he was correct when he said he didn't leave me; he left Haven. What exactly was I expecting him to do, relapse so he could come back? I knew I wasn't thinking rationally. Reluctantly, I picked up my phone to FaceTime him, hoping he was alone. He immediately picked up.

"Hey you…." he said, happy I was calling him.

"I'm so sorry, Josh. I'm a complete bitch," I began.

CHAPTER 10

$\mathscr{J}$t looked like any other fancy apartment building on Manhattan's Upper East Side. Freshly groomed shrubs along the archway, sparkling with white lights, marble floors throughout the lobby, crystal chandeliers hanging. Although soft music was playing throughout, all I could hear was the thumping of my heels against the floor.

"May I help you?" the doorman greeted me.

"I'm Calista Reed. I'm here to see Joshua Knight," I answered politely.

"Ah, yes, Ms. Reed, he's been expecting you. I'm Oscar. Follow me." He led me into the elevator and brought me to the thirty-second floor. As the door slid open, he held it for me as I got out and motioned his head to the last unit. "Mr. Knight is down the hall. Enjoy your evening."

I slowly made my way over to his apartment. My heart was racing a bit, and my palms were clammy. I was excited and nervous at the same time. Sure, we were now speaking all the time again, but it had been three months since I had last seen him in person and since we had the astral experience. It's like seeing a guy after having a dirty dream about him, except he knows you had one. When I knocked on the door, he opened it pretty fast. I assumed Oscar had given him a warning I was on my way up.

Dressed in a black t-shirt and dark gray basketball shorts, his beard now groomed to more of a five o'clock shadow, he stood in front of me, smiling ear to ear. He swung the door open wider, "Come in," he said excitedly. "How was your trip home? How was your ride in? When do you start working? How was traffic?" he started rambling out questions a mile a minute as I took in his apartment. His living room was incredible, all glass overlooking the city. An entire wall was a built-in TV displaying music videos he had playing. On the other end was a massive fireplace that blended in with the glass so well it appeared as if the flames were dancing in the air. A sliding door led out to a balcony overlooking the city. There was a black leather couch across from the TV wall, a matching loveseat parallel to the fireplace, and a gray marble coffee table between them. The place was incredibly classy. He either had extremely good taste or an amazing interior decorator.

"This is quite the place," I commented, my eyes fixated on the fireplace, mesmerized by the flames.

"Thank you," he said.

"And you say I'm bougie?" I said, suddenly annoyed at all the times he's made fun of me.

"Oh, come on, I was just kidding. I mean, you knew I had money, right? That rehab wasn't cheap."

I stood silent for a minute. Suddenly I felt like I was in some guy's house I didn't even know. I don't know why I felt that way, but I did.

"My ride in was fine. Traffic wasn't bad," I said, addressing his questions. "Can we step out and get some air?" I motioned to the balcony door. He rushed to the door and slid it open, waving with his hand for me to go first. He followed behind and shut the door as we sat on two cushioned seats separated by a glass table.

"I start my job next week," I said, going back to his questions. He nodded in acknowledgment.

"Cool, what's the movie about?"

"It's a true story. Based on the Broadway actress that was all over the news a few years ago," I answered.

He tilted his head like he was trying to remember for a minute, then said: "Oh right, what was her name?"

"Bianca Evans," I replied.

"Right, Bianca Evans," he said. We stayed silent for a moment; the conversation was getting very awkward. I don't know why I felt so intimidated around him, I was used to rich guys; he just hadn't struck me as one of them the whole time. He was different, so humble and modest, it was hard to imagine him so well off. But he was right, as usual. I knew he had money, and Haven was unbelievably expensive.

"Yeah, so it seems like an easy gig, New York-based, six months at most. Blonde hair, green eyes, I fit the mold," I let out a nervous laugh. I rested my elbows on my knees and looked over at the skyscrapers, the neon lights illuminating the billboards, the loud blaring of sirens and horns from below, a completely different scene than I had grown accustomed to with Josh. I felt like I was with a stranger. My breathing became heavy, and I could feel my forehead dampening with sweat. I pushed my hair behind my ears. "Do you have water?" I asked.

"Yeah, of course, sorry. I should have offered before. Come," he said as he led me back into the kitchen. The kitchen was also enormous, a huge island in the middle with tall bar seats and stainless-steel appliances; it attached to a dining room with a colossal marble table that could seat at least twenty people. He reached into the fridge and retrieved a bottle of water as I sat on one of the stools. "I, um, I got you a juicer," he said uneasily.

"You got me juicer?" I repeated.

"Yeah," he gave a nervous laugh. "I didn't really know what we would do. You know we can't, like, go to a club or bar or anything, so I thought we never did try that celery juice."

He pulled a fancy machine off the countertop and placed it in front of me, then went into his fridge and started displaying different types of vegetables. "I got celery, carrots, beets," he listed as he placed them one by one in front of me. I could tell he was getting anxious, scrambling for something to say. I sat motionless, looking at the vegetables, also racking my brain for words. He took his vape out of his pocket and took a pull.

"Maybe I should go," I finally said. He shoved the vape back in his pocket, sprung around the side of the table to where I was sitting, and put his arms around my chair on both sides of me. Then, looking directly into my eyes said in a pleading tone: "Please don't go. It was stupid to get a juicer, I'm sorry. I just didn't know what we were going to do...."

"It's not the juicer," I assured him, shaking my head.

"Then what is it?" he asked, his arms so close to me that all I could envision was them around me that night as he held me up in the rain.

"Can I take a pull of your vape?" I asked.

He straightened himself up, reached into his pocket, and handed it to me.

I took a hit of the vape and looked down at my lap. "What's wrong, Cali? Talk to me."

"It just feels different," I said, spinning the vape around in my hand, not moving my gaze from it.

"Is it the money? Would you like me better if I was broke?" I know. It sounded just as stupid to me too.

"No, I don't know what it is. It's just weird. Being here, in real life, with you. With actual things, with access to anything we want...."

He pulled the stool next to me closer, took the vape from me, took a pull, and passed it back. "You know, I was so nervous about you coming here. I was fine the whole three months I've been out of Haven, I really was- until tonight. Then I was in that stupid grocery store buying those damn vegetables, all I was thinking was I could really use a shot to take the edge off."

I let out a sigh of relief, and I took another pull on the vape and looked up at him. "Yes, that's exactly it. I could use something to take the edge off."

He reached over and took my hand, his thumb running up and down my palm. His touch immediately sent heat through my veins and put me at ease as I closed my eyes and took in the moment. Realizing he was soothing me, he ran his fingers from my palm up to my wrist, then up my arm, and pulled me into him. I got off my chair and followed his lead until I was nestled between his legs, wrapped in his arms, my head on his shoulder, as he held me tightly and ran one of his hands up and down my spine and his other firmly gripped my head into him. Running his fingers through my hair, the smell of musky cologne intoxicated me.

"That's what you have me for," he whispered. I lifted my head and looked into his eyes; our lips were so close I could practically taste him. His gaze shifted to my lips, like he wanted to kiss me but wasn't sure if he should.

"How do you do that?" I muttered.

"How do I do what?"

"Close your mind so I can't read it?" I whispered.

He smiled as he gently bit his bottom lip.

"Why are you trying to read my mind?" he asked.

"Because I want to know what you're thinking," I said.

"Why can't you just ask me what I am thinking?"

I put my hand on his chest. At that moment, it would have been easier to read his mind than hear him say the words I knew he was thinking. I was a liability.

"What are you thinking?" I hesitantly asked.

He ran his hand down my cheek and gently pushed my hair out of my face. "I'm thinking you're gonna be a massive pain in my ass," he laughed.

I slapped his chest. "Hey, come up with your own lines!"

"And to answer your question, I have trained my mind to always be in the level of subconscious state. No one can get into it once your mind is in that state," he answered. "You want to go for a run?"

I took a step back. "I don't think I am in the proper attire to go for a run," I said, looking down at my distressed jeans and five-inch heels. His eyes ran down my body slowly as he smirked, making it evident he was enjoying what he was looking at.

"No, you're definitely not. You want me to call you a car?" he asked, sounding defeated.

I sat back down on my chair. "No," I said, shaking my head and looking at the vegetables. "Let's make some juice!"

He let out a laugh. "It's okay; it was a dumb idea. We don't have to…."

I held my hand up to stop him from speaking as I stood up and started looking around his kitchen. "Where do you keep the utensils? How do we make this crap? You have a recipe?"

Forty minutes, a lot of chopping and a considerable mess later, we sat there with two tiny glasses of brownish-looking thick liquid that we both held out in our hands, examining them with a look of disgust on our faces.

"I was expecting it to be bigger," he commented.

"That's what she said," I joked.

"No, for the record, 'she' has never had that complaint," he winked. Finally, there was my old, sexually inappropriate, sarcastic Josh.

"Ready?" I asked, holding up the glass in the toast position.

"To new beginnings," he said as he clinked my glass with his.

"To new beginnings," I repeated as I put the glass to my lips. He swallowed his drink in one gulp. As he put the glass down, a look of revulsion crossed his face. Josh covered his mouth and held his other hand up to try to stop me from drinking mine, but it was too late. The second the horrid taste hit my tongue, feeling as if I was going to gag immediately, I ran to the sink to spit it out. He grabbed a bottle of water and started rinsing his mouth out.

CHAPTER 11

y eyes gradually opened as I stretched my body out, gently running my hands along my sheets, taking in the luxurious touch of my teal satin sheets under my skin, as bright as the ocean. I reached over to my nightstand and pressed a button, opening my room-darkening blinds. Watching in awe as they slowly rolled open, displaying New York City and allowing in sunlight. I felt it. I was home. I pushed myself up in bed and stretched my body out as I looked around my room. The light gray marble furniture matched perfectly with the linen and a soft, plush loveseat to the side of the dresser. Abstract art hung on the walls, and plants in every corner. Attached to the room was a rather large bathroom that led to my dressing room.

Changing out of my nightgown, I threw on a pair of jean shorts and an olive-green t-shirt. Tying my hair into a ponytail, freshening my makeup, and completing the look with a large pair of sunglasses, I grabbed my purse and headed out.

The restaurant was only a few blocks away, and I tried my hardest not to be noticed as I walked quickly to meet Debbie. "You look fantastic!" she greeted me as she stood to hug me.

"Thanks," I said as we sat at an outside table, which she had already secured off to the side. "Also, thank you for having my apartment redone while I was…" I struggled to find the correct word.

"Away," she chimed in. "You were away on a mental break, a vacation. That is what we are telling everybody. And no problem," she winked as she studied her menu. Debbie had been my agent for years. An older woman, well put together and aged like a fine bottle of wine that Hollywood's best plastic surgeons had restored. She had taken the liberty of having the rather large bar in my living room reconstructed into a very big display case wrapping around the wall, show-casing various pieces of artwork I had collected throughout the years as well as awards and Oscars I had received. It was a nice gesture and a pleasant surprise to walk into, rather than a fully stocked bar.

I still couldn't get Josh's apartment out of my head. Who would have known how much money he had? Sure, my apartment was hot, but his was gorgeous. It must have cost him twice the amount mine did. The waitress broke me out of my thoughts. "Can I take your orders?"

"I'll have the avocado toast and a coffee," Debbie ordered, handing her back the menu.

"I'll have the same," I said, passing my menu to her.

"This movie will be good for you," Debbie said. I nodded.

"I know; I'm looking forward to it. I need to get back into it."

"How have you been otherwise? I guess you haven't been home long enough?" she asked.

"Fine. I met someone there; he actually lives in New York. I was hanging out with him last night until like three a.m., the reason why I didn't wake up until noon today," I laughed.

She leaned her elbows into the table. "Do tell. What does he do? Is he cute? Good in bed?"

I started shaking my head as the waitress came back with the orders. "No, no, nothing like that, we're just friends. But he's a real cool guy. It's nice to have someone that gets what you're going through, you know? We um, well, we made juice last night," I laughed as I took a bite of my avocado toast.

She curled her lip and scrunched her nose. "I'm sorry, you made juice? Is that what the kids are calling it these days?"

"Yeah, like actual juice. We.... never mind, I guess you had to be there," I said.

"Sounds like fun," she said sarcastically.

Finding myself not wanting to explain, I could already see Josh and I would need to get a better hobby than making juice. Something to talk to people about, or they would start thinking I was getting weird. After lunch, Debbie and I went shopping for hours and spent the day together. It was nice to be able to do everyday things again. I didn't get back to my apartment until later that night.

"Good evening, Ms. Reed," my doorman, Logan, greeted.

"Hey, Logan," I cheerfully said as I headed up to my apartment. I walked in, taking in the view; it had been so long since I was in my own place. Grabbing clean clothes, I headed into the shower. I stood under the water as I washed my hair, feeling so relaxed. I felt happier at that moment than I had in a while. I was back home. I had my life back. I felt healthy, and I had a new movie role. Things were looking up. And Josh was there, in New York. Humming to myself, I got out of the shower and threw on a pair of shorts and a tank top. It had suddenly occurred to me it was almost ten p.m., and I hadn't eaten anything since that avocado toast during lunch. My stomach now rumbling, I made my way to the kitchen, rifling through the refrigerator to see what Debbie had it stocked with.

There were some fresh cold cuts; I took out the turkey and mayonnaise, remembering the day Josh had taken me hiking for the first time and given me his sandwich. As I dug through the bread drawer, I picked up my phone to text him. Then it occurred to me. It was after ten p.m.; maybe he was with a girl or something, he'd been back home for three months. I didn't know if he was dating anyone or had a girl-friend. That had never come up. I put the phone back on the counter and shuffled through the drawer for a butter knife. I reached into a cabinet to grab a plate. I could feel drops on the back of the plate as I turned it over to put the bread on it as if it were still wet. As I placed the container on the counter, I reached into the bread bag to take a piece out when I saw movement on the plate from the corner of my eye. My attention immediately went to the dish as I stood paralyzed, watching the water droplets move on their own as if someone was controlling the water.

I watched the droplets as they deliberately moved towards each other, forming the number four. My heart sank into my chest, and the hair on my arms stood as goosebumps rose. Memories of the night 542 days being traced on the mirror inundated back through my head. I dropped the bread to the floor. I waited a few minutes to see if anything else would be written, but that was it, just four. I quickly picked up the phone to FaceTime Josh in a panic. After three rings, he picked up.

"Hey you," he greeted, smiling.

"Are you alone?" I asked.

"No, I am currently hosting an orgy, but the good news is I have a king-size bed, and there's a spot for another, so you're more than welcome to join," he winked. "Of course, I'm alone. Who would I be with?"

"I don't know. You're a good-looking guy. Maybe you have a girl there," I answered.

"Ah, so, the truth comes out. You think I'm good-looking!" he joked. I shook my head in a frenzy. I had no time to flirt with him.

"Can I come over?" I asked, annoyed.

"Sure," he said.

I hung up, called a car, and made my way to his place.

His smile immediately turned to concern when he saw the look on my face once he opened the door.

"Are you okay? You look like you've seen a ghost. Wait— *did* you see a ghost? Was it William?"

Walking right past him like I owned the place, I sat down on his couch and frantically started telling him the whole story. When I finished, he sat there staring at me in silence.

"Do you think it was him? The kid?" he finally asked.

"I don't know, but I'm freaking out. I wasn't prepared for this today."

"Okay, to be fair, we haven't been 'prepared' for any of this shit," he said. "We need to look into what four could mean in all of this. So now that's the second time four came up because it's also the middle number in 542," he pointed out.

"And the sum of 1111 and 22, in Twin Flames," I added.

"That's true also," he said, rubbing his eyes. I looked at the clock.

"Speaking of…," I said, as he looked up at the clock. 11:11 p.m.. "What do you think that means?"

"I think the universe is telling us it's time to sleep. It's late. Some of us didn't have the luxury of sleeping in late. We'll continue tomorrow," he said, yawning. He stood up to take my hand. "C'mon, I'll show you the guest room."

I shyly looked down. "What's wrong?" he asked.

I put my hand in his and let him pull me up. I looked into his eyes. "I don't want to be alone," I said, right above a whisper.

"Oh," he said quietly. "You can sleep in my bed if you want."

I followed him into the bedroom; as I crawled into his bed, he went into his bathroom to change. He returned in shorts and a t-shirt and got in also. We laid apart, both facing the ceiling. "I'm getting scared, Josh," I admitted.

He turned his head to look at me. "Don't be scared. We got this. At least we're in this together. We're going to figure all this shit out, I promise," he said.

I moved in closer to him and rested my head on his chest. He ran his hand up and down my back, trying to comfort me. Once again, the second his fingers touched me, he immediately put my body at ease. I ran my hand along his chest up to his neck, where my fingers lightly traced the neckline of his t-shirt. He shifted his head to look at me, his eyes piercing mine, his lips so close I could feel his breath on me. He closed his eyes for a second, let out a deep breath, and then looked back at me. His eyes flowed down to my lips.

"You're killing me, Cali," he muttered.

"You want me to leave?" I asked.

As if he couldn't control himself anymore, his lips were pressed firmly against mine, his tongue in my mouth as he ran his hand from my face down to my shoulder, rolled me over, and got on top of me. He took his lips off mine for just a minute, pushed my hair out of my face, and said: "Absolutely not," before his lips were back on mine.

The kiss started slow and sensual but progressed into more within seconds. His hands ran down my body as he lifted my shirt above my head. I clutched his hair between my fingers, grasping at his t-shirt, trying to pull it off him. He lifted himself above me on his knees, raised his shirt above his head, and threw it to the floor. Taking in his hard, defined body, the flames of his tattoo inked into his bicep seemed to glisten in the moonlight peering through the shades.

Suddenly, as we became more intimate, the calmness he had implanted in me started rapidly changing. I was somehow becoming angered, and I was getting visuals before my eyes of multiple times Josh and I have had sex as if this wasn't our first time. Some were filled with lust, some anger, some just horrid. My emotions were swiftly changing. My body was uncontrollably reacting to his touch as if I had some sort of bad drug reaction. Then, out of nowhere, I swung a closed fist and punched him in the face. He stopped for a second, confused and out of breath, and he held his lip, blood covering his hand as I pleaded with him not to stop. Perplexed, he continued as I violently threw another punch in his direction, and he caught my arm in midair.

"Should I stop?" he asked, panting.

"No!" I insisted.

Afterward, I calmed down again as he pulled me into his chest, still out of breath and with a look of shock on his face.

I ran my hand softly down his chest until I rested it on his heart. I felt a heavy pain run through me. "What did you see?" I asked.

"I suspect the same thing you did," he said. I tenderly stroked his heart, absorbing his anguish as if my hand was a sponge, taking it all into me. His entire body crumbled beneath me as he let out a soft moan.

"Don't stop," he whispered.

"I'm a healer, remember?"

"Yes, I remember," he said.

"Talk to me, Josh," I begged. "This clearly wasn't the first time we've been together."

"No, I guess it wasn't."

"Why are you hurting? What happens to us?" I asked.

He shook his head. "I don't know. We obviously have a

past and a future. What's in that future? I really don't know. All I know is where I am right now, and that is here, in my bed with you, and I am loving being here in this instant. So can we just be in this moment, right now, tonight?"

I ran my thumb along the dried blood on the bottom of his lip and kissed him. "Yes, we can."

I watched him as he slept, his arm clutching his pillow. He wasn't kidding; he did sleep like a baby. I delicately ran the back of my hand over his cheek, careful not to wake him. He awoke something in me no man ever had before. I craved his touch and yearned for his embrace; something in his kiss drove me absolutely insane. Wanting more of him yet pushing back simultaneously, a whirlwind of emotions entangled within me. I was intrigued and terrified at the same time. I knew I couldn't love anyone, so what was the sense of getting so close to someone when it would ultimately come to a bitter end? It wouldn't be fair to him. He didn't carry the same burden I did. He didn't have to live with the weight of the constant curse. So why would I get close to someone that I could potentially hurt so bad? I contemplated going home for a second, but then the visual of the four on the plate came rushing back into my head.

I crept out of his bed, careful not to make a sound, as I grabbed his t-shirt off the floor and pulled it over my head. I quietly made my way into his guest room and went to sleep.

CHAPTER 12

$\mathcal{I}$ woke up the next morning to the aroma of eggs and fresh coffee filling the air. Rubbing my eyes, I climbed out of bed and headed into the kitchen, where Josh was in front of the stove cooking. Sensing my presence, he turned around to look at me.

"I'm never washing that shirt again," he commented, smiling. I smirked slightly and sat on one of the stools as he filled two plates with eggs. He put one down in front of me and sat down across from me. I stared down at the food in front of me as he took a bite.

"This is not necessary," I said, pushing the plate away from me.

He stopped chewing and looked from the dish back to me, confused. "You're not hungry?" he asked.

"We don't need to have breakfast because we had sex," I said frankly.

"Now you have something against breakfast? We've had breakfast like a zillion times. We can't have breakfast because we had sex?"

"Why do guys feel the need to exaggerate with the word a 'zillion'? You know how much a 'zillion' would have to be?"

He took a sip of his coffee and returned to his food, ignoring the statement.

"You want coffee or tea or something?" he asked.

"No, thanks," I answered.

"Was my bed uncomfortable?" he asked.

"No, why?"

"Just curious why you slept in the guestroom," he asked.

"I mean, I don't know. What were we going to do? Cuddle?"

He put his fork down and rested his elbows on the table. "I don't know, sleep?" I stayed quiet. I didn't really know what to say to him. There was an awkward silence before he got up and started clearing off the table. "Come on," he said as he finished cleaning up. "Let's go figure out what this number four means."

I got up and followed him into the living room as I sat on the couch, and he sat on the loveseat and buried his head in his phone. "I found something interesting this morning that I want to show you. Have you ever heard of something called numerology?"

I shook my head as I peered over to look at his phone screen. "No, what's that?"

"It's the belief that numbers have a mystical relationship to one or more coinciding events. That numbers actually play a significant role in everything from birthdays to random numbers we see, and often relate to paranormal, astrological, and similar divine beliefs," he explained.

"So, numbers are actually signs from the universe?" I asked.

"Yes, sort of. But more than that. Let's talk about the astrological aspect for a minute. So, my birthday is March twenty-second, and yours is January second, making me an Aries and you a Capricorn, right?"

"Right," I conceded.

"Not according to numerology. It is believed that our birthday sets a life path number at birth, predetermining our destiny. We are both in this life with a mission, or a life path, based on our birthday."

"So, our birthday is actually a life path number?" I asked, getting confused.

"No, our birthday *calculates* to our life path number. You add up all the digits in your birthday until you get down to a single digit. That single digit is your life path number. Unless you're an eleven, twenty-two, or thirty-three, all three of those numbers are master numbers."

He got up from the loveseat and sat next to me on the couch, pulling up the calculator on his phone and displaying the screen for me. "Check this out. My birthday is $3+2+2+1+9+8+4$, which equals twenty-nine. Then $2+9$ equals eleven," he held the phone up, displaying the eleven. "$1+1$ is two, but I'm an eleven, which is a master number, so it doesn't need to be broken down to a single digit."

"What am I?" I asked, getting excited with his discovery. He cleared his calculator and started again.

"$1+2+1+9+9+0$ equals twenty-two." He held up the phone to show me.

"I am a master number also? And we happen to be eleven and twenty-two, like Twin Flames," I said in revelation.

He nodded. "Yes, but $2+2$ is also four." The vision of the plate came back to me.

"No way, I bet everyone comes out to some master number. This is too coincidental," I said, disbelieving.

"According to this, there are no coincidences. I've calculated everyone I know, and they don't."

"What does this all mean? Like what does a master number symbolize?" I asked.

"Depends on the number. For instance, here's mine," he opened an article he had saved on his phone and started reading out loud. "Eleven or two symbolize the power of illumination and free will. You are inspired by relationships and experiences and have the power of intuition. You have greater potential to learn than other numbers and the determination to steer away from negativity, hatred, war, and destruction. At times, you may not grasp where your power is coming from and become frustrated, but once you accept the ability, you will become a leader. Eleven is the number of inspiration and fame."

"Looks like you may go viral after all," I laughed. He smiled and then pulled up another article.

"Now, a twenty-two. The most balanced number of four, the most powerful number on the chart. You came into this lifetime for a specific purpose. You were born with the gift of 'the knowing.' You are a master achiever, diplomat, and organizer. Very few twenty-twos or fours reach their full potential; your greatest weakness is self-doubt. You were brought into this lifetime to accomplish a specific goal, and once you recognize what that is, it will benefit many on a high level."

I bit the side of my lip. "This is sounding more and more like the end of the world," I said nervously.

He cupped his face in his hand. "I don't know about that, but look at this." He pulled the calculator back up on his phone. "542 days. 5+4+2 equals eleven."

I leaned back against the couch. "Okay, so everything is leading back to eleven or twenty-two. Got it, Twin Flames. We're here together, figured that part out. Now what? Everything is pointing to this greater purpose, the 'reason.' We haven't figured out what that is," I said, frustrated.

He put his hand on my knee. "Relax, we will. Look how

far we've already come, and it's only been six months." I put my hand over his as he looked at me with genuine care. Then, my gaze shifted from his eyes to his bruised lip. I ran my thumb across his lip.

"Your lip is pretty messed up," I said.

"I got punched in the face last night," he said. I inched closer to him and sat on his lap, facing him, my legs around him. I placed my hands on his face, leaned in, and tenderly kissed him. He let out a small sigh, ran his hands down my shoulders to my arms, and pushed me back slightly, his eyes trailing down my body, then meeting my glare again.

"Just so we're on the same page, is sex still on the table?" he asked.

I ran my hand down his chest and leaned into his ear. "I don't care if sex is on the table, the floor, the couch, or the bed."

His smile widened. "There's my feisty fairy!" he said, lifting me and carrying me towards the bedroom. "No sleep or food. Got it. Worth the sacrifice!"

"You may want to restrain me," I commented. Josh carried me into his bedroom and dropped me on his bed.

"Not a bad idea. Wait here; let me go see if I have a rope or something."

Afterward, we lay exhausted as I started tracing his tattoo with my finger. "Why the flames? Is it because you're an Aries?" I asked. He cleared his throat uncomfortably.

"I've always had a fascination with fire," he simply answered. I studied his facial expression. There was clearly more to that statement than he was letting on.

"Fascination with fire?" I repeated. He took a deep breath and put his hand over mine.

"You really want to know?" he asked.

"Of course," I answered. I threw his t-shirt back over my head and followed him as he led me into the living room. He sat on the loveseat and patted the spot next to him, indicating I should sit. I sat beside him, eagerly watching him, excited to hear what would come out of his mouth. He nudged his head towards the fireplace, implying I should look at it. I looked from him to the fireplace as I watched the flames dance in the air.

"I can control fire," he said. I let out a laugh.

"Yeah, okay."

He looked at me, then to the fireplace. He held his hand up in the air, moving his fingers as if he were grabbing the flames, then twisted his hand and pulled it up. I watched in disbelief as the fire seemed to follow his direction, rising as his hand did.

"No way, that's a trick. You have a controller or something," I said, my eyes not moving from the fire. He lifted his other hand, placed them together, and then pulled them apart as I watched the blaze split in two. One veering left and the other to the right. I shook my head and chuckled. "Still not buying it." He put his hands on his lap, leaned over, and kissed me lightly.

"You think I would lie to you?" he asked.

"No, but you're playing around. That can't be real. You didn't do that."

"So, you think something can trace 542 in a fog, that you can believe. Yet, you can't imagine I can control fire?" he asked. I stayed silent, just glaring at him as the reflection of the flames seemed to dance in his eyes.

"Show me," I said softly, almost hypnotized by his stare.

He turned back to face the fire, his hands motioning in the air again. The sparks followed his fingers as he appeared to break a piece off, and above it, form the letter C. Bringing his finger back down, he repeated the same motion, now drawing an A with the fire. He continued until the name CALI was above the fire, appearing to be dancing, glowing orange and yellow. I stood motionless, watching as my name flashed before my eyes, New York City in the shadows. He looked at me for a reaction, as I remained motionless, mesmerized by the blaze. He waved his hand as if wiping a whiteboard clean, and the fire burst into tiny droplets of flames, dropping back into the pit.

We both sat silently as I mentally tried to wrap my head around what had just transpired. Finally, I looked over at him.

"Say something," I said.

He let out a breath and turned his entire body to face me as he placed his hand on my knee. His face getting very serious now, he leaned in. "This after sex food ban? Is that just breakfast? Are you going to want to eat dinner, or are you still fasting?"

CHAPTER 13

*A*s Josh ordered us food from an Italian restaurant nearby, I went to take a shower. His bathroom was elegant, all marble, with a huge glass shower and a hot tub in the middle of the room. It had a nostalgic feeling to it, like I had been in that shower before. Standing under the water, humming to myself, it occurred to me suddenly what it reminded me of. His bathroom was almost identical to the one in San Diego, the night everything started, the night that changed my world upside down. I held on to the wall for support as my mind brought me right back to that hotel room.

It happened when I was getting out of the shower. I remembered it vividly. It was as if I were back in that space.

I heard a squeaking noise suddenly. I couldn't figure out where it was coming from by scanning the room. I continued getting dressed and heard the noise again, louder this time. I started walking around the bathroom. Nothing. Again.

A small horizontal straight line was drawn on the mirror, and I was positive it wasn't there before. Almost as if it were handwritten by someone in the fog. I had stared at the mirror motionless in shock for a second as I saw an image of myself, my own blonde hair and green eyes staring back at me. Then the squeaking noise happened again, only this time I watched as a vertical line was drawn under the first line. I stood paralyzed as goosebumps emerged on my arms and the hairs on my arm stood straight as a circular motion came next. Five. The number five was sketched in the fog on the mirror.

This can't be happening. Cali, you're losing your mind, was all I was thinking, but the squeaking noise wasn't subsiding. It was getting louder. I dropped to the floor and sat against the bathtub, watching as the tracing continued. The next number formed was a four.

A chill wracked my body. I wanted to run, but couldn't move. It was like one of those bad dreams where you are being chased, but your legs will not take you where you need to go. It didn't matter how fast you ran; you went nowhere. That is precisely how I was, completely unable to move. I couldn't take my eyes off the mirror. The screeching seemed to get shriller and more distinct with every number. Two.

I pulled my knees into my chest and closed my eyes tightly. I covered my face with my hands and started rocking back and forth. "You're high. This isn't happening. You're high. This isn't happening," I kept chanting, over and over to myself. I finally stopped speaking but didn't open my eyes immediately. I waited to hear if the noise of the tracing had stopped. I stayed quiet to listen for a few moments. Silence. Okay, maybe it was just a hallucination, a bad batch, I had rationalized. I am going to look up, and nothing will be there, I really thought.

Slowly, I spread my fingers and peered through them towards the mirror. My eyes widened in disbelief. I lifted my head and stared at the mirror. Clear as day, written in the fog, was the message: 542 Days.

Now here I was, in Josh's shower in the middle of July. Seven months after the incident occurred, almost 220 days into the 542. My mood quickly changed from relaxed and calm to anxious and paranoid. I shut the faucet off and climbed out of the shower. I pulled a clean t-shirt Josh had given me over my head and opened the toothbrush he had left. He must have done quite a bit of "entertaining," considering he had an entire box of extra toothbrushes. As I brushed my teeth, I couldn't help but wonder if he was seeing someone or had a girl in his life. He never mentioned being romantically involved with anyone, but he was gorgeous, and apparently rich. It was hard to imagine him *not* having a girl. I looked at myself in the mirror as I ran a comb through my tangled, wet hair. I remembered the day I met him when he told me how gorgeous I was. Looking at my reflection, I realized he must be used to dating models considering his line of work. Did he really think I was that pretty?

When I made my way to the kitchen, he was sitting at the table already with the food on plates, patiently waiting for me to eat. I sat across from him, examining my grilled chicken Caesar salad as I poked it with my fork. "How long have you been able to do that for?" I asked as if we had just left off a conversation.

He looked up at me in between bites of his chicken parmigiana sandwich. "Do what?" he asked.

"The fire," I elaborated.

"Oh, since I was a kid. I've never shown that to anyone before."

"Were you scared? I mean, it can be dangerous. What if you get mad or something and accidentally burn down a house?" I asked.

He laughed and shook his head. "I can't create fire, Cali. I can just control it, make it move. It's not like I can shoot it out of my hands or anything."

Realizing how foolish that sounded, I laughed. Of course

he couldn't make fire. That wasn't possible, or was it? Everything was happening so fast that I found myself wondering if this was all really occurring or if I was losing my mind. I was only two years younger than my mother was when she lost it. Was any of this really taking place, or was it a figment of my imagination? I continued eating my salad in silence.

"Did I freak you out?" he asked, a hint of regret in his voice. I could tell he was second-guessing himself for showing me. I stood up, wiped my plate off, put it in the sink, and then went over to his.

"Are you done with this?" I asked. He nodded, still looking at me with remorse in his eyes. I put his plate in the sink and went back over to him, pushing his legs apart and standing between them as I wrapped my arms around his shoulders. He ran his hands down my waist until they rested on my lower back.

"There is nothing you could ever tell me that will freak me out," I said, assuring him, running my hand down his chest. He let out a small breath of relief as he smiled, and his lips met mine. He pulled me closer, and I felt his scruff against my face.

After another incredible session, he watched me as I picked the t-shirt up from the floor, put it back on, and rubbed my arms for warmth. "There are extra comforters in the guest room closet if the air conditioning is too high," he said.

I walked back over to the bed and climbed in as he held the blanket up for me, and I snuggled myself into his chest. "For your information, I was planning on using you for warmth," I said.

He pulled me in closer to him and wrapped his arms around me. "Oh, good, because for your information, I was planning on eating breakfast in the bathroom tomorrow," he said.

He rolled over to face me, his hands slowly moved up the back of my shirt, and he tugged me closer to him.

"Are you cuddling with me?" I asked.

"Nooo," he said in an exaggerated tone. "I was simply planning on feeling you up all night." He buried his head in my shoulder as his hands wandered up and down my back, and I found myself unconsciously tracing his tattoo with my finger once again. Moving his hand down to my leg, he pulled it up around him and drew me in closer as his lips merged back into mine. He did this thing with his tongue, where he somehow rolled it in my mouth. I don't know how he did it, but when he did, I lost all control of my senses. He had me hypnotized as I pulled my lips off him and buried my face in his chest.

"Josh, when was the last time you had sex with a woman?" I blurted out.

"Last night," he mumbled, burying his face back in my shoulder. I pushed him a little.

"Not with me, a different woman," I said. He lifted his head and looked directly into my eyes.

"Oh, other than you!" he said sarcastically. "If I answer the question, can we drop it and move on?"

"Depends on your answer."

He rolled his eyes. "The night before Haven. I knew I was going into rehab. Got it all out of my system," he said and dug his head back into me.

"You've been out for three months," I said. He let out a sigh.

"Can we not do this?" he asked pleadingly.

"Why not?" I asked. He picked his head back up and looked at me again.

"Look, I know what you're thinking...."

"Are you reading my mind?" I interrupted.

"No, I don't need to read your mind to know what's going through it. You think I haven't had sex with another woman because I am falling in love with you. And you're nervous that you are leading me on because you don't have the capabilities of loving me back," he said. He wasn't kidding. He was spot on. I raised my eyebrows, signaling that he was correct in his assumption. "Look," he continued. "I haven't slept with another woman because I haven't met another woman that I had the desire to sleep with. Plain and simple. Is it because of you? - maybe, maybe not; I really don't know. I do know that I am fully aware of your issue, and I am a grown-ass man and can make my own decisions as to who I do or don't sleep with."

I ran my hand down his face. This guy always knew the right thing to say. "Look at that. The little icicles around your heart must be melting a bit if you care so much about hurting me," he laughed.

"I do care about you, Josh. You're my best friend."

He put his hand on his chest as he leaned back, squinted his eyes, and let out a gasp. "Best friend? Damn, that's worse than the friend zone. Next, we'll be polishing each other's toenails and joining book clubs together."

"I don't read," I said, laughing.

He wiped his forehead, pretending to be wiping sweat. "Thank God!"

CHAPTER 14

$\mathcal{I}$ felt a breeze across my face as I inhaled the scent of freshly picked daisies. I followed the scent to the master bedroom. It was all solid oak furniture, a white canopy around the king-size bed in the middle of the room, brass headboards, and a large mirror over the dresser that matched perfectly. In the right corner of the room was an altar of some sort, where a mess was laid out. My heart fell to the pit of my stomach as a dark energy came towards me, illuminating the altar. As I slowly approached it, the heaviness in my heart became stronger, and my senses warned me of danger. I ran my hand along the wood of the table, spilled out resins all over and old apothecary bottles, each holding different liquids.

To the left of me, I felt his presence as I turned towards him in fear. The same man who had been hovering over me, beckoning me to stand. "What have you done?" I asked, afraid to hear the answer. He turned around to look at me, his evil eyes seething into mine, as he walked towards me. I flinched a little as he held his hand out and touched my cheek, his massive body towering above me.

"What do you mean, my love?" he asked.

My eyes shifted to the altar, then back to him. He nodded in recognition as if he were proud of himself. "Just a little spell," he answered, grinning.

"What type of spell?" I asked as I backed away from the table.

"Darling," he began, inching closer to me, "You've never questioned my magick before. Why the sudden interest?"

My heart raced. He had done something terrible; I knew that much; I could feel it in my body.

"Lucas, what have you done?" I asked again, my voice cracking a little.

"Nothing more than secure the promise you've already made to me," he said. "Do you remember that, Claudia? The night we married? The oath you gave me, your word? To be mine, and only mine, always?"

My insides were screaming. He couldn't be serious. His hand wandered down my waist as he pulled me towards him. "Do you recall that, my beloved?" he asked me, his lips so close to my ear I felt his huff on me. His deep voice sent shivers down my entire body.

"Surely, you're attempting to be humorous?" I asked.

He shook his head. "No, no, I am quite serious. Now you have no choice but to be with me and only me. You couldn't love another man if you tried," he chuckled. "But, that shouldn't affect you since you've already made that vow to me. You did say until death do us part, did you not?"

His lips touched mine, making me wince. He ran his thumb across my lip as his eyes followed. I nodded my head in agreement. He smiled. "I was merely ensuring it because Claudia, you will be mine—always until death does us part. In this lifetime and every lifetime. I will find you every single time."

I bolted out of bed, dripping in perspiration as my body shook in fear. "Holy shit!" I screamed out. Josh immediately got up and threw his arms around my waist, pulling me into him.

"What happened?"

"That is one scary dude! I need drugs, Josh. I need something. A drink, a Xanax, please, anything," I felt my eyes fill with tears. He pulled me into him as he rubbed my back gently.

"You don't need drugs, Cali. Relax, calm down," he said, as his hands heated my veins and tried his hardest to sedate me.

"There was a guy," I said frantically. "The same one from the other memory. He put a spell on me, Josh. A love spell."

He pulled back with a look of shock on his face. "Well, that was stupid. That's like magick 101. The first thing we read, love spells backfire," he said.

"He said he's coming for me, in every lifetime. Josh, maybe he's the one who wrote 542," I felt the tear trickle down my face as fear consumed me. He reached out and wiped the tear from my face.

"What else do you remember?" he asked.

"Lucas, his name is Lucas, and he is big! He was my husband."

"Your husband?" he exclaimed. "So, wait, there's a paranormal kid and a crazy ex-husband who is a witch?"

"I don't know. Can guys be witches?" I asked.

"That's pretty sexist. I can control fire, and I'm a guy," he said, insulted. "What kind of powers does he have? How big is big? I'm a pretty big dude. Is he bigger? Do I need a gun?"

"I don't know what he can do. All I know is that he is terrifying. And he said he was coming. Oh, and he called me Claudia."

He took out his phone and started documenting everything I was saying.

"Maybe it's a good thing that it's a spell and not a curse. We can break a spell, no?" he asked, trying to reassure me.

"I don't know. I guess we have to look into this," I answered. "We really need witch friends."

He laid back down in bed and yanked me to him, pulling me into his embrace. "Go to sleep. It's late. We'll figure this out. I am here with you, he's going to have to come at me, and I can handle myself," he said confidently.

The next morning, I woke up in his arms, still rattled from the dream before. This guy, my old husband, apparently, was still taking up space in my head. I couldn't shake the feeling of disgust when he touched me.

"I can't stop thinking about him," I said quietly to Josh. He ran his hand down my back.

"That's what every guy wants to hear when he wakes up next to a beautiful woman, that you can't stop picturing another man," he said.

"I'm serious; you don't understand the hatred I felt for him. Now I need to know what possessed me to marry him in the first place. I wish there were a way I could put myself in some sort of state so I can go back."

He sat up, rubbed his eyes, and then turned his body to face me. "Are you suggesting time travel?" he asked, trying to hold back laughter.

"No," I said, realizing how ridiculous that sounded. "The way we were able to astral project and ended up in a different plane…."

"Which we still haven't figured out *how* we did that," he interjected. He got up from the bed, retrieved a clean t-shirt from the dresser, and pulled it over his head. He ran his fingers through his hair, attempting to fix it.

"Well, I'm just saying. There must be a way to put our

minds into a different state, almost like...." I sat up, trying to think of the correct word. "Recollection. How can we make our minds regain lost memories?"

"You've done that. I have not. You're the twenty-two and four; you are the one with the gift of the 'knowing,'" he said.

"And your third eye is open. You said it yourself when you taught me Reiki. So, you're powerful enough to do it. We both are, collectively, at least. There has to be someone who can help us," I said.

"That's different. That's a premonition, not recovering lost memories. You're seeing things that already happened; I know when something is going to happen. Plus, you're talking about finding recollections from a completely different lifetime. Who would help us with that? How would we even ask that question to someone without sounding completely insane?" he argued, pulling his joggers up to his waist. I eyed him up and down, suddenly realizing he was getting dressed.

"Why are you getting dressed? Where are you going?" I asked. He came over to the bed and sat down next to me, pushing my hair out of my face.

"I'm afraid to say it," he said, sighing heavily.

I bolted up and looked at him. "What? Tell me," I insisted, putting my hand on his thigh. "I told you last night; you can tell me anything." He put his hand over mine and squeezed it a little.

"You know when something is going really well, and you know the next thing you say can potentially mess everything up?" he asked. I took a deep breath and closed my eyes. Josh was the furthest thing from shy. If he was afraid to say something, it was going to be bad. Really bad. My heart accelerated as I opened my eyes to look at him.

"Just say it, rip it off like a band-aid." He opened his mouth, but then bunched his lips together. "What? Just say it!" I begged, now desperate to hear what would come out of his mouth.

He let out a deep breath. "I'm starving. Do you want to go eat breakfast?" I let out a sigh of relief and playfully slapped his arm.

After breakfast, he came with me back to my place. I was nervous walking in as the plate with the water still sat on the counter. He walked over and examined it. He dipped his middle finger slightly in the water and rubbed it against his thumb.

"It's definitely water. You watched this number form?" he asked. I nodded. He took a picture of the plate and put it in the sink, then walked around the apartment, carefully looking in every corner as I followed behind him. "I feel like I need a proton pack," he said jokingly.

"What's that?" I asked. He paused for a minute and looked at me, shaking his head in disbelief.

"*Ghostbusters*? Come on. You're an actress. How do you not watch movies?"

Grasping he was kidding, I let out a laugh. "Silly me to take you seriously for a minute."

He opened the door to my balcony and stepped outside. He looked over at the buildings in a daze as he wrapped his arms around his chest. I entwined my arm in his, my gaze following his to the skyscrapers. He looked down at me for a second, then his attention went straight back to the scene.

"Crazy, isn't it? We have like the same view," he commented. "How long have you lived here?"

I thought about it for a minute. "About five years," I answered.

"For five years, we have literally been a few blocks away from each other, and yet we meet on a deserted island in a rehab facility," he said.

"Trust me, it's better we met there," I said, pulling him back into the apartment.

"Why do you say that?" he asked.

"Me and you, in our heyday? We would have got into so much trouble together," I laughed, sitting on the couch as he walked over to my display case to look at the awards. I pointed at the stand. "That used to be a fully stocked bar."

"Impressive," he said, pointing at the trophies, as he walked over and sat next to me. "And yes, we would have gotten into a ton of trouble together."

I ran my finger along his bottom lip. "Your lip is completely healed," I observed. He leaned over and kissed me.

CHAPTER 15

For the next two weeks, Josh and I returned to our normal routines. Well, as normal as it could be, considering we were basically new people—sober people. Josh had already had three months to get acclimated to his new lifestyle; now, it was my turn. Upon waking, I would meditate every morning, do an hour's workout, then go to work. I was nervous I would fall back into my old habits while filming a movie, but instead, it proved to be a good distraction. It was a relatively easy gig, with no stunts, no special effects, just a twelve-hour day of shooting. Josh and I spent the weekends with each other at my place or his. The sex was incredible, although I still had to be restrained because I had the issue of not being able to control my anger. It was some kind of weird phenomenon neither of us could figure out, but it only occurred during intercourse. It wasn't his lips or tongue that did it. It was specifically during the act, the second we started, a mixture of rage and passion erupted within me that I had no control over. I was incredibly attracted to him, and there was no denying that. Just his touch alone was able to get me aroused, sometimes even something as small as a look he gave me.

He came to watch me film one Friday after getting out of work, dressed in jeans, a light blue button-down shirt, and dress shoes. I almost didn't recognize him.

"You look good," I said flirtatiously. I approached him, eying him from head to toe.

"Casual Friday," he said, with a look of excitement on his face.

"Why do you look so thrilled? Never seen a movie being filmed?" I asked as I came up to him.

He shook his head. "No, I haven't, actually, but I have a surprise for you," he said, boasting.

"It isn't a juicer, is it?" I asked.

"No," he laughed and looked down at his watch. "But we need to hurry because they close at ten p.m."

We jumped into a cab and headed downtown. As we got out of the cab, we stood in front of a tiny shop. The storefront displayed an assortment of crystals in all different sizes. Some were exhibited like pieces of art; others were made into jewelry. A giant Buddha sat in the middle. One particular article caught my eye. It was clear crystal, with pointed pieces sticking out that illuminated a rainbow lighting around it. I walked up to the window to get a better look, pointing at it through the glass to show Josh. "Look how pretty that is. What is this place?"

"It's a metaphysical store," he answered. "I researched it; they have a bunch of stuff here that can help us."

He opened the door to hold it for me as I walked in, a bit apprehensive. The bell chimed as I walked through, and a soft, sweet, musky scent immediately hit me, suddenly putting me at ease. I had never smelled anything like it, almost like a rose, but not quite.

We strolled around the store, looking at all the items. The

aisles presented all different types of stones, some different shapes as small as a quarter, other pieces larger like you would see exhibited at a museum. A bookshelf against the wall in the back, holding various types of books about everything from dream definitions to spell books, others about Reiki and Pranic Healing.

Going back to the aisles to look at the stones, I touched a piece that grabbed my attention. I held it in my hand, feeling the round edges. Polished and shiny, it looked like a dark green, but studying it in-depth, depending on the position I held it in, it shone in different pigments of color. I felt a vibration run through my arm, as if I had a rubber band wrapped around my wrist that was cutting off my blood circulation.

"That's called a labradorite," an older female voice said behind me. Josh and I both turned around to look at her. She was a short older woman, with vibrant red hair and warm brown eyes, with a bunch of beaded bracelets on her wrist, similar to the stones around the store. "That's one of the most powerful protection stones. It creates a shield of protection around your aura, to protect against negativity and bad intentions," she explained.

"It's beautiful," I commented.

"Yes, it's one of my favorites. You know, they say the crystals find you, not the other way around. If it called to you, then you need it," she said. I looked down at the stone in my hand, turning it around and examining it. Her eyes shifted from me to Josh, then back to me. "Have I met you before?" she asked.

I let out a laugh. "No," I said, shaking my head. "I'm an actress; you probably recognize me from movies."

She came in closer to me, glaring into my eyes. "No, that's not it. It's your aura. You radiate a very powerful presence."

She then looked up at Josh. "You do too. Not as much as your wife, but strong nonetheless."

He waved his pointer finger back and forth from me to him. "Oh, we're not married. We're friends," he explained. She let out a small grunt and chuckled.

"Ah, I see. So, what brings you both here today? What can I help you with?"

Josh's eyes scanned the store to assure no one could hear him, then leaned down to get closer to her. "We need to break a spell," he said uneasily. I studied her facial expression, waiting for it to change to doubtful, but instead, her eyes shimmered with curiosity.

"What kind of spell are you trying to break?"

Josh looked at me to answer as if he couldn't even say the words. I smiled nervously and looked back at the woman. "A love spell," I answered.

"You do know love spells backfire," she warned. We both nodded in acknowledgment.

"Yes, we didn't set it, but I believe it is on me, and we need to get it off," I specified.

She signaled for us to follow her to the books in the back. She shuffled through the shelf, retrieved a paperback, and handed it to me—*The Mystery of Magick.*

"This should help you, especially if you're both beginners. It tells the history of magick and Witchcraft and has spells in it as well. Some simple, some more complex. It has everything from binding to removal of hexes." Binding. Suddenly, my mind catapulted back to San Diego, to the massage therapist who told me all those things the day of the mirror occurrence. Her words came back to me suddenly: *"This morning, something told me to bring this in today,"* she said as she made her way over to her counter. *I heard her rifling through her pocketbook. When she returned, she held a long, skinny stick, covered in a white powdered resin. "It's sage. Do you mind if I burn it over you? It will help clear the negativity and unblock anything that may be attached to you. I believe you are bound."*

"What exactly does 'binding' mean?" I asked.

"It means someone put something on you to prevent you from doing magick," she answered.

"Would a love spell do that? If it backfired?" I asked.

"No, it would be a completely different spell." Great, so now I had two curses on me. Who could have possibly done this to me? A few months ago, I didn't know any of this stuff. Who would have? I stood in silence, looking at Josh for some reaction, but he was intensely listing to everything she was saying.

"What if someone did that to me? Is it a curse? Is there some way to remove it?" I asked.

She motioned with her hand to follow her and led us to the counter. A clear display sat under the register, exposing all different types of herbs, some in bundles and some loose, almost like small rocks, submerged in their own dust. It looked just like the resins laid out on Lucas' alter in the past life recollection. She reached under, pulled out a bundle, and placed it on the counter. "I would start with something like this. It's white sage. You can cleanse yourself and your space. You can also use it to cleanse your stones," she said, extending her neck to motion to the labradorite I was holding. That's exactly what the massage girl used on me. My attention shifted to an incense burning on the counter, a stream of smoke rising from it, which was the aroma I inhaled when walking in.

"What is that?" I asked, pointing at the lit stick.

"That is dragon's blood; it is used to intensify any spell. It's extremely powerful, and I wouldn't suggest it for a beginner, although something tells me that you aren't a beginner, even if you think you are."

"Recollection," Josh uttered as if the thought just came

into his mind. "Do you have something to help us recall lost memories, specifically from past lives?" She went around the counter and headed back towards the stones as we followed behind. She pointed to a box displaying a dark bluish-purple crystal.

"Lapis lazuli," she stated. "Also known as the Stone of Truth. That will help open your third eye. But I would cleanse your space before trying to do anything. Take one that calls to you."

"My third eye is open, and I can't see the past," Josh said.

"Just because you *haven't* doesn't mean you can't," she answered.

I reached in and took one out, holding it in my hand and feeling the same pulsation go up to my arm. "Why do I feel a vibration when holding any of these?" I asked.

"The earth forms crystals, and they all have different sensations. Also, they hold and store energy, which is why cleansing them before use is important and setting your intention to each stone."

"How do we cleanse them? Just put the sage smoke over it?" Josh asked.

She nodded. "That's one way. Some you can run under lukewarm water; the most efficient way would be to set them outside under a full moon. The moon's energy will cleanse and charge them." She kneeled and grabbed a white square plate made from a crystal similar to the one I had noticed in the window. "This is selenite. It does not require cleansing. You can set your crystals on them overnight, and the energy from the selenite will do the work."

"And setting intentions?" Josh asked.

"After cleansing the crystal, hold it in your hand and close your eyes. Imagine exactly what you want the stone to do for you, then affirm it out loud."

I reached out and took the slab from her. Then I brought

her to the window and pointed at the piece that had caught my eye. She identified it as an angel aura quartz, which she explained was used to purify and balance your chakras, aid in meditation, and connect with divine realms. Josh and I both looked at each other. We were on the same page-astral projection. I took the piece and walked over to the counter as Josh continued picking out things that called to him. I observed the woman wrap each stone in tissue paper and bag them. Josh returned with a handful of items he had chosen, and she proceeded to wrap his up as well.

After ringing us up, she handed him the bag. "Good luck, it was a pleasure meeting both of you, and I am sure I will see you again."

CHAPTER 16

*A*fter shopping, we returned to my apartment and sat in the living room, our new items on the coffee table. Josh immediately started researching how to use sage and cleanse the apartment properly.

He stood up. "Okay, open all the windows. There needs to be openings to let all the negativity out," he instructed. Walking around the apartment, I opened the windows in every room and cracked the door to the balcony. "So, you need to start at the doorway. You are going to put the smoke in every corner of the house and inside all the closets, cabinets, and anything with an opening. Begin clockwise around the entire house, then come back around counterclockwise."

I picked up the sage bundle and went to the kitchen drawer to find a lighter. Then, standing in front of the front door, I held the bundle in one hand and lighter in the other, reluctant to light it.

"What if I do this wrong? What if it backfires and brings negativity in?" I asked. He buried his head back in his phone.

"It doesn't say anything about backfiring. But we're just

cleansing the apartment, it's not really a *spell* per se, so I don't think it can theoretically 'backfire,'" he assured me.

I went to light the sage, then paused again.

"Should I say something?" I asked. He tilted his head and scrunched his eyebrows.

"Yeah, probably. And out loud, remember when we read about Witchcraft, it said that a spell needs to be spoken out loud."

"You just said it wasn't a spell!" I argued. He stalked closer to me, sensing my apprehension. He held his hand out.

"Give it to me, and I'll do it," he said. I went to hand him the bundle, then pulled it back.

"It's my apartment. Maybe I should do it," I reasoned. He took a step back.

"Okay, go," he said. Once again, I brought the lighter to the sage, then halted.

"I just thought of something. What if William is the one who did the four? He's not bad or negative. I felt protected around him. Am I going to force him to leave?" I asked, nervous that I would push him out. He stared at me for a second, thinking about the point I had just made. Then he shook his head.

"No, you are asking the negativity and ill wishes to leave, aka your psycho ex-husband. I don't think you'll push the kid away. Oh, one more thing. It says you should ask your spirit guides and protectors to be with you as you do it, and then give gratitude when you finish."

I took a deep breath and thought about what to say for a minute. "How's this: please clear this space of all negative energy and any ill wishes. Remove all evil entities and protect this house and everyone who enters it."

He nodded. "Yeah, that sounds good. Now light the damn thing already and cleanse this bitch," he said firmly.

Slowly, I held the lighter to the tip of the bundle and

watched as it lit on fire. "Will my spirit guides and protectors, be with me as I say this prayer," I said aloud as I watched the burning sage form a cloud of smoke. Then, deliberately walking around the room, I smudged the smoke in every corner of the house as he instructed; he followed behind me while I repeated the chant over and over. When I finished, I expressed my thanks, moved the sage around my body, inhaled the smoke, and then did the same to Josh.

"How do I put this out?" I asked, now standing in the middle of the room. "I don't feel like I should douse it under water."

"Like a cigarette, I guess," he answered. I walked out to my balcony and blotted it into the ashtray as I lit a cigarette and sat on the chair. Josh came outside and sat next to me, inhaling his vape. We sat in silence as we smoked, and I carefully placed the rest of the sage back into the paper bag it came in. Walking back into the apartment when we finished, I immediately felt a difference in the area. A crisp, clean fragrance of musky menthol engulfed me, and I felt like a weight was lifted off my shoulders. I sat down on the couch as Josh followed my lead.

"How do you feel?" I asked, turning my body around to face him.

"Lighter," he said. "If that makes sense." Suddenly, I started laughing uncontrollably. He looked at me, confused. "What are you laughing about?"

I put my hand over my mouth, trying to control my laughter. He threw his hands up in the air in annoyance. "What? What's so funny? Did the smoke make you high?" he pressed.

"I'm just thinking, this time last year, if someone had told me that in a year I'd be standing in my apartment with some random dude, putting smoke into corners of my house, I'd ask them what *they* were smoking and where I could get some," I said, still laughing.

"Some random dude?" he asked, sounding insulted, as he dramatically backed his body away from me.

"Okay, some hot random dude," I said, leaning my face toward him until my lips were right near his. "Better?"

His eyes shifted to my lips as he slowly merged his with mine. "A little, but maybe hot Twin Flame is more fitting." He pulled me onto his lap as I wrapped my arms around his shoulders.

"Fine, hot Twin Flame," I whispered as my tongue lightly traced his ear.

The next morning, I lay in bed restless while Josh slept peacefully. Looking at the clock, it was only 6:20 a.m., and I felt like something was calling me into the living room. Still in a daze, not yet fully awake, I stumbled into the living room to look at the items from the metaphysical store still on the table. I sat down on the couch without thinking as if they were calling to me and inspected every item we bought. Josh had picked some lovely stones also. I placed them all on the selenite slab. Holding the angel aura quartz in my hand, I remembered back to the lady explaining it helped with the divine realm. I took out my phone and started researching astral projection to see if anything we purchased could help us shift back into that state.

When Josh awoke an hour later, he found me sitting on the couch, creating a list.

"You look busy," he commented. I looked up from my phone.

"I know, I know, you're hungry," I guessed.

"Are you reading my mind?" he asked.

"No, I don't need to read your mind to know you're always hungry," I laughed. I held up my phone to show him. "I created a list of crystals and resins we can use to help us with astral projection. Why don't we go for breakfast and then go back to that store? I feel like we were kind of rushed last night. I want to take my time and look around," I suggested.

He agreed, and after we showered and dressed, we made our way downtown.

The bell chimed as we walked into the store, the similar pleasant aroma from the day before greeting us. The same woman greeted us no sooner than we made our way to the crystals.

She touched my arm, and I felt a flush of warmth run through my body. "I'm so glad you're back," she said. I turned my head to see behind me, to assure she was talking to me.

"Me?" I asked.

"Yes, you, come with me," she said as I followed her to the register. "What is your name?" she asked.

"Calista," I quietly said as I watched her shuffle through a handful of small papers. Curious about what was going on, Josh immediately came by my side.

"Calista, that's a beautiful name. My name is Barbara," she began. She held out the documents to show me. "Every night when I close up, I take all the receipts from the day and put them in an envelope. This morning, I realized I forgot one— yours. The two of you were the last customers of the night."

Josh and I looked at each other and then back at her, eager to hear where she was going with her story. She continued, "This morning, when I realized the discrepancy, I looked for the receipt. I found it over here," she pointed to the side of the register and held out an item to show me, "and this was on top of it. When I picked it up, there was a very protective, feminine energy around it. I think it's for you."

I reached out and took the item and observed it in the palm of my hand. It was a beautiful clear glassy light pink gemstone, polished and shaped into a heart, with a gold clasp around it to hang from a necklace.

"What is it?" I asked.

"That crystal is called morganite. It's associated with the heart chakra. It symbolizes compassion, inner strength, and unconditional love," she explained. My heart fell to the pit of my stomach as I held the heart in my hand. "Is there something in particular that made you come back today?"

"I have a list," I said uneasily, now remembering back to the morning, waking up so early and unable to go back to sleep as if the crystals in the living room were calling to me. "I woke up at 6:20 and couldn't go back to sleep."

"Does the number 620 mean anything to you?" she asked, resting her elbows on the counter and leaning towards me.

"June twentieth is my mother's birthday," I uttered right above a whisper. Josh reached over and took my hand in his in an attempt to keep me calm at the mention of my mother.

"Is your mother alive?" she asked, with a tone of compassion indicating she already knew the answer.

"No," I said. "And to answer your earlier question, my real name is Morgan. I changed it when I became an actress, but that's the name my mother gave me."

Barbara came around the counter, walked over to the jewelry display, and picked out a black rope necklace to hang the charm from. She reached out, took the heart from me, and placed it through the rope.

"Well, Morgan, now I know this was meant for you. Wear it well," she said as she gave me a sincere, warm smile and handed me back the necklace.

CHAPTER 17

*J*osh and I stayed in the store for a good hour, filling our baskets with everything I had put on my list and new goodies. We followed Barbara's original advice and bought anything that called out to us. He also purchased a slab of selenite for his house. We ended up back at his apartment after cleansing our new crystals and studying the best potential ritual we could perform to break the love spell. I wore the necklace that I was now convinced did, in fact, come from my mother, which made me realize all the more why we needed to break this hex. If she was showing up now after all this time, there had to be a reason behind it.

We found a simple protection spell, which seemed to be the most straightforward and least likely to backfire. The only problem was, it was most effective under a full moon. Unfortunately, the next full moon wasn't until six days, so we were in a holding period until we could do it. I was nervous about performing magick, but Josh seemed to think my nerves would settle down a bit when it came down to doing it.

"So, we are going to try to do this tonight, astral project?" Josh asked as he lay beside me in bed. His fingers lightly caressed up and down my back, leaving behind a trail of goosebumps.

"Yes, but I think we should sleep in separate rooms," I suggested. He agreed, and I went into the guest room with my new supplies. I placed the lapis lazuli stone on the nightstand next to me and carefully lit a piece of myrrh resin we had purchased to help aid in spiritual awareness. It didn't take long for me to fall under.

I expected to awake on our mountain like we had the last time, but that wasn't quite where I ended up. Instead, I was in a village-like area around the same time as my past life recollections. Definitely the seventeenth century, only I was in a place I didn't immediately recognize. It was an old cottage in desperate need of some repairs, small and quaint but unkempt. Not dirty, just as if the owner didn't have much money to keep it in good shape. The furniture was mixed-matched, and the paint on the walls was peeling. It didn't have a bad vibe to it; in fact, it was quite the opposite. I felt safe and protected in the small lodge. I slowly walked into the living room, where a shag rug lay across from a fireplace, blazing heavily, a beat-up brown armchair across from it, and a beige couch parallel.

"Josh?" I whispered as I headed towards the fireplace. It didn't appear as if anyone was around. I recalled the time when Josh had made a ball of fire and burnt down the tree on the mountain to prove he was in a different realm. I held my hand out towards the fire and motioned my hand to the left, watching the flame follow my lead. Then to the right. The fire was clearly following my direction, proving I was in another realm. I stared intensely at the blaze when I felt someone's hands come behind my waist and wrap around me. His touch immediately put me at ease, as my body instinctively followed, and I laid my head back on his shoulder as he kissed the back of my neck.

"Hasn't anyone taught you not to play with fire, my love?" he whispered. I slowly turned my body around to face him. He wasn't very tall, with an olive skin complexion, black hair, and brown eyes with a goatee. I didn't recognize him, but my body uncontrollably reacted to his touch. He stroked my face as he cupped my cheek in the palm of his hand, his thumb tracing my lower lip. I was drawn to him like a magnet; my lips immediately planted on his as I felt a wave of desire run through my entire body. His hands traveled down my back as I wrapped my arms around him, following his every move.

His lips moved from mine down my neck until he was untying my dress from behind. He pushed me slightly to the rug as we both made our way to the floor. His kiss felt so comfortable and familiar as he removed my dress, and I ran my hands eagerly through his hair. I let my hands slide down his chest until I unbuttoned his shirt and pushed it off him. He sat up on his knees, gazing down at me. He had to be in his late thirties, maybe even forty, but he looked well for his age and was in very good physical shape. My heart raced with anticipation as I watched him undo his belt. His tongue went from my neck to my lips as I passionately kissed him back. It never once occurred to me to ask him his name because, at that moment, I felt as if I had known him my entire life.

As he grew more passionate, I clutched his hair through my fingers as my breathing became heavy. Then, suddenly, I watched him start to fade before my eyes. I closed my eyes tightly, saying out loud, "no... no... no!" when unexpectedly, I felt like I was falling. I woke up gasping for air in Josh's guestroom. I put my hand on my chest and felt my heart racing. I sat there for a few minutes, collecting my thoughts before walking into the kitchen to get water. Josh was sitting at the table, drinking a cup of coffee. "What time is it?" I mumbled.

"After nine, you slept late," he said. I reached into his refrigerator, grabbed a bottle of water, and walked into the living room. I plopped down on the loveseat, staring at the fireplace. I couldn't get this new guy out of my head. He certainly wasn't Lucas, but he was also extremely familiar. Josh came in and sat on the armchair across from me, placing his coffee cup on the coffee table.

"So that was an epic fail," he said. I looked up at him, unsure if I should tell him what had happened. He looked at me in revelation, obviously recognizing something had transpired. "Did something happen with you?" he asked.

"Yes," I simply said. He stayed quiet, staring at me, waiting for me to tell him. "I was in an old cabin, somewhere around the same time as the other memories. There was a guy, but it wasn't Lucas."

His mouth hung open as he studied my facial expression. "What guy?" he asked.

"I don't know."

"What did he say?" he asked.

Still trying to process what had happened, I finally said,

"He didn't say anything, really. I was playing around with the flames in the fireplace to test if I was really projecting. He told me not to play with fire, then he called me his 'love,'" I answered.

"His love? How many ex-husbands do you have?" he asked, laughing until he realized the seriousness in my tone. His smile quickly changed to a look of concern. "What happened?"

I folded my hands in my lap and looked down as I rotated my thumbs around each other. I wouldn't look up at him. I just watched my thumbs wrestle each other. "We had sex."

He bolted up from the chair and stared at me with a look

of shock on his face. "Are you kidding me right now?" he asked loudly. I also stood as I made my way to approach him.

"You don't understand, Josh. I think it was you."

"Me? No, Cali, it definitely wasn't me. I would have remembered banging you out in any realm, same as I did last time."

"He was so comfortable, so familiar. I can't explain how I felt around him. Have you ever felt like a piece of you was missing, and then out of nowhere, someone comes along, and you suddenly feel complete? I had butterflies in my stomach, and my heart felt heavy around him, but in a good way…."

"That sounds a hell of a lot like love," he interrupted.

"Really? Is that what love feels like?" I asked.

"Yeah, that's what love feels like. So, you're telling me that you had sex with some dude last night in a different plane, and now you're somehow in love with him?" as his voice was getting louder, the flames in his fireplace rose. I watched the sparks, then looked back at him.

"Josh, calm down. You're making me nervous." He looked from me to the fireplace and then back at me.

"Relax, it's in glass, nothing is going to happen."

"Listen to me," I tried to rationalize with him. "I really think it was you. Like past life you, same as how I look different and have a different name…."

He rolled his eyes and started laughing, pacing back and forth in the living room like that was the stupidest thing he had ever heard.

"So, let me get this straight. You're telling me that some guy shows up, you sleep with him, somehow fall in love with him, yet it was *me*, and I don't remember it? Sorry Cali, that's a hard pill to swallow."

I walked toward him and extended my hand to touch his

arm, but he pulled it back. I looked down at the floor, he was clearly upset, and I couldn't even look at him like that.

"I'm going for a run," he said as he stormed out of the apartment, slamming the door behind him. I sat back down on the couch, not sure what to do. Josh and I had never fought before. We weren't even a couple; this was all new territory for me. I contemplated leaving, but instead, I went into his bedroom and laid in bed.

CHAPTER 18

I must have fallen asleep because I woke up to Josh's lips on my neck and his arms tightly around my waist, pulling me closer to him. "You didn't leave," he whispered into my ear, relief in his voice. I turned around to face him as he held on to me firmly.

"I wasn't sure if I should go," I said.

His lips immediately attached to mine. He let up for just a second to say, "If you're ever not sure if you should leave, the answer will always be 'stay,'" before he kissed me again. I ran my fingers through his hair as he buried his head in my chest.

"I'm so sorry," he muttered.

"You have a jealous side, huh?"

He shook his head, still submerged in my chest. "No, I really don't." I tugged his hair lightly, just enough to have him look up at me.

"Technically, we're not together, so I could have slept with someone yesterday. Would you be mad?" I asked. I watched his face lose color as his eyes shifted towards the ceiling.

"Did you?" he hesitantly asked. I put my hand over his heart; his body crumbled into me as I healed his pain.

"No, I didn't. I haven't slept with anyone since you," I said. "But seems to me like you do have a bit of a jealous streak."

He let out a breath. "I never did before; it's you. There's something about you, I can't explain it, but you make me crazy," he said. He rolled over to his back and pulled me into his chest.

"You were gone for a long time," I said.

"I went for a run; then I felt like I really needed a drink. So, instead, I went to a diner, ate a burger, and had a huge shake. Now I feel gross," he groaned, patting his stomach.

I ran my hand from his chest down to his stomach. He pulled back a little and turned his head to look at me. "Look, I was thinking a lot while I was running. I don't hang around you because I am trying to make you fall in love with me. I hang around you because you make me happy. Because no matter what type of day I'm having, when you walk into the room, you instantly brighten my mood just by smiling. I am fully aware that you aren't capable of falling in love with me…."

"We're going to break the spell," I interjected.

He nodded. "Yes, we are, but that doesn't guarantee you're going to fall in love with *me*, and that's okay. But I do hope you fall in love with someone because you deserve to feel that." He paused for a minute to gather his thoughts. "As far as this new guy, I know you believe it's me, but I really don't think it is. When I was at the diner, I researched a bit. Did you ever hear of a psychic attack?"

"No, what is that?" I asked.

"It's like a mental assault. When someone can get into your head, usually by a curse or a hex, whoever that is can manipulate your mind to believe you're seeing or feeling something you're not. I think it's Lucas. He is disguising himself as something you desire, want, or need. He's messing with your head."

"So, what do we do? If it's really him, I mean," I asked.

"We need to make sure we do the protection spell under the full moon on Thursday night. If this guy shows up again, then maybe you're right; maybe it is me. I hope you are right, but my gut tells me you're not."

"Do you believe you're my Twin Flame?" I asked.

"Yes, a hundred and ten percent," he quickly answered.

"So, then, we are destined to meet every lifetime. Isn't it weird we haven't seen you yet? Why wouldn't this guy be you?" I argued. He stood silent, processing what I said.

"There's something I haven't told you." He finally said. I backed away from him. He was holding back information this entire time. I felt myself start to get angry as my mood quickly started changing, and my hand uncontrollably turned into a fist. He reached out and stroked my cheek, his touch almost immediately calming me. He pushed my hair out of my face and looked directly into my eyes. "I must have been twenty-one or twenty-two when I first saw you on TV. That show you did when you were younger, you had to be like fifteen or sixteen."

"My Life?" I asked.

"Yes," he said, nodding. *"My Life.* It was on TV, and when I saw you, my heart stopped. I knew two things the minute I laid my eyes on you. You were the girl I was meant to be with, and you were going to break me."

I reached out to touch his chest. "Josh…"

He held his hand up to stop me from continuing my sentence. "The point is, when I saw you that day at Haven, your hand all banged up and bloody, I knew who you were, and I knew what I was walking into. I could have easily turned around that day and walked away, but I *couldn't.* I physically could not bring myself to walk away from you, even knowing what you may do to me."

"Even if that were the case then, it may not be now. We are going to break this curse. Maybe you're wrong. Maybe you have only seen one version of multiple outcomes that could happen," I justified.

He put his forehead against mine and pulled me into him. "I hope so," he said.

I felt gutted. My heart literally hurt for him. I wished so much, at that moment, that I had the ability to love him because he was the one who deserved it. I leaned into him and kissed him.

"For what it's worth, I am completely and utterly addicted to you," I whispered. He smiled as he kissed me back, his fingers digging deeper into my waist.

"It's worth a lot," he answered.

CHAPTER 19

The next five days felt like five years, waiting anxiously for the full moon. Josh met me at my apartment after I got off work. We stood on my balcony staring at the full moon glowing in its radiance, floating above the skyscrapers. I reached out and took his hand in mine as he gazed up at the brilliant white mass.

"How many times do you think we've stood under a full moon together?" I asked. He looked down at me and flashed a heartfelt smile.

"I have no idea, but I do know it's not our first and won't be our last," he answered.

"You ready to do this?" I asked nervously. He nodded, and we walked inside my living room. I carefully lit the sage bundle and cleansed the area around the couch, asking once again to clear it of any negativity and ill wishes. Then I placed black sand into the abalone shell I had purchased and carefully lit one piece of frankincense and one piece of myrrh. Resting it in the sand, I watched as the smoke formed a hefty cloud and leaned in to inhale the aroma. Josh let out a soft sigh as he exhaled, and I watched his body relax as he sat

way over to him as he guided me by the small of the back into the restaurant.

We followed the hostess as she led us into a back room with a private table against the wall. As classy as the atmosphere was, it was hard to pay attention to because I was too enthralled by what Josh looked like in a suit. The hostess pulled my chair out to let me sit down as I took my sunglasses off and slid my hood back.

"Let me take that for you," she said as I slipped out of my coat. "Sir, would you like to check your coat?"

"Sure," he said, taking his suit jacket off and handing it to her. As she walked away, a waitress approached us.

"Good evening Mr. Knight, Ms. Reed," she began, nodding her head from him to me. "Can I get you started with a drink? Perhaps the wine menu?"

I looked down at my silverware; I could picture what a glass of wine would feel like running through my veins for the first time after being sober for ten months. I felt his stare on me as he cleared his throat. "No, we'll just have a bottle of Pellegrino, please," he ordered.

"Absolutely, let me get that for you," she said as she handed each of us a menu. He placed his menu on the table and leaned across it to be heard.

"I'm sorry about before. Today was a little crazy at the office."

The waitress returned promptly and filled our glasses. "I'll leave you two some time to look over the menu. Would you like to put in an appetizer?"

He looked over at me. Under the dim lighting of the chandelier, his eyes seemed to sparkle an even brighter blue. He looked so amazing, and I was having a hard time focusing. I felt like I was with an entirely different man. I was losing myself in fantasy, imagining holding him by the navy and yellow tie he was wearing, picturing him on top of me.

Finally, he smiled slightly and gestured to me, "Whatever she wants."

The waitress looked at me for my order, and I snapped back to reality. I quickly glanced at the menu and just started rambling items out randomly. "Um, we'll do the gyoza, tuna tartare, the scallops...." I looked up at Josh as he was trying his hardest not to laugh at me, realizing I was nervous.

"Anything else?" the waitress asked. Josh leaned back on the couch, his arms wrapped around his chest as he squinted his eyes and bit his bottom lip. He knew I was getting turned on, and he was toying with me.

Are you in my head? I thought, already knowing he was reading my mind.

He grinned, his dimple becoming more prominent. *I sure am*, he answered silently.

"No, that's it for now," I politely said to the waitress.

"Excellent choices," she commented as she walked away.

I leaned over the table to get closer to him as I rested my chin in the palm of my hand. "What did I tell you about reading my mind?" I asked sternly. He let his hands fall to his lap and laughed at my annoyance.

"I'm sorry, but the look on your face, I just had to. You look rattled, Cali. Are you tense?"

I stood up and went to his side of the table, sliding next to him on the booth. I ran my hand from his knee up to his thigh. I tilted my head towards him so that he could hear me. "I'm loving the suit. Who are you wearing today?" I asked as if I were interviewing him on the red carpet. He sensually licked his lips and bowed back into me, so close I could feel his breath on me.

"Armani," he said, being coy. *That's not funny*, he warned telepathically, as he motioned with his eyes that the waitress was returning. Seeing I had switched seats, she placed the plates of food on the table and then took my setting from the previous seat and put it in front of me.

Who's laughing? I silently asked. *You seem to be turned on....*

"How can I not be? You know what you do to me," he whispered as he gently took my hand and tried to remove it. I held it steady while he looked at me with an expression mixed with arousal and concern.

Don't mess with me, he silently said.

I sucked in my bottom lip and grinned as I rubbed his leg under the table.

Do you have any idea what I am going to do to you later? He asked.

Whatever it is, I hope the suit stays on, I teased. He straightened himself up and leaned towards the table.

If I knew you liked suits, I would have had them flown to Haven sooner, and we could have saved ourselves months of sexual tension, he answered.

The waitress started making her way back to us; as she came over, she realized our appetizers weren't touched. With my hand still on his thigh, I paused. She seemed clueless.

"Oh, I'm sorry; I will give you some more time," she said. As she turned to walk away, I continued what I was doing.

Once I realized he couldn't take my teasing anymore, I grabbed a scallop with my fork and placed it in my mouth. Tasting the vinaigrette, the light, wet texture touched my tongue as I chewed slowly and looked at him. He stared at me as I swallowed my food and pointed to the plate.

"This is delicious. You need to try it," I said casually.

CHAPTER 20

"*W*hat is this?" I asked later as I sat up in Josh's bed, holding a book he had given me in my hand. The title read *Bounded by the Bond*, a plain black cover with white lettering. I quickly flipped the pages; it was a relatively long book, over 400 pages. I opened to the front page. Embedded in the dedication, it said, *In loving memory of Jayden.* "Didn't we go over this? I don't read. This is what you lured me here for? To give me a book?"

He sat down on the bed next to me and planted a kiss on my lips. "No, I lured you here for the amazing sex we just had. But yes, this is what I told you I got for you."

I looked down at the book again, a memory flurrying back to me. My heart fell into my stomach when I could picture myself and my sister in the shelter after getting kicked out of another home. The husband had flipped out when he caught my sister with this exact book. They were a very religious family, and this book spoke about Witchcraft. He had insisted she worshiped the devil, and I remembered her fascination with this book as clear as day. I dropped it on the mattress, not even wanting to touch it.

"What's wrong?" he asked.

"This book. Where did you find this?" I asked.

"I went into a metaphysical store near my job. The woman working there suggested it to me. Have you read it?"

"Okay, for the second time, refer back to the 'I don't read' statement," I said, my tone slightly harsh.

"You evidently have some weird feelings about this book, so how do you even know about it?" he asked.

"My sister," I began, then stopped myself. I could picture her crying that day, apologizing to me profusely for getting us kicked out of another home. "She was obsessed with this book; she would read it over and over. It was the only thing she made sure she had with her everywhere she went, that and a picture of our mother. It's about Witchcraft, no?"

"Yes, but not entirely. It's a story about two sisters, actually. Yes, they were witches. One of them had a son, who died, I guess, in his first life? I don't know. This is what the woman told me; I didn't read it. Anyway, the kid had a karmic debt attached to him, and in every lifetime he would come back, he would die at an early age. The sisters would try to save him, over and over every lifetime, but every time they did a spell in one lifetime, it affected another terribly. Kind of like that movie *The Butterfly Effect*."

"I've never seen it," I said.

"Seriously, *how* are you even an actress?"

"What's a karmic debt?" I asked.

"It's when you did something bad in a past life and didn't pay it back, like the law of karma, except it carries over until you pay it back. Anyway, every time they were reborn, they would learn about this later in life. They would do spells to remember earlier in their next lifetime, but nothing ever worked. They kept ending up with bigger problems when they were reborn. So, when the lady told me about it, I thought maybe you could read it, get some ideas on how to recollect lost memories."

"Is it based on a true story or fiction?" I asked.

"Is anything ever really 'fiction'?" he asked. "How do all these authors come up with this stuff? Don't you think they all have a bit of real-life experiences or occurrences?"

I stared at the book in silence, afraid to move it. He rolled his eyes in frustration and came over to take the book. As he held it from one side, I grabbed the other to stop him from getting it. Before long, we were playing tug of war with the book.

"I obviously suck at getting you stuff, so just give it back," he said, irritated.

"No, I want it. Really, I am going to read it," I said. He let go of the book, and I held it in my hands, examining it for the writer's name. "There's no author on here."

"Yeah, that is a big mystery. She said no one really knows who wrote the book, just that it's been around for centuries," he said. I stood up, put the novel in my pocketbook, then climbed back on his bed and kissed him.

"Thank you, I will read it," I said.

"I mean, I don't want to make you do homework or anything. No big deal if you don't, it just seemed like something maybe you would want to read, so I got it for you."

I smiled. "Seriously, that's very sweet of you. Thank you, I will read it."

I recognized the place immediately. I was in Lucas' house, my home, technically. It always had the same smell, the scent of freshly cut flowers. I found it surprising that I once enjoyed the scent of flowers because of my hatred for them in this life. I carefully walked through the hallway, trying not to make a sound. I didn't sense Lucas anywhere and hoped it would stay that way, so I could explore. I followed the aroma to the kitchen, where a glass vase of freshly picked roses was in the middle of the table. The kitchen was well put together, painted in a light shade of yellow, and the entire house suggested money, proving Lucas to be a very wealthy man. A porch door from the kitchen led to a large yard with a massive garden of flowers. The property was at least two acres long, with a barn and a stable across the field, presumably part of our property, along with a guest house. I nearly jumped out of my skin when I felt a presence behind me. I slowly turned around to see a teenage boy standing with dark black hair and grayish-blue eyes. He looked like a miniature Lucas; only he had an innocent vibe to him.

"You frightened me," I said, holding on to my chest as my heart raced. The sudden realization that I knew exactly who he was, our son. I stood staring at him, dumbfounded, while he continued speaking.

"My apologies. You called for me, Mother?"

"Yes," I said, now having no control over what was coming out of my mouth. "Elijah, I need you to do something for me. Do I have your word?" I asked.

"Of course, Mother," he said politely.

"If I were ever gone, I need you to promise me two things…."

"Gone? Gone where?" he interrupted me with concern in his voice.

"Anywhere, no particular place. You know our kind is frowned upon," I said. His eyes shifted to the ground as he nodded. "You must promise me that you will never let anyone know of your powers; can you assure me that?"

He nodded again. "Yes."

"Second, do I have your word you'll look after your

father?" His face dropped as his eyes shifted up to me, resentment in his stare. "He's not a bad man," I said.

"He's not a good one either," he argued.

"He's a good father," I reasoned.

"He's not a good husband," he said.

"Well, then, I suggest while you're giving gratitude, you include in your blessings that he wasn't made your husband." He let out a defeated breath.

"Yes, mother," he reluctantly answered. He plainly did not think highly of his father. However, he still consented and reassured me that he would obey both promises.

"Thank you, now go do something fun before you wake up a man and can no longer enjoy carefree things." He smiled at me with love and headed towards the yard.

Waking in Josh's room I watched him sleep peacefully, clutching his pillow. How I went into that state, I am unsure, but this time it felt different. I wasn't frazzled or scared, more curious than anything else. Closing my eyes, I tried my hardest to return to that house.

CHAPTER 21

The next morning I woke angry at myself that I didn't end up back at Lucas' house. "Shit!" I blurted out loud as I hit the mattress in frustration. Josh slowly started opening his eyes.

"Good morning to you too," he said sarcastically as he gradually sat up, rubbing his eyes. I got out of bed and started gathering my clothes to get dressed. I still had to get home, shower, and get dressed for work.

"It's not you," I said as I pulled up my jeans. "I had another recollection last night. I was back in Lucas' house."

He looked up at me in disbelief. "So, the spell didn't work?" he asked, disappointed.

"He wasn't there, but there was a kid. A boy. He was our son. Mine and Lucas' son," I said.

"Your son? Is it the same kid? William?" he asked.

I shook my head as I pulled my shirt over it. "No, he was younger, maybe thirteen or fourteen. And he looks nothing like William. Good-looking kid. He looks just like Lucas," I said.

Josh rolled his eyes. "Now Lucas is 'good-looking?'" he asked, using air quotations.

"I never said he wasn't. I stated he was terrifying; there's a big difference. You're not getting jealous again, are you?" I asked, half kidding.

He stood up and put his t-shirt on. "No, clearly you have remarkable taste in men," he said, signaling at himself. I stood on my tippy-toes and kissed him.

"Evidently," I said. "I have to go to work, though. I will tell you all about it later. You're going to come to my place after work?"

He nodded. "Yeah, I'll see you around nine," he said as I left to get to my apartment. I rushed to get myself ready and made it to the set with five minutes to spare. As I watched Natalie, my makeup artist, apply my makeup through the mirror's reflection, I couldn't help but imagine what her life was like as the last ten months of mine fluttered through my head. Natalie was slender, around my age, with a roses sleeve tattooed up her arm. She was very pretty, with blue eyes, and changed her hair color almost monthly. She happened to be rocking a purple style on that particular day.

"Do you have a boyfriend?" I asked, trying to distract from the visual of Elijah stuck in my mind. She paused, applying my mascara for a minute and tilted her head, most likely shocked I was showing any interest in her personal life.

"I've been seeing someone for a few months now. Nothing serious, more like casual sex," she answered. "You?"

I watched through the glass as she returned to making up my eyes. What would I call Josh? Well, I couldn't exactly say I met my Twin Flame, and we were going through some sort of spiritual awakening. "Same," I simply answered. Unfortunately, the awkward banter wasn't serving as a diversion as I had hoped. I sat silently for the rest of the session until I was called to the set. The set was decorated like a rooftop; the backdrop was a New York City skyline. I approached my co-star, Hunter. I closed my eyes for a second and took a deep breath, trying to break free from my mental fixation on Elijah to get into character. As soon as the director, Richard, yelled "action," I said my lines:

"If I remember correctly, you told me you'd give me whatever I wanted if I showed up, not the reverse."

Hunter smiled, raising his eyebrows and reciting his lines. "You're right. I did promise you anything. Did you decide what you wanted?"

"Yes." I stood and reached down to him. "I want you to dance with me." Pulling him up, he started shaking his head.

"I don't dance," he said abruptly. I opened my mouth to say my next line when I saw a shadow appear behind Hunter from the corner of my eye. I stood still while the figure came closer. As it stalked nearer, I could clearly see his face, grayish blue eyes, and short dirty blonde hair. My heart stood still as William stood directly behind Hunter. I couldn't move; I remained frozen in place.

Richard's voice rang through my earpiece. "Bianca—'You said *anything*,'" he reminded me of my line. I opened my mouth to speak, but nothing came out as I stood paralyzed, staring into William's eyes. "Cut!" Richard bellowed as he came out to the set and approached me.

"You okay?" he asked. I slowly redirected my focus from William to Richard.

"Yes," I said.

"Okay, take it from here," he said as he walked back off. "Action!"

"You said *anything*," I said aloud, still looking past Hunter at William. Hunter stood up, placed one of his hands around my waist, and intertwined the fingers of his other hand through mine. Still, I couldn't move. "Cut!" Richard yelled again, this time with aggravation in his voice. He stomped back over to me dramatically. "Calista, it's literally one more line, and then we're done. 'I want you to dance with me right here to my favorite Christmas song before they start talking about banning it for being inappropriate.' Cue *Baby It's Cold Outside*, and that's it. Are you okay? Can you do that?" he asked.

"Yes," I quietly said as I nodded. Once again, he made his way back to his chair and yelled action.

"I want you to dance with me right here, to my favorite…." I began and was quickly interrupted as William came closer to me and spoke.

"Help me," he pleaded. My heart fell into the pit of my stomach as the hairs on my arm stood up. I stared at him in astonishment when he said it again. "Help me." I am sure a commotion was taking place behind me as Richard grew more irritated, but at that moment, I only saw something no one else could—William. My brain immediately returned to my last memory of my mother, crawling into her bed after I dreamed of him.

"Did the boy come back tonight?" she had asked.

I nodded into her chest.

I remember sensing pain in her chest as she held my head to her heart and clutched my hair in her fingers.

"Did he ask you to do anything?" she asked. Did he ask you to do anything?

I snapped back to reality. "Help me," he repeated, now for the third time. Tears filled my eyes as I grabbed my pocketbook, ran off set, and sat on the stoop outside, shuffling through my pocketbook for my cigarettes. My hands were shaking as I tried to pull the lighter up and light the cigarette. Rain poured down as I cupped my hands around the cigarette to avoid it from getting wet.

It was raining so hard; the wind and water made it challenging for me to get the lighter to ignite. I started rocking back and forth, trying desperately to light it. The rain soaked it as I threw it on the floor and reached for another. As my hand touched the pack in my pocketbook, the book Josh gave me the night before caught my eye. I stopped crying for a minute and held the book in my hands as I read the title, *Bounded by the Bond.* I looked up, stunned that it had stopped raining long enough for me to light the cigarette. I finally got it lit and took a large puff as I opened the book to the dedication page: *in loving memory of Jayden.*

The memory of my mother flooded me, and I started crying again, feeling like I was losing my mind. I watched a droplet of rain hit the book. I looked up; it had begun raining again. I quickly shut the book and threw it back in my pocketbook to avoid getting it wet when something suddenly occurred to me. Forcing myself to stop crying for a second, I looked up and watched the rain immediately halt. It appeared as if every time I cried, it would start raining. Like my emotions were somehow affecting the weather. Memories started flashing before my eyes; being with Josh on our mountain, getting injured in that same spot, the car accident the night of the DUI—it was *always* raining. I put myself back into a state of distress, and let the tears fall down my face as the rain resumed again. Choking back the tears, I stopped crying. The rain ceased. Holy shit, I was making it rain! Josh could control fire, and I could control water. I looked back down at the book. I knew what I needed to do; I needed to see my sister, she would have answers.

A private jet went out that night as Josh and I made our way to Tennessee to visit my sister, Chrys.

"Is there anything I can get you?" the flight attendant asked. My eyes were closing from exhaustion as I looked hopelessly at Josh.

"Can we put our seats into bed position?" he asked.

"Of course, Mr. Knight. I will open them for you as soon as we get to safe flying altitude."

Josh reached out to me and pulled me into him as I laid my head on his chest and fell asleep. Before long, I was in the cottage, staring at the same shag rug and fireplace. I slowly turned around to see my mystery man, his brown eyes gazing at me as his hands gently touched my face. He pulled me into his embrace and whispered: "Claudia, I've been waiting for you."

a limo was waiting for us at the airport when we landed. "You sleep okay?" Josh asked as we headed towards Chrys' house. I looked down at my lap, feeling my cheeks get warm. I couldn't tell him about the recollection, not yet. I knew he thought it was Lucas, and I was under some sort of psychic attack; I didn't want to argue. Not right before I saw my sister, the meeting itself would be awkward enough. I hadn't seen her in eleven years. I just nodded. "Fill me in on your sister," he said.

"She's a jealous bitch," I replied, not looking up. "Divorced, no kids, not very social; she kind of always kept to herself. She didn't handle my mother's death well, and she hates that I went to Hollywood. She feels like she should have been the one to go, not me. I'm sure she will throw that in my face at least a dozen times, so be forewarned."

"Ah, sibling rivalry at its finest," he commented. Josh was an only child. Although I had thought he was fortunate when he told me that, he argued it was lonely, especially when his parents were never around, and he had a nanny taking care of him most of his life. I was curious to see if he still felt that way when he met my sister. The limo stopped as the driver came around the side and opened the door for me. I climbed out and slid my sunglasses down the bridge of my nose to look at the house. Josh got out behind me. It was a rather large house on the massive property covered in grass. She must have had two acres of land. There was a long, gravel walkway leading to the house, and I could hear animals chatter in the background.

"I don't think we're in Kansas anymore," I muttered, almost under my breath.

"Actually, I think we are," Josh said as he looked over at me. "And finally, you've seen a movie!" A silhouette of my sister stood in the doorway, studying us. Releasing a deep breath, I clung to Josh's arm for support.

"Let's go do this," I said as I carefully stumbled along the gravel pavement, still holding onto him. Chrys didn't take her eyes off me as I tried to walk across the walkway with difficulty. She said nothing as she opened the door and waved us in. I wiped my feet on the welcome mat below me as dirt and small pebbles fell from my shoes. She looked me up and down.

"This is Tennessee, not the set of *Sex and the City*. You couldn't wear tennis shoes?" she asked sarcastically. I was taken aback by the southern twang she had acquired. I took my sunglasses off.

"I must have missed that memo," I responded. "And they're called sneakers."

"Who's your friend?" she asked, her attention now going to Josh.

"This is Josh," I introduced. He extended his hand to shake; she hesitantly reached out and shook it. She led us through the carpeted living room. Although all her furniture appeared in good condition and relatively new, she had a very different style than Josh and me. Her house was filled with warm colors to create a cozy, comfortable vibe. Paintings of animals, especially horses, that I knew she had done herself hung on the walls. I could spot my sister's artwork a mile away. She led us to the kitchen, where a glass table sat with four wicker chairs as she opened her refrigerator and retrieved a pitcher of iced tea. She poured two glasses and put them on the table before us as we sat down. Then she poured herself one and sat at the table. I took a sip as a bitter taste hit my tongue and tried my hardest not to make a face of disgust.

"What is this?" I asked.

"It's iced tea," she replied.

"Why isn't it sweet? It's the exact opposite," I complained. She went into the cabinet and came out with a bowl of sugar and a spoon.

"We don't put sugar in iced tea here. That's sweet tea," she said, sliding the bowl to me.

I filled the spoon up with enormous amounts of sugar as I emptied three scoops into the cup. Stirring my tea, I looked up at her. "When did you get such an accent? You were born in California," I said, unamused.

Josh reached across the table and pulled the sugar bowl to him.

"I've been here for eleven years. You know, the same amount of time it took you to get so glamorous," she said, waving her pointer finger up and down my body. "After you stole my spot in *My Life*." I rolled my eyes and sighed as I looked over at Josh.

"Here we go. Get it all out now; tell him the whole story about how I 'robbed you' of your success," I said dramatically.

She looked over at Josh. "I was nineteen years old, which made Morgan sixteen…" she began.

"My name is Calista," I interrupted.

She shook her head. "No, it's not. It's Morgan. And Reed? Come on, where's your originality? What a boring name you chose for yourself." She took a sip of her tea without taking her eyes off Josh. "Did she tell you our real last name?" she asked him.

"No," he answered, looking from her to me awkwardly.

"It's NaPalespo," she said proudly. "It's a powerful last name, unlike *Reed*," she said, curling her lip up at me. "Do you even know what it means?"

"No, I don't; please enlighten me. What great significance does the name NaPalepso hold?" I asked. Josh leaned in, now very intrigued by what the name meant.

"It derives from Greece, and in English, it means 'to fight,'" she said slowly, for dramatic effect. Josh slumped back in his chair, disappointment on his face.

"I'm going to be honest with you; I was expecting better with that lead-up," he said.

"What?" she asked him, annoyed.

"I mean, the way you said, 'do you even know what it means,'" he repeated, mimicking her tone. "I was expecting something like 'to die without mercy,' or something way cooler than 'to fight,'" he explained. She wrapped her hands around her chest and leaned back on her chair.

"Anyway," she continued. "Morgan and I had just got our own place after we had been shuffled around from foster home to foster home. I always did very artistic things. I draw, I write, I would act. I signed up for an open casting to audition for the role. I was so excited; I practiced my monologue for a month. Except, pretty little Morgan over here decided to tag along."

I rested my elbow on the table and leaned my chin into my palm, tapping the side of my face with my finger, impatiently waiting for her to finish the story. Chrys and I looked completely different; we didn't even appear as if we could be sisters. She had dark brown hair and hazel eyes. She stood about five inches taller than me and was much curvier. She would constantly blame everything I've ever had on my "looks."

"I didn't even get to audition. The director took one look at Morgan and decided she was the perfect candidate. He told her he would 'groom' her on how to act. Tell him, Morgan, tell him how well Henry 'groomed' you," she said, using air quotation marks. My body cringed at the name Henry, while I involuntarily pictured his hands all over my body.

"I just wanted out," I said coldly. Her eyes shifted quickly from me to Josh.

"Are you okay?" she asked him.

He took a sip of his drink. "Yeah, why?" he asked.

She put her elbows on the table and leaned over towards him. "I'm an empath," she said.

He swallowed his tea. "And what's an empath?" he asked.

"I can feel people's emotions, almost like a sponge. They stick to me. I just felt a wave of jealousy come from you when I mentioned Henry…. and look, there it is again."

He clenched his jaw as he looked at me uncomfortably and cleared his throat. "I get the jest of the story. I don't need the details," he said.

"So, Morgan tells me y'all started dabbling in Witchcraft. She was born with extraordinary gifts she refused to acknowledge her whole life. I heard you have some abilities as well," she said.

"I guess," he simply answered. Picking up on his discomfort, she dropped the subject.

"Y'all must be tired from your trip; let me show you to the guest room, and we can hear all about it tomorrow," she said. We stood and followed her lead up carpeted steps as Josh carried the suitcases. She opened the door to a room. Very simply furnished, there was a small bed with a night table on each side, a decent-sized dresser, and an old tube TV sitting on top of it. My mouth hung open as I looked at the size of Josh, imagining us both cramped in the tiny bed.

"Is that a twin-size bed?" I asked.

Chrys let out a laugh. "No, it's full. Relax, princess, there isn't a pea under the mattress either. You'll be just fine."

CHAPTER 23

*J*osh rolled the suitcases in and gently closed the door; as I paced the small room, my hands squeezed up in tight fists. "Ohhh, she infuriates me," I said in a loud whisper through clenched teeth. Josh plopped down on the bed.

"I like it; it forces you to cuddle with me," he said, smiling ear to ear. I pointed at the tube TV on the dresser.

"I mean, what is this? Did she buy it at a garage sale? I feel like I'm in 1983 right now," I ranted.

"I think it's cozy," he said, extending his arms up towards me. "Aw, come here, my bougie little princess," I crawled into the bed next to him and laid my head on his chest.

"It smells like moths," I complained.

"How do you know what moths smell like?"

"I'm guessing like this," I said as I ran my hand along the comforter. "Is this wool?"

He let out a laugh. "Explains the moths."

"Ugh, who uses wool blankets anymore? Feel this. It isn't even comfortable!"

He stroked his hand up and down my back. "Maybe she

made it. She said she's artsy. I couldn't care if it was wool, satin, silk, or a bed of burning coals I was lying on if you're lying on top of me."

I couldn't help but smile as I moved my finger in a circle around his chest. "You're one spoiled bitch, huh?" he laughed. I slapped his chest.

"Please, you're worth more money than me," I said.

"And yet, I have no problem laying on wool," he answered.

"I told you she'd bring up the *My Life* thing. And trust me, she'll find a way to do it again."

"How would you feel if you wanted something so bad, then someone came out of nowhere and took it from you? 'Accidentally' at that," he asked.

I thought about it for a minute. "I don't know; no one has ever taken what I wanted," I said.

"Maybe someone needs to," he joked. I bit my bottom lip and ran my hand down between his legs.

"Or perhaps I should take what I want," I said in a flirtatious tone. He pulled my hand off him.

"Don't turn me on. I was afraid to point this out to you, but...." he motioned behind him to the wall. "No headboard, nothing to tie you to."

"Ugh," I sighed as I sank my head back into his chest.

He closed his eyes as his hand still routinely rubbed my back. As I lay on his chest, my mind returned to the other nights recollection.

"Claudia, I've been waiting for you," he said as he held me tightly.

I looked into his brown eyes while his fingers gently grazed my face.

"I can't do this, Jacob, not yet." He took me by the hand and led me to the fireplace as he pulled me down to sit on the shag rug and put his arm around me. I leaned my head into his shoulder and stared at the blazing fire as he ran his fingers through my hair.

"We said today," he reminded me.

"I know, but I can't. I just can't leave my son," I said.

"We'll take Elijah with us. Surely, he sees how Lucas treats you. I cannot imagine he would object."

"Lucas would hunt me down, even more so if I took his son from him," I said.

"My love, you deserve to be treated like the queen that you are, even if the king himself doesn't see it."

"One day, Jacob, I promise we will be together. I am certain of it."

His name was Jacob, and obviously, I was in love with him. It was the only time in my life I had an idea of what love felt like. I felt so protected and comfortable in his presence. As I watched Josh drift to sleep, the curse on me tortured me. I wished I could feel that way about Josh, and I was sure he was wrong about the psychic attack. Jacob was him; he had to be. I wondered if we could somehow perform a ritual that would make Josh remember his past lives so he could see for himself. As much as I hated my sister at that moment, I couldn't wait to see what input she had on the situation.

The piercing sound of crowing shot me out of bed. I went to the window to see where the noise was coming from.

"What the hell is that? A rooster?" I asked Josh, irritated. He slowly sat up in bed and ran his fingers through his hair.

"Sure sounds that way," he said.

"Seriously? They're really a thing?" I asked as I laid back down in bed. He fell back and turned his body to face me.

"Of course, they're a thing. It's an animal. What did you think, they were some sort of urban legend?" he laughed. I let out a sigh and hung my head in exasperation. This was going to be a long few weeks ahead of us. "Would you like me to set them on fire for you?"

"Yes, please," I said.

He raised his eyebrows. "You know I can't create fire, but you would honestly want me to burn a bunch of innocent roosters? You're a monster!"

"Oh, please. I've watched you devour chicken wings; you're no angel," I answered, swatting him with my pillow.

"So, I can control fire, and you can control water; how cool is that?" he commented. "You know what happens when you mix fire and water?"

"No, what happens?" I asked. He paused for a minute.

"I have no idea; science was never a strong subject of mine. But it sounds like it would be pretty badass, no?" I yawned and stretched my body.

"We are going to get no sleep in this place," I said.

"Speaking of those chicken wings…."

I touched his stomach. "You're hungry, aren't you?" I asked.

"Yes, ma'am," he said, in his best imitation of a southern accent. We made our way down to the kitchen, where Chrys was sitting at the table drinking coffee. A warm, sweet aroma filled the room, mixed with the scent of fresh coffee. I watched Josh's face light up.

"Morning," she greeted.

"Good morning," I mumbled.

"It smells amazing. What is that?" Josh asked. Chrys got up, went to the oven, and pulled out a tray of freshly baked golden-brown pastries.

"Biscuits," she said. "Y'all hungry? Do you want me to whip up some eggs?"

"No need, I'll just have butter," Josh commented.

"No, I am good," I said. She placed the biscuits in a basket and placed them on the table as she went into the fridge to get the butter. She set the table and sat down.

Josh sat beside me as he buttered up a biscuit and took a

bite. "This is so good!" he commented. "Did you make the butter?"

Chrys stopped chewing her biscuit and looked at him as if he had three heads.

"Come again?"

"Did you make the butter?" he asked, pointing at the butter dish with his knife.

"No, I didn't make the butter," she said as if that were the most ridiculous thing she had ever heard.

"Oh, I don't know. I thought you guys made your own butter here," he said. "Do you have coffee?"

She shook her head in disbelief. "Yes, mugs are in the cupboard."

Josh got up, reached into the cabinet, pulled out two cups, and poured coffee for each of us. "Do you have milk?" he asked.

Chrys put her biscuit down on her plate. "Yes, if you go in the yard, into the barn, there are two cows there. Make sure you pick the female one. It's really simple; you just slightly tug," she said, as she moved each of her hands simultaneously in a jerking motion. "One at a time. Shoots right out."

Josh's mouth hung open as he stared down into his coffee. "It's cool. I'll drink it black," he said casually. Chrys let out a loud laugh.

"I'm yanking your chain," she said, laughing hysterically. "It's in the refrigerator, middle shelf. Where the hell y'all think you are?" He rolled his eyes and let out a sigh as he went to the refrigerator, got the milk, and sat back down next to me.

"Now, let's talk about what you came for," she said.

CHAPTER 24

*C*hrys sat up straight in her chair and got very serious. "So," she began, looking at Josh. "From what Morgan has told me, she can control water, and you can control fire, correct?"

He nodded. "Yeah, pretty much."

"That's interesting. I can control air." A flashback of the winds blowing with the Ouija board from our childhood raced through my mind. "That is three out of five of the elements."

"Earth and spirit," Josh said proudly.

"Yes, those are the other two, earth and spirit. I see someone has been doing their homework," Chrys answered. "Water and fire are complete opposites, so now I'm wondering about the issue that you two have when you...." she formed the fingers on her left hand into an O shape while she inserted her right pointer finger back and forth through it.

Josh made a grimacing face and looked at me. "You told her about that?"

I threw my hands in the air. "What? It was relevant information!"

Chrys rested her chin in the palm of her hand and stared off, deep in thought. "And the boy? What does he look like?"

"He's very thin, maybe seventeen or eighteen years old. Really short dirty blonde hair and grayish-blue eyes," I answered.

"That's interesting. I have had a teenage boy following me around since we were kids. It was one of the reasons I was so obsessed with that book. He's about the same age but looks completely different from what you described. Same color eyes, but very dark hair and husky. His name is Andrew."

"That sounds more like Elijah, not William, but he isn't husky. He was thin also," I said.

"So, wait; you both have teenage boys following you around?" Josh asked. "I just thought of something. Do you guys ever feel like you're dead?"

At that moment, Chrys and I must have really looked like sisters because we shot him the same look as if that was the craziest thing we'd ever heard.

"No, can't say I have. Have you ever thought you were dead?" she asked.

"I haven't before now but hear me out. I'm thinking of that movie, *The Sixth Sense*. What if we all died somehow, and we're the spirits, and the kids are actually the ones alive?"

Chrys wrapped her arms around her chest and looked at me. "Who is this guy?" she asked, annoyed.

I looked over at Josh, then back to Chrys. "He's um, well, he's.…"

"I'm the Twin Flame," he jumped in. She tilted her head and looked at him.

"Oh, you're the Twin Flame? Why don't you go sit in the living room and leave the witches to talk," she said sarcastically.

Josh rolled his eyes and went over to the couch in the living room.

"I despise the word 'witch,' you know," I said.

She turned her attention to me. "Why's that? That is what you are, what you were born as."

"Witch just sounds so negative and ugly. Am I supposed to adopt a black cat now and get excited over Halloween?"

She let out a sigh. "Halloween is actually a very important holiday. It's called Samhain. It is when the veil to the other side is at its thinnest. Where we honor those who have passed," she said defensively. "And don't worry, Morgan, no one thinks you're ugly. That's apparent."

She got up and poured herself another cup of coffee. When she sat back down, she took the chair next to me instead of the one she was originally sitting in and leaned into me to whisper. "Your friend, Josh.... he isn't the sharpest tool in the shed, huh? I hope he's at least good in bed."

I smiled at the idea that my sister was trying to gossip as I leaned closer to her. "He's harmless; he's actually very smart. And yes, he's amazing in bed."

A huge grin crossed her face, and it started to disappear as she looked over at him in the living room. "Why is he looking at us like that? Can he hear what we're saying?" she whispered. I looked up and saw Josh peering in, smiling at us.

"Oh shit," I muttered. "I forgot to warn you; he can read minds. So can I. Well, I can only read his, really."

"So, he can hear what we're saying?" she asked, amazed.

"Yes, even though he's promised not to read mine. But theoretically, if you're comprehending what I am saying, then I guess he can hear what we're saying through you." We both looked back at him as he shrugged, clearly pleased with what we had to say about him.

"Can I come back now?" he hollered into the kitchen.

"I guess so," she said as she waved him back in. He came

back and sat down across from us, still beaming with a cocky grin.

"Get over yourself," I said. "So, what exactly is in this book?" I asked Chrys.

"It's about sisters Fiona and Ruby who are trying to save a boy. The boy was originally born to the first sister, Fiona. He did something terrible in that life and was born with a karmic debt. They never figured out what it was that he had done. Every lifetime they are reborn, they find this out and try to help him, but they get something wrong every lifetime. For instance, he was born to Ruby instead of Fiona in the second lifetime."

"So, he became the nephew?" I asked.

"Yes. With that being said, growing up, I always assumed this would be my son, or nephew, depending on who is who out of the sisters. But neither one of us has children," she said.

"So, what if he was just born to someone randomly?" Josh chimed in.

Chrys shook her head. "No, not possible. He'd have to have the same DNA. Also, that wouldn't make sense because now there are two boys, not just one. We both have a different boy following us; therefore, it can't be connected." We all sat in silence, racking our brains. "I wish Mom was here. She could help us."

I rolled my eyes and bolted up from my seat. "Seriously? Still? Why are you so obsessed with her? She's gone. It's been thirteen years. When are you going to get over it already?"

Josh sat up straight, sensing a fight was about to happen, as Chrys got up from her chair and inched closer to me. "Probably never. That's what happens with normal people when they lose their mother. It's a terrible thing. You are straight-up demon spawn; how do you not give a shit your mother is dead?" she yelled.

"Why should I? It was a selfish thing she did. She left us all alone, with no one to take care of us. We lived horrible lives because of her; moving from foster home to foster home. We were abused and went to sleep hungry. How do you idolize someone like that?" I shouted back.

"She wasn't well, and honestly, she'd be rolling in her grave right now if she could hear what you were saying. She adored you. You were by far her favorite. She gave you extra special attention. You were the extraordinary one; you were the pretty one, you were the...."

"Stop!" Josh firmly said as he stood, hit his fist on the table, and raised his voice. "Enough already, the both of you. I get it. You don't like each other, fine. You both have different views on your mother's death, okay. But we have a very serious situation here. Cali got a message, a creepy, real deal, hardcore message that said 542 days. We are now over 400 days into that! So, I want the both of you to go to your damn rooms and read this book as if it were written about you!"

Chrys and I stared at him in shock that he had become so authoritative. I had never seen him get so angry before. I followed her silently as she headed towards the steps. She suddenly stopped in her tracks and looked at me. "Is it me, or is he kind of sexy when he gets mad?" she asked.

"Now!" he demanded.

CHAPTER 25

*W*hile it only took Chrys half a day to finish the entire book, it took me an hour longer to get through it, but when we were both done, we reconvened back in the kitchen. She started preparing dinner as Josh and I sat at the kitchen table again.

"I think it is us," Chrys announced. We both looked up at her.

"I thought you said the kid had to have the same DNA? It confirmed that in the book," I reminded her.

She nodded as she dipped chicken cutlets into batter and placed them on a plate to prepare to fry. "He does. But, we're only thirty-one and twenty-eight; we can still have kids. I don't think he was born yet. The book specifically mentions that even though they keep messing up, they find out earlier and earlier in their lifetimes about him. In the book, they are both in their thirties, so that proves to be accurate with you still being in your twenties," she explained.

"So why are there two of them?" Josh asked.

"I think we're both seeing different versions of him. You're seeing William, and I am seeing Andrew. The book is dedicated to Jayden, and I think they're all the same boy from different lifetimes. The fact that you're seeing Elijah leads me to believe that you're Fiona and I am Ruby. If that is the case and history does repeat itself again, he will be my son this lifetime, based on the assumption the last spell didn't work either."

"Has Andrew asked you for anything? If Elijah was my son, that means William was my nephew. Why is he asking me for help and not you?" I asked.

"Well, according to the book, you were the more powerful one. Maybe you're the only one who could help him," she shrugged. "Or maybe because you're the one who gave him his soul. I don't know. I'm just speculating here."

"Okay, so if this book was, in fact, written about both of you, then who wrote it?" Josh asked.

"I have no idea, but that's a good question. Whoever wrote this book may be able to help us if we can figure that part out," she said.

"We may actually have enough time now if he wasn't born yet," I said excitedly.

"Yes, maybe, except you're bound. We need to get that hex off you first," Chrys answered.

"We did that spell already. We think it worked," Josh said. Chrys remained silent as she looked down at the cutlets and started putting them in the frying pan one by one. I looked down at my lap.

Josh straightened himself up and looked from her to me. "What does she mean she doesn't believe it worked?" he asked me. I shot a look at Chrys, who stared at Josh as if he had just violated her.

"You can't just go around reading people's minds!" she said, embarrassed.

"What does she mean it didn't work?" Josh asked again.

"I had another recollection the other night when we were on the plane," I said quietly.

"What? Why didn't you tell me?" he asked, growing visibly upset.

"Perhaps it's that wave of jealousy you keep giving off," Chrys snapped back, defending me. He didn't answer her. Instead, he just stared at me, waiting for an answer.

"It was him, the other guy, the one you believe is a psychic attack from Lucas. His name is Jacob, and I was having an affair with him. We were supposed to run away together. I backed out at the last minute," I said. Josh sat back in his chair, glaring at me in shock.

"And you lied to me about it?"

"I didn't lie to you. I just didn't tell you. Yet. I was going to; I was looking for the right time. I do believe he's you, Josh. Here's another thing, every time I am with him recently, we are always sitting in front of a fireplace. You can control fire; you don't think that is a sign?" He took his vape out of his pocket and took a hit.

"I don't know what I believe, but you can't just hold back information from me. And for your information, Chrys, I am not jealous of this guy Jacob. I am concerned. I think Lucas is playing with her mind. But either way, we need to get this curse off her. Who could have done this and why? That woman, Barbara in the metaphysical shop, said it would be a completely different spell, not the love spell that backfired," he said.

"I agree with you that the binding is likely not Lucas," Chrys said. "But whoever it is must be very strong to be able to do this to you, considering how powerful you are." She loaded the cutlets on a plate and brought them to the table. I got up, went over to the cabinets, and began setting the table. She looked at me, surprised I was helping. "Thank you," she said. I nodded in acknowledgment, and we all ate in silence.

Later that night, Chrys had gone to the market, and Josh was in the bathroom. He called out to me and asked me to bring him a towel. I went into the closet in the hallway, shuffling around for a towel. As I reached in to retrieve one and took it off the shelf, a shoebox tucked behind the linen caught my eye. My curiosity got the best of me as I pushed the towels out of the way and grabbed the box. On the front of it was a label with the word "Mom" written in permanent marker. I remained there staring at the box for a minute, debating whether or not I should open it. No, it's not mine, I finally decided and went to the bathroom to give Josh the towel. He stood there shirtless in his boxer briefs.

"Are you still mad at me?" I asked. He took the towel from me, placed it on the sink, leaned over, and kissed me.

"No, you know I can't stay mad at you too long," he said as he pulled me into him. "But we need to be honest with each other and not hold back important information."

"I know, I'm sorry. I won't hold anything back again," I said as I kissed him back. The kiss started out slow but got more passionate within minutes. His lips wandered down my neck as he whispered in my ear, "Take a shower with me."

I backed away from him, shaking my head. "No, no," I argued.

"Come on," he said, pulling me back to him and making an exaggerated pouting face. "It's been a fantasy of mine to get you in the shower."

He ran his hands up and down my body as he continued kissing me, trying his hardest to seduce me.

"You can't restrain me in the shower. It's too dangerous. I am going to slip and bust my ass," I argued. He reached across to the faucet and turned the water on, his lips never leaving my body. He began lifting my shirt above my head.

"I'll hold you; I won't let you fall," he promised. As much as I thought it was a bad idea, my bare breasts against his chest made my body feel differently. I gave a mischievous smirk as I opened my jeans and slowly slid them off. His smile widened as he bit his bottom lip, and his eyes strolled up and down my body. He slid off his boxer briefs and then extended his hand to help me. I climbed in as the water poured down our bodies, and he vehemently kissed me.

His fingers dug firmly into my hips to support me. I nervously waited for my rage to show itself, but it didn't. Instead, the more passionate he became, and I felt the warm water trickle down my body, the more aroused I got and needed to touch him. I pulled myself back and turned around, draping my arms around him.

I ran my fingers through his wet hair as I pulled him closer to me. I didn't take my lips off him. "I love feeling your arms around me," he mumbled through his kiss. I wrapped my arms tighter around his shoulders.

We both stood motionless, out of breath, as the water poured down our bodies, and he pulled me into him. "I think the water is calming you," he said. I lifted my arm towards the shower head and waved my hand as if I were parting the water. Half of the flow veered off to the right, as the other half went to the left. He stared up at the water flowing around us but not touching us. His eyes lit up in excitement. "That's amazing!" he exclaimed.

CHAPTER 26

*J*osh lay sprawled out on the bed, still in his boxer briefs, gazing at me and smiling like a kid who had just got into a bowl of candy. "You're awesome," he said.

I raised my pointer finger to my lips. "Shhh," I hushed him as I slowly opened the door and peered out. I stretched my head out to the hallway listening for evidence if Chrys was home. Josh shot up in the bed.

"What are you doing?" he asked.

"Hush," I said in a loud whisper as I headed into the hallway. I tiptoed back to the closet, got the shoebox labeled Mom, and brought it into the room. I gently shut the door and sat on the bed with my legs crossed and the box in front of me. Josh looked down at the box and then up at me, a look of shock on his face.

"What are you doing?" he whispered loudly. "Is that your sister's?"

I turned the box around to display the label. "No, it says 'Mom,' and she's my mother also, so technically, it's common property," I said. I went to open the box, but he put his hand on top of it, preventing me from taking the lid off.

"Cali, this isn't a good idea. Don't go rummaging through your sister's shit. She's going to know," he warned.

"How is she going to know?" I asked, annoyed.

"She's a witch!" he answered. I rolled my eyes and let out a sigh.

"So am I," I snapped back. "And according to the book, the more powerful one, so relax. What is she going to do? Bind me? For all we know, she could have been the one who put the hex on me, to begin with." He took his hand off the box and crossed his legs also, the package now sitting between us. I gradually took the lid off and nervously peered in, unsure of what I would find. I shuffled through the contents and took out a stack of pictures. The first one on top was my mother with a good-looking man. He looked to be in his mid-thirties, clean-shaven and well-dressed, with dark hair and light eyes. I passed the picture to Josh.

"That's her, that's my mom," I said. He examined the picture with sorrow in his eyes.

"She was pretty. You look a lot like her. Is this your dad?" I took the picture back from him and looked at it again. I didn't remember ever seeing that man before.

"I don't know, maybe."

"What happened to your father?" he asked. I racked my brain to find any reminiscences of my father but was drawing a blank.

"I don't know. I don't remember him," I finally said as I continued flipping through the photographs. I smiled as I came across one of my mother, squatting down in the field she loved, with my sister and me to each side of her. It must have been taken shortly before she died. Most of my better childhood memories took place in that exact field. I kept rifling through the box, finding an assortment of healing crystals in pink, green, and blue. A substantial purple piece, still holding its vibrancy, and a matching necklace and bracelet with the same stone buried beneath the others. I held the larger one in my hand to display to Josh.

"Is that an amethyst?" he asked.

"Looks that way. Guess she really liked amethyst," I said, as my attention snagged by an envelope. I put the crystal back and reached for the envelope. Inside were two smaller individual ones, one marked "Chrys" and the other "Morgan." The cursive writing brought back a memory of sitting on my mother's lap as a little girl. I could hear her voice vividly as she held my hand and guided it to form the letter M. *That's how you write an M,* she had said. I delicately opened the envelope, trying my hardest not to damage it, and took out the letter. My heart stopped for a second as I stared at my mother's letter. I hadn't seen it since my sister read it to me as a kid. I silently reread her note.

Dear Morgan,

My beautiful, special baby girl. There are so many things I want to say to you, but I don't know where to start. I want you to know that I love you so much and know that you are going to do incredible things in life. You are going to grow up to be an amazing, powerful, and talented woman. I want you to know that when you experience your first kiss, your first love, your first everything in life, I will be there with you smiling not only for you but with you. Although my body may not be there, my spirit and heart will always be. I know you will grow up hating me, and I am truly sorry for that. I hope that when you look into the eyes of your son, you realize the unconditional love I have for you, and you find it in your heart to forgive me. I only wish you love and happiness in life. I love you with all my heart and soul.

Love, Mommy

What a load of bullshit. I handed the letter to Josh to read and held the one labeled Chrys in my hand as I felt his stare pierce me.

Don't, he said silently. I put the envelope back in the box.

"What happened to you not reading my mind?" I quipped.

"Only when needed," he said. He handed me back the letter. "I don't want to read this. This letter is yours and only yours, same as that's Chrys'," he said sternly.

"Yet it's in *her* closet," I said sarcastically. "Don't guilt-trip me. She's obviously read my letter. But I don't even care what hers says." I pulled the letter back from him, placed everything back in order exactly as it was, and returned it to the closet.

I came back into the room; Josh watched me intensely as I sat down next to him on the bed.

"Go ahead, tell me how evil I am," I said.

He pulled me into him and kissed my forehead.

"You're not evil. I get it. You have a lot going on you don't understand, and you're just trying to find answers," he said, lying down and pulling me into him. "But it's late. Come on, beautiful, get some sleep."

I woke up the next morning to the same squealing of roosters. My eyes shot open as I stared at the ceiling, and Josh groaned.

"How about if I light a match? Can you somehow control it to move in that direction and set them on fire?"

He rolled over to face me. "Now you're being evil," he said. "I'm going to have to find a pharmacy or something to get you earplugs."

We went downstairs, where Chrys was seated at the table drinking her coffee. I went to the coffee maker and poured a cup for myself and Josh as we sat across from her. I took a sip of my coffee, trying to wake myself up.

"So, Cali and I had sex in the shower last night," Josh

uttered nonchalantly. I nearly spit out my coffee as Chrys looked from me to Josh and then back at me.

"You did what, now?" she asked.

"Josh!" I scolded.

His eyes shot wide open as he pushed himself backward in his chair. "What? I thought we could talk about it if it were pertinent information?"

"*We* can talk about it," I said strongly, waving my finger back and forth between myself and Chrys. "*You* cannot. She doesn't need to hear your version!"

"You had sex in my shower?" she asked me, disgusted.

"Wait, my *version*? I didn't realize we had different 'sides' to the story," he said, using air quotations.

"You had sex in my shower?" Chrys said again.

"Go to the living room," I said to Josh.

He wrapped his arms around his chest and started tapping his foot impatiently. "No way; now I want to hear your *version* of the story."

Now put on the spot, I looked at Chrys.

"You had sex…"

"Yes, we had sex in your shower," I admitted. "I'm sorry, I wasn't going to, but he does this thing with his tongue when he kisses me; that kind of puts me in a trance….."

"Oh, so you like that, huh?" he chimed in, now leaning into the table.

"See, this is exactly why you can't be part of this conversation! Yes, I like that….but, Chrys, something incredible happened. When the water hit me, it somehow calmed me. I didn't have anything but passion and lust. No fury, no rage…."

She rested her elbow on her chair's armrest as she bit her thumbnail, processing what I had just told her.

"I got it!" she said as she jumped up from her seat, bent down to the bottom cabinet, and got a pot. She put a little water in it, placed it on the stove, and turned the flame on high. "Come here," she said eagerly. We both went to the stove and waited until the water came to a boil. "What happens when you put water on fire?"

"It boils," Josh answered.

"Correct, it boils. You can control fire; she can control water. For some reason, when he enters you, he is making your blood actually boil!" Josh and I leaned towards the pot to better observe the bubbles forming and the steam rising. Chrys went over to the sink and filled a glass with water. She came back to the stove and poured it into the pot, making the boil come to a stop. "The more water you put in, the longer it takes to make it simmer."

"The night of the astral projection, you made it rain," Josh remembered.

"Great, so now instead of tying me up, you can just submerge me in water," I said sarcastically.

CHAPTER 27

As restless as I was, I fought the urge to squirm as Josh quietly slept. Finally, after repositioning myself for an hour and trying to get comfortable, I grabbed my cigarettes and quietly made my way outside to the yard. I sat on a rocking chair on the porch as I stared off at the grass. The weather was beautiful, and the stars were so bright, without all the New York City smog blocking them. All the animals had gone to sleep, except the chirping of crickets that rang through the air. I nearly jumped out of my skin when I heard Chrys' voice behind me.

"Can't sleep either?" she asked as she sat in the chair next to me.

I shook my head as I took a puff of my cigarette.

"You know what's the worst part of being an empath?" she asked.

"What's that?"

"Josh can hear what people are thinking. I can *feel* them. The pain, the sorrow, the anguish, the anxiety...."

"I'm sure you can feel good emotions too, though, right?" I asked.

"Yes, I can. You know he's in love with you," she said.

I took the last pull of my cigarette and held the butt up in the air. "You have an ashtray?" I asked, avoiding her statement. She went inside and came back with a plastic cup filled halfway with water and handed it to me. I watched my cigarette sizzle as it hit the water.

"He hasn't read the book, has he?" she continued.

"No," I answered.

"So, he has no idea you have the ability to make men fall in love with you?" she asked. I sat back on the chair as I made it rock back and forth with my foot.

"You're assuming I'm Fiona and not Ruby," I said. "We don't know that for sure."

"Oh, we know that," she said through a smirk. "Makes so much sense, even at that audition, how Henry was so drawn to you." I wanted to jab her for bringing up Henry again, but I didn't.

"Even if that is true, I am bound. My powers are useless," I simply answered.

"Your magick is useless, which is why your protection spell didn't work. The abilities you were born with have nothing to do with that. Your aura is white. It is the rarest color, as you also read. It's what gives you the ability to heal, to fall into a state of meditation so easily. You're in a closer spiritual state than others because your crown chakra is open. People are naturally drawn to you; you make them feel better in your presence. They feel comfortable enough to tell you their deepest, darkest secrets. Vulnerable enough to fall in love with you. The same way you are still able to control water, despite the hex," she explained.

"And what about Nathaniel?" I said, mentioning Fiona's boyfriend from the book. "He fell in love with Fiona on his own; she didn't use her abilities on him. Same as Josh and I assume Jacob."

"Why didn't you read my letter from Mom?" she asked. I stopped rocking and looked at her in surprise. "Oh, come on, you New Yorkers think y'all are so slick. You really think I'd leave that box in the linen closet, not expecting you to snoop around?"

"Why'd you leave it for me to find?" I asked.

"I felt like you should read it," she answered.

"I read my own. Yours wasn't mine to read," I said.

"Josh stopped ya, huh?" she laughed. "Do you want to know what it said?"

I lit another cigarette. "You smoke too much," she commented.

"Is that what it said?" I asked mockingly.

"No," she said, as she leaned her body in closer to look directly at me. "It said to help you. When the time came, that you would come to me for assistance, that you couldn't do it alone. She begged me to help you."

"Was that man our father?" I asked.

"Yes, my only memory of him is when he left us. You were just a baby. He left us all alone," she answered. "Too bad he was a dick; he was good-looking, no?"

I let out a laugh. "Yes, he was. Have you ever tried to find him?"

She nodded. "I did. When I was in my early twenties, that is when I really started researching the family. By the time I found him, he had already died, alone. No wife, no other children, he had nothing."

"I'm sure that would sound a lot sadder if he hadn't abandoned us in the first place," I said, expressionless. "Did he even know what she did? Did he know she died, that we were by ourselves?"

She shrugged her shoulders sluggishly. "I don't know; I was hoping to get those answers from him, some type of closure, I guess, but I was too late. There is something else I found, though, when researching the family."

I put my second cigarette out and leaned in closer to her. "What?"

"The name, NaPalepso. It's her maiden name. Mom must have changed our names when he left. I don't have our birth certificates; I have no idea where they are. But I did find out she has a sister."

"Mom has a sister?" I exclaimed. "Is she alive? Did you meet her?"

"Yes, she is alive. Her name is Laura, and she still lives in California—Santa Monica. She is seven years older than Mom was. And no, I never reached out to her. I never felt I needed to. It's not like she came to our rescue, either. I am certain she knows what happened to her sister. She was likely at the funeral for all we know," she said.

"I have a house in Malibu. It's like a forty-minute drive to Santa Monica. I think we should pay her a visit," I suggested. "And that's a fantastic point—where the hell was she? Maybe she has our birth certificates. Clearly, Mom knew I was going to ask you for help. She also knew William would be asking me for help. She obviously had abilities as well; maybe this Laura bitch can fill in some of the missing pieces."

"So, you want to just show up on her doorstep unannounced? Hey, we're your long-lost nieces?" she asked, not convinced that was a great idea.

"Yes, that is exactly what I want to do. Give her no preparation, no time to come up with excuses. Just roll up on her," I said.

"'Roll up on her,'" she repeated, holding back laughter. "You asked me where I got the southern accent from; when did you become *so* New York?"

I also laughed, realizing how funny that sounded when she said it aloud.

"Okay, but first, we need to do a real protection spell on you. And not an easy one, like you chose. We will use candle magick," she said.

"That sounds very *witchy*," I said skeptically.

"Morgan, you're a witch. Whether you like the word or not, it's what you are. Candle magick is more effective," she answered. "The protection spell won't be too difficult; unbinding you will be harder. Maybe after we meet Laura, we'll have some idea of who could have done this to you."

"And the boy? What are we going to do about him?"

"I don't know that yet. We need to figure out who wrote this book. Whoever that author is, obviously knew us in our last life. They knew exactly what rituals we performed, how they failed, and the ramifications that followed. And more importantly, the one we did last lifetime in detail."

"Why is there nothing mentioned in the book about past life memories? Is this the first time I have had them? Have you had any?" I asked.

"No, but think about it, what was the last spell they did in the book?"

"Recollection," I realized.

"Exactly, recollection, to awaken sooner to try to save him in time. And it worked. So well, in fact, you're having flashbacks of your other lifetimes," she said.

CHAPTER 28

The smell of freshly picked flowers made me realize I was in Lucas' house as I walked through the corridor, examining everything around me again. Old, framed pictures hung on the walls in bronze frames, a chandelier dangling with large candles hanging from them. The house was tranquil, and it appeared as if no one was home as I made my way to the gigantic property in the back. My bare feet stepped through the grass and felt comfortable in the atmosphere for the first time. Rows of various flowers in the garden seemed to stretch out for hundreds of yards. I stooped down to get a better look at one beautiful flower that caught my attention. It hadn't quite bloomed yet, but it was the prettiest shade of pink I had seen. Just as I reached over to touch one, I heard Elijah behind me.

"Do you need a hand, Mother?" he asked. This time I wasn't alarmed by him, as I turned around and saw him standing over me. Instead, I felt incredibly comfortable and protected in his presence, much like I did with William, which led me to believe Chrys was on point with her prediction that they were all the various versions of the same boy.

"Where is your father?" I asked, almost whispering. I followed his gaze as he looked toward the guest house on the other end of the property. He stretched his neck to motion to it.

"It is his hosting night. He is entertaining the ladies," he said uncomfortably. My mouth dropped a bit as I realized that our son was well aware of his affairs like it was common knowledge. "Let me get a vase for you," he offered, changing the subject; he disappeared inside and returned with a glass container filled with water. He squatted next to me and held the bottle towards me as I pulled some flowers out from the root and placed them in the vase. "I like this one," he smiled, pointing over at an underdeveloped flower similar to the one that drew my interest. "It will bloom nicely." I reached out to grab it for him and placed it with the others.

"How often does your father entertain the ladies?" I asked. He looked at me, surprised, as if I should know the answer.

"Every fortnight," he replied, pointing at another flower. "How about this one?" Seeing him try so hard to distract me from growing upset over Lucas warmed my heart.

"Yes, that is lovely; good choice," I said.

I smiled as he leaned towards it, pulled it out, and arranged it with the others.

I woke up abruptly to the same screeching of roosters again. Josh looked over at me and let out an exaggerated yawn as he stretched his body. "Don't say it; we are not setting them on fire."

"Damn, I was having a recollection," I said, frustrated. His forehead creased as he looked over at me uneasily, afraid of what I was going to tell him.

"Was it Jacob again?" he asked hesitantly.

I shook my head. "No, not this time. Elijah and I were picking flowers while Lucas was.... well, I guess sleeping with other women," I replied.

"So, Lucas wasn't there?" he asked after I explained the entire memory in detail.

"No, but he's around. He'll show up again. I am positive about that. Chrys is certain the spell we performed didn't work," I said as I got up from the bed and started putting on clothes. "We had a long talk last night while you were sleeping." I filled him in on most of the conversation Chrys and I had the night before about my family's history, the plans to meet our Aunt Laura in Santa Monica, everything but what she said about him, and the similarities I shared with Fiona. He threw on a clean pair of joggers and a t-shirt, and we went downstairs to meet Chrys in the kitchen, who was cooking eggs.

"Do you wake up this early every day?" I asked as Josh headed straight to the coffee maker to make us cups.

"Yes, ma'am," she said.

"Don't call me ma'am. It sounds so old," I said. Chrys laughed like that was the funniest thing she had heard. As I gathered plates and set the table, she dished out the eggs and sat down.

"I would love to wake up to freshly cooked breakfast every morning," Josh teased and winked at me.

"Then hire a cook," I retorted as he joined us at the table, placing a cup of coffee in front of me.

"So, we're going to do the spell today, yes?" she asked hopefully. I nodded.

"Yes. If you are the one who's going to do it, do you believe it will work this time?" I asked.

"I do," she answered, washing her eggs down with coffee.

"And what about the moon cycle? It doesn't matter that the moon isn't full?" Josh asked.

"That's true. The spell would work more efficiently if the moon was full; however, we don't have time to wait. As long as we do it properly, it should be successful regardless," she said.

When we finished eating, we followed her up to her bedroom. Also furnished very simply, there was a queen-size bed, surrounded by night tables and a flat-screen TV on the dresser facing the bed. I thought it was decorated it nicer than the other rooms, all in violet and gray. She had an altar in the corner, similar to the one in Lucas' house, only more modern. Her style surprised me. She did well for herself as an accountant, but lived very modestly.

She opened the drawer to the altar and retrieved a clear case display bearing all sorts of healing crystals, then reached under the table, took out a box, and opened it. She reached in and handed me a white pillar candle and a Swiss Army knife. The candle was rather large and had to measure at least six inches of plain white wax. "I want you to carve on one side 'protection' going down the surface of the candle and your name on the other," she instructed.

Taking care not to slip and cut myself, I inscribed the words and handed the candle back to her. She placed it on a saucer in the middle of the table and surrounded the candle with five stones. As we watched, she lit a bundle of sage and smudged all three of us, along with the stones and candle.

"These stones all hold different metaphysical properties," she explained. "Fluorite for protection," she began, holding up the shiny green stone and placing it strategically next to the candle. Next, she went to a light pink one and held it up. "Rose quartz for love and healing." Then, a brown one, with hints of black running through it. "Tiger's eye to enhance your third eye," she said as she placed her finger between her eyebrows, pointing at where the chakra was located. She held up a plain back one, "Tourmaline for grounding." Last, she placed a completely transparent glass-looking stone, "And a clear quartz to intensify the potency of the crystals." Once she aligned them to her liking around the candle, she lit the wick, chanted a prayer out loud three times, and asked Archangel Michael for assistance. When she completed the spell, she thanked him and gave gratitude to her spirit guides.

"Do not under any circumstances let this candle go out," she warned. "It needs to burn through, and once it goes out on its own, we will bury all of the remains and the crystals in the backyard."

"I used a fluorite bracelet when I did my spell; I was told it aids in removing a hex," I said.

"It helps, it is one of the most protective stones," she answered.

"Who is Archangel Michael?" Josh asked.

"He is the archangel of protection; I ask for his assistance only when necessary. I don't like to overdo asking for aid or take advantage in any way," she looked from Josh to me. "I think it's pretty vital at this point, no?" We agreed with her as we headed back down to the living room.

"Once the candle goes out on its own, we will go 'roll up,' as you put it, on Laura," she said. Plans were made for Chrys and me to go to California in four days, our best estimate of when the candle would go out, while Josh would go back home to New York.

"Do I get to ride on your jet?" she asked excitedly.

"Of course," I answered. I turned to Josh, "Do you want me to order you one?"

He let out a laugh. "No, it's quite alright, thank you. I am not high maintenance, nor does anyone care who I am; I can fly commercial."

CHAPTER 29

*C*hrys followed me through the front door of my Malibu home and stood still in the foyer, paralyzed in awe.

"You want a drink or something?" I asked, turning to her as I noticed she was motionless in shock.

"You live here?" she asked slowly.

"Only half the time, I am mostly in my New York house now," I said. "Are you going to come in or just stand at the entrance?"

She slowly walked in, her eyes scanning the entire place. It was a tremendous space on a cliff overlooking Los Angeles. An open floor plan made the house appear even larger than it was, with expensive pieces of art hanging on the walls and a long, winding staircase that led to the six bedrooms upstairs. She strolled through the living room into the kitchen, apprehensive about touching anything.

"Relax, it's just a house," I said as I went into the refrigerator and took out two bottles of water. She sat down at the table.

"I have never been in a house this nice," she admitted. "It's straight out of a movie. Who takes care of it when you're in New York?"

"I have people for that," I answered nonchalantly.

She opened the water and took a sip, staring into the living room. "Private jets, mansions in Malibu.... just when I thought I was over you stealing my part in *My Life*, here I am wondering why you and not me?"

I sat down at the table across from her. "Oh, will you stop it already? I didn't steal your part or your life. Can we drop that? Even if I did get the role you wanted, nothing prevented you from auditioning for another TV show, so can you let it go? You seem pretty content with your roosters and homemade butter," I said.

She started shaking her head vigorously. "I didn't make the butter!" she said, irritated. I couldn't help but laugh; it was so easy to get under her skin.

"Relax, I'm kidding. Now let's have a serious conversation about Laura. What exactly are we going to say to her when we show up?"

"We are going to explain to her who we are and why we are there. We want to know exactly what missing pieces she may know about Mom," she explained.

After we both showered and dressed, we headed out to the rental car; I tossed her the key and jumped in the passenger side.

"How long did you lose your license for?" she asked as she started up the car.

"Three years," I said as I opened the sun visor to look at myself. "The judge went easy on me."

"Must be that inviting aura," she said sarcastically. I flipped through the radio stations until I got to my favorite nineties' alternative.

"Oh, hell no," she said as she started messing with the

channels and landed on a country station. Annoyed, I put the channel back to alternative.

"We are in my town now; leave the country where it belongs," I said. The argument over the choice of music served as a good distraction on the ride because it seemed like a lot less than forty minutes by the time we pulled up in front of Laura's house. We stayed in the car for a few minutes, staring over at the house. It was a typical California house, decent sized and well maintained. Finally, I slid on my sunglasses.

"Let's go," I said as I opened the car door. She hesitated for a minute, then got out and followed my lead as I marched to the door and rang the bell. A well-put-together woman in her early sixties appeared as she opened the door dressed in yoga clothes with her hair tied back in a ponytail as if she had just returned from the gym. She had dark hair and eyes, with an olive complexion, the opposite of my mother, who was fair-skinned with blonde hair and green eyes. She looked us up and down.

"Can I help you?" she politely asked.

"Are you Laura NaPalepso?" Chrys asked.

"How do you know that last name?" she asked.

"Is it you or not?" I asked impatiently.

"That's my maiden name. It's Everhart now. And you are?"

I slid off my sunglasses and looked directly into her eyes. Her face immediately went from confused to shocked. "Do you know who we are?" I asked.

She opened her mouth to speak, but nothing came out as she eyed me up and down. Finally, she nodded. "You're Calista Reed! From the movie *The Golden Train*!" she exclaimed, starstruck. Thankfully, she recognized me for *The Golden Train* and not *My Life*; I wasn't ready to deal with another remark about it. I pinched the bridge of my nose and shook my head in disbelief as Chrys asked if we could come in. She opened the door to let us in, still staring at me in shock.

"Please sit," she excitedly said as she led us to the sofa in the living room. Although the living room was nicely decorated with modern accessories and leather couches, there was a dark energy to the room I couldn't get past. I looked over at Chrys, who must have felt the same vibrations; she signaled to me with her eyes that she felt uncomfortable as she held on to the fluorite bracelet on her wrist.

"Can I get you guys something? A drink or something to eat, maybe? Did I win a contest or something?" she started anxiously asking a ton of questions.

"Not exactly," I said, unamused. "We have some questions for you."

"Does my sister look familiar to you? Other than from the movies?" Chrys asked hurriedly. Laura shifted her interest from Chrys to me, and studied me for some sort of remembrance as to who I could be.

"Have we met before? Do I know you?" she asked, confusion in her voice.

"I'm not sure. You might. You definitely know my mother or *did*, I should say. Olivia NaPalepso," I said simply. Her face lost all color as her eyes went from me to Chrys, then back to me. She stood up suddenly.

"What do you want?" her voice changed from enthusiastic to agitated almost immediately.

"Answers," I said. She stalked closer to me to get a better look, staring directly into my eyes.

"Yes, now that I get a closer look at you, you look exactly like your mother. Are we done here? I have a lot to do…" she said as she waved for us to get up.

"That wasn't the question we need an answer for," Chrys stated. "We want to know everything you know about our mother. I am sure you are aware she is no longer with us. She had abilities, unexplainable gifts that we are trying to...."

"Your mother didn't have *abilities*," she snapped. "She was ill. She was delusional, and it's tragic what happened to her, it's very sad, but I really need to get going...."

"When did she first know she had these abilities," I asked, ignoring her blatant plea for us to leave.

"Your mother started developing issues as a teenager, much younger than both of you, maybe twelve or thirteen. But listen, I have to run," she said, still trying to get us to stand. Chrys shot up from the couch and approached her.

"We're not leaving until you answer our questions, unless you want to call the police and have us removed," she said confidently. I was taken aback and impressed at the same time by her firmness. Laura sat back down across from us, staring at us with a stone-cold expression on her face.

"What exactly do you want to know? Are you into this Witchcraft bullshit too? Because I will not tolerate conversations like this in my house. Unlike your mother and obviously her children, I have a realistic view of life. I do not believe in fairy tales or magic...."

"Where are our birth certificates?" Chrys asked. She threw her hands in the air.

"You're asking me that? How the hell would I know that? I can tell you I know you were named after healing crystals, based on the 'powers' or 'gifts' as you put it, that your mother believed you both possessed. Morganite," she said, looking at me. "And Chryscollca," she said, shifting her eyes to Chrys.

"And our father? I know he died but who was he? Why did he leave us?" Chrys's second question.

She let out a deep breath as she looked down at her lap. "Your father's name was Frank, and he adored your mother. He begged her to get help, but she refused. It became too much for him, for everyone in the family. In the end, your mother had no one but the two of you," she answered.

"Help for what?" I asked.

"Look, I know you girls have some sort of disillusion about your mother's mental wellbeing; that's apparent because you're even referring to it as 'gifts.' Your mother heard voices; she had visions of things that didn't exist. She suffered from hallucinations."

"What kind of visions?" Chrys asked.

"She thought she could see the future," she said, with melancholy in her voice. "She finally stopped talking about it until Morganite was born. Then she had a vision that haunted her every single day. It disabled her. She kept you both close to her at all times, especially Morganite. She stopped leaving the house and wouldn't talk about it. She became agoraphobic. Your father pleaded with her to tell him what she thought she had seen, but she refused to tell him. She believed that she was a witch, and if she said it out loud, it was destined to come true. She claimed she had no way of identifying a true psychic vision and convinced herself that if she said it aloud, she would make it manifest. Your father tried very hard to get her to see a psychiatrist, but she refused. She was terrified she'd be put away," she said. "It finally became too much for him to handle, and he left her. Your mother had a lot of secrets."

"And you? Where the hell were you?" I asked, now standing up, feeling my anger rise. Laura also stood to be eye level with me. "Do you know how we grew up? Do you know what we went through? Even if you truly believed she was sick, why didn't you step in and help her kids?" I looked around her house. "It appears as if you do well for yourself, so what exactly was it that stopped you from helping two innocent children?"

She came closer to me as I watched her grow irate.

"Because I got tired of cleaning up your mother's messes. I had done my part in her life; I have sacrificed many things to help her out," she said defensively. "Much like your father, I too gave up."

I let out a snarky laugh and shook my head in disgust. "I'm over this conversation. Let's go, Chrys," I said as I headed towards the front door. Chrys stood in place, not moving. "Let's go," I firmly said as I waved her to come to me, jerking my head towards the door.

"Morgan, cool down; we need to know more," she argued.

"Know more of what? What a piece of shit our mother's own sister is?" I said as I pointed my finger at Laura. "If I stay here one more second, I am going to lose my shit and get arrested for assault, so I'll wait for you in the car," I said as I stormed out. I rushed to the car, desperately trying to get in. I started patting my pockets and shuffling through my pocketbook, looking for the key. But, of course, Chrys had it. *Shit!* I put my sunglasses back on and sat on the hood of the car, my arms crossed over my chest as I slowly rocked back and forth, trying to calm myself down. I regretted my decision to come along with Chrys and let Josh go back to New York. I found myself wishing he were there to calm me down.

CHAPTER 30

*C*hrys came out a few minutes later, dangling the car key in the air as she approached me.

"You forgot you don't have the key?" she asked. I rolled my eyes, annoyed, and slid off the hood, going around to the passenger seat.

"So, what did our wonderful Aunt Laura have to say after I left?" I asked as I climbed in.

She let out a sigh as she started the car. "Nothing relevant, but I swear she is hiding something. Something just didn't feel right in that house."

"I agree; something was absolutely off with her. I mean, she seriously let two innocent kids basically live on the street," I said, not hiding my annoyance.

"And once again, you'll make this about you. Even knowing all this, you still have no empathy for your mother?" she asked nastily. I pulled down the sun visor and studied myself in the mirror to distract from the conversation. I might have felt worse for my mother if we hadn't lived such horrific lives. But I just couldn't. I still had too much hatred in me. I brought Chrys out shopping, and we went to a high-end restaurant that night for dinner. I figured I should enjoy my last night in California before returning home to New York. She advised me to do a daily protection spell, similar to the one I initially did, using the white light meditation, but this time to make sure I put the same beam around William as well. Now that he had appeared in the present, she was nervous Lucas could get to me through him.

When I got home, I had to return to the set and finish the movie's last scene I had walked out on. Richard was quite annoyed with me, but it wasn't too bad other than his attitude. After filming ended, I decided I needed a break from acting for a bit. Too much was happening, and a mental break was quickly in order.

I had my interior decorator convert one of my apartment's rooms to a meditation area. Josh and I got a kick out of going to metaphysical stores to buy crystals to decorate the room. The space looked fantastic once completed. All soft earth tone colors, the walls a light blue, the furniture a warm brown. End tables in every corner, exhibiting healing crystals and plants. A giant plush beanbag in the center of the area accompanied by a Himalayan salt lamp, a diffuser, and a happy Buddha statue gave it a very feng shui vibe.

I couldn't wait to try out the new space when I woke up the next morning. I enthusiastically went into the room and turned my diffuser on as I made myself comfortable on the bean bag, sitting straight across from the Buddha statue. Putting on soft music, I closed my eyes. Taking calculated deep breaths, I inhaled the scent of eucalyptus, lavender, and frankincense as it spilled throughout the room and put me at ease.

It couldn't have taken longer than five minutes before my mind entered a state of subconsciousness. I could feel the concrete steps below my bare feet as I slowly made my way up and opened the door to the cabin. William was already there. Sitting upright on his mat as if he were waiting for me. Inching my way towards my mat, I kneeled as he turned his head to face me.

"You're back," he said, with a slight smile indicating he knew I would be.

"Is that okay?" I asked as I studied his facial expression. A blue light illuminated his aura, making it seem like he was glowing. He had a tattoo on his bicep of some sort of tribal evil eye and one on his forearm of a hamsa hand.

"What is that?" I asked, pointing at the ink, realizing I had never noticed it before. He explained that both symbols were a sign of protection, and I told him about the bubbles of light I would place around both of us. We sat in silence as I followed Chrys' instructions, putting us in barriers.

"Now close your eyes, and go back to your happy place," he whispered to me when I was through. "The most peaceful place you have ever been." Instinctively, I obeyed. When I opened my eyes, my location had changed; I was no longer in the cabin, and William wasn't with me. Instead, I was back in the past, on top of a roof that appeared to be a barn. I wasn't startled, though. Instead, I was incredibly relaxed, sitting comfortably, staring off at the land in front of me.

It was a very serene view, looking at the town from above. The field of flowers, similar to the ones at mine and Lucas' house, stretched out for miles. With the chatter of birds and other animals lingering through the air, I felt in the most peaceful state I had in a long time. I shut my eyes again, inhaling the scent emulating from the flowers, as I felt one with nature, and it was soothing me even more. I could feel gentle hands around my waist and his breath on my neck as I leaned back and rested between his legs. At first, I assumed it was Jacob, judging by how I felt wrapped in his embrace, until he softly spoke, and I suddenly realized it was Lucas. The sensations I had around him were different this time, though. I didn't have hatred or fear; instead, I felt warm and protected. I was incredibly comfortable, warped in his body and didn't want to move.

"I love how enchanted with the meadow you become," he whispered into my ear as he kissed the back of my neck. "Your eyes seem to sparkle as you gaze at them."

"I believe those were the first words you uttered to me when you found me up here. Do you remember that?" I asked

"How could I not remember the day I met the love of my life? And now you see, I spoke with sincerity," he said.

"Amazing, isn't it? How we both happened to come to the same place when we needed to unwind?"

"It was fate, darling. You are my destiny," he muttered.

"I could stare at these flowers for days," I said in a daze.

"Well then, I shall make sure you have your own garden of flowers, every type of bud you could desire."

"I would love to have my own garden," I admitted as I intertwined my fingers through his.

"I will make it my sole purpose to give you everything you desire," he promised.

My eyes popped open as I realized I was back in my meditation room. Still mesmerized by Lucas' memory, I reached for my phone, only now feeling the warmth. I shut off the music and called Josh.

He came right over, and we sat in my living room as I explained the occurrence to him.

"So, even after Chrys did her spell, and you had just put yourself in a bubble, he still came through? He must be insanely powerful," he stated, annoyed.

"It was different this time, opposite of how I felt before. I assume it was before we got married. It was almost like a memory inside a memory, if that's possible," I said.

"I think at this point, *anything* is possible," he said. He took my hand in his. "How do we know that was a real memory, and he isn't just toying with your head?"

"I mean, I did marry the guy. I assume I must have loved him at some point. Maybe the spell did work, and that is why the better memories are coming through now," I suggested.

"Or maybe it was just the mind frame you put yourself into. You were in a deep state of meditation. Maybe it brought you back to a similar time you were in the same headspace. William did tell you to go to the happiest place you remembered, right?" he asked.

"Yes, he did. The roof we were on, the barn; it wasn't the first time we had been there. I was so comfortable there, like you said—I was in a completely different zone."

He ran his thumb in a circular motion in my palm, sending heat waves through my body.

"It would be so much easier if we could just get the whole story at once, instead of these piece-meal visions you're getting," he said.

"I wish I could somehow take you with me to see what I see through your own eyes," I said. "Do you think it's possible to put you in the same state so you can see my recollections?"

He rested his forehead in his hand and massaged his temples, thinking about what I had just suggested.

"The only thing I can think of is trying to astral project again. We need to practice, and we need to somehow keep these other dudes out of your mind while we do it," he let out a laugh.

"What?" I asked.

"Nothing," he said, shaking his head as if whatever his idea was had been completely ridiculous.

"Tell me," I said, sliding closer to him on the couch. He

stayed silent. I put my hand on his thigh and slightly rubbed him. "Tell me!"

He placed his hand over mine and looked at me. "It is just a little crazy," he admitted. "It's like I'm competing for your attention in an entirely different plane."

CHAPTER 31

*J*osh stayed at his place, and we both set up our night tables to prepare to "go under," as we called it. Placing the myrrh and Lapiz Lazuli across from me, along with a diffuser releasing sandalwood, as Barbara had suggested when she helped guide us through the process when we went back to the metaphysical store. I tried to put myself back in the yearning phase I must have been in with Josh when I traveled the last time. I laid in bed, desperately attempting to recreate the feeling I had that night that Josh left Haven, my craving for him, and how desperately I wanted to see him in my dream. Worry kept me from drifting off as fast as I should have, but finally, I fell asleep. When I awoke, I was on our mountain, and like last time, he was standing by our blanket.

I made my way over to him as his face lit up. "It worked!" he excitedly said as he bent down and kissed me. "Are you going to make it rain again?" he asked, raising his eyebrows up and down quickly, with a mischievous smile on his face. I teasingly slapped his arm.

"Don't be a horn ball, Josh; we have important things to

do. We have some people we need to find," I said as I slowly walked around the area, inspecting everything. He stood in place as his face turned from excited to disheartened.

"Cali, this is *our* spot. We're not going to see them here," he said suddenly. I walked back over to him, gawking at him, grasping that he was correct. I slumped down, disappointed, on our blanket and crossed my legs. He followed my lead and rested across from me in the same position. "Now what?"

I racked my brain for an idea. "The last time I was able to have a memory within a memory," I said as I reached my hand out to him. He extended his and rested it in mine. "Maybe if I can get us to the house, you can see through me. It's worth a try." He nodded, as I closed my eyes and strategically tried to get myself back to Lucas' house. I pictured everything from the items in his house to the scent of the flowers. "Don't let go of me," I whispered, not opening my eyes. Suddenly, I felt as if I were falling fast; I clutched his hand tighter and forcefully squeezed my eyes to try my hardest to prevent myself from waking. When the falling sensation halted, I gradually opened my eyes, expecting to be back in my bedroom. I was taken aback when it wasn't my room I was in; instead, it was a place I didn't recognize at all.

Sitting in the damp grass, I slowly stood up. Realizing that I was in a dark open field, my eyes scanned my surroundings thoroughly, looking for him. "Hello?" I yelled out. "Josh?" Nothing. Miles and miles of moist grassland ahead of me. I looked down, and I was barefoot. Now in the same white sundress and alone in the dark. I had somehow made it back, only Josh was nowhere in sight, and this was new territory. The air was so clear, and you could see the stars so perfectly, that it was evident I wasn't in New York. As a matter of fact, the sky was clearer than any place had been, period. Almost as if the stars were closer to earth than usual. I started walking, not really sure where I was headed. I came to a waterfall, passing trees and beautiful flowers unlike anything I had ever seen before. The brilliance of the stars shimmered off the water, making it appear to glow purple, with just a hint of teal through the trees behind it. Instinctively I walked into the river until I was knee-deep. I closed my eyes as I felt the stars beam down on me, and the room-temperature water instantly put me at ease. I was in a meditative state, letting the peace and tranquility sink in until it completely consumed me, almost forgetting why I was even there in the first place. A sudden presence made me realize I wasn't alone. I spun around nervously, not sure if it were Jacob or Lucas I would come eye to eye with.

His affectionate brown eyes reassured me immediately as my body naturally fell into Jacob's embrace. He swept his hand down the side of my face as he pulled me into his kiss. I sensually ran my fingers down his arm until his hand entangled with mine, and I pulled him back towards the waterfall.

The fresh, clean water fell over our bodies, drenching us both as our kiss became more intimate. His lips trailed down to my neck as I gripped the back of his drenched shirt. He reached down, pulled my leg up around his waist, and supported me. I progressively opened my eyes to take all of him in as I watched him start to fade. I tugged on his shirt tighter, determined to try to stay with him when I felt like I was falling once again. When I landed this time, I was in front of a typewriter, at a desk in a room with a dim light shining on the paper, and I was typing the last page of a book. I read and retained every word. I could see each letter clearly as if I were really writing until I typed "The End."

My eyes abruptly shot open as I heard the intercom and Logan's voice come through, and I was back in my room.

"Ms. Reed, Mr. Knight is here for you," he announced.

"Of course, let him up," I answered, still half asleep. Frazzled, I slipped out of bed and lethargically opened the door in a stupor to see Josh standing there, with a look of concern on his face. He quickly walked in.

"I called you like twenty times! I lost you, and when I woke up, you weren't picking up the phone. I panicked," he frantically rambled. "You were just gone! You closed your eyes and told me not to let go, but then you just disappeared."

My heart raced swiftly; the memories were still fresh in my head as I tried to process what had happened. I didn't say anything to Josh. I just walked into my office, opened my laptop, and started typing every word I had retained from recollection. The last page of a book I had been writing. When I finished, I went back to the living room, where Josh was still sitting on the couch. I explained everything that had transpired and the numerous memories I had recovered.

"What kind of book was it?" he asked after hearing the entire story.

"I don't know, I just know the ending, and it isn't a happily ever after," I answered.

"How did it end?" he asked hesitantly. I was silent for a moment, remembering when Laura had said that my mother had been afraid to say her visions out loud to avoid manifestation. He gaped at me, keenly awaiting an answer.

"It was a tragedy," I finally stated. "A romantic tragedy."

His lips parted as he inhaled a deep breath. "Was it you?" he asked tensely. I shook my head.

"No," I said. "I don't know who the woman was, but she was left mourning and in pain."

"Was it from the past? You said there was a typewriter; is it possible it was Jacob or Lucas who died?"

"It was the past," I conceded. "Just not *that* past. It was more like the twentieth century, not the seventeenth."

He rubbed his forehead and looked distressed. "How many lifetimes did you have?"

I sat down next to him on the couch. "Well, judging by the

different variations of the boy, we know there are at least four," I said. "Elijah, William, Andrew, and Jayden. Assuming Chrys is correct, and they are all the same kid."

"If that is true, there is a version of you we are missing," he said.

"And you. There is Jacob, Nathaniel, and now this new timeline; we're both missing in one."

"Do you think Lucas and Jacob may be different forms of the same guy? And somehow, they both show up at once? Maybe now that Chrys did an effective spell, you're really separating the two lives?" he suggested. I stood up, reached my hand down to him, and pulled him up to me.

"I don't know. I'm tired and can't even begin comprehending it now," I said. "I am glad you came here, though. Please come sleep with me."

CHAPTER 32

*J*osh and I weren't "dating." We didn't have that title, at least. Sure, we always hung out and had sex, but I wouldn't have called us a couple. I wasn't seeing anyone else, and I was confident he wasn't either, we spent most of our free time together, but we didn't do couple things. We rarely went out to dinner or on dates; we didn't hold hands and didn't really do anything that a couple would normally do. We didn't do much other than research the happenings in the last year and a half. It had been a year and three months since I met him and a year and a half since the message on the mirror. 541 days, to be exact.

He didn't make a big deal about it when he asked me out to dinner that night, but I knew why he did. Neither of us had any idea what we were waking up to the next day. He took me to a fancy steak house on the Upper East Side, a very romantic spot. He looked amazing, dressed in slacks and a light blue button-down shirt that matched his eyes perfectly. I wore a short black cocktail dress. It was nice to get dressed up to go somewhere for a change. He had reserved a private table in the back, candlelit, where we could be alone. Old brick walls made it a very cozy atmosphere, with soft music playing throughout the restaurant. I guess it would have been typical for a couple to do if they were unsure if it was their last day on earth. At that point, I don't think either of us knew what to expect when we woke up the next morning, if we even woke up at all. I recalled the time at Haven when he suggested the message could possibly mean the end of the world, and I couldn't help but worry about whether or not he was correct.

He didn't say much as he studied his menu, but I could feel it; the uncertainty he was feeling was radiating from him. My mind went to Chrys for a minute, thinking of the time she told me how she could feel everyone's emotions and now realizing how horrible that could be.

"Have you decided what you wanted, sir?" the waiter politely asked. Josh looked at him and spoke for the first time since we sat down other than to order a bottle of Pellegrino at the start.

"I'll have the lobster tail and filet minion, medium rare," he said as he handed the menu back to the waiter.

He took the menu from Josh and then turned to me.

"And for you?"

I looked down nervously at the menu. What would I eat as my last meal? Should I go all out and get the lamb chops with mashed potatoes? I hadn't eaten like that in years. Then I reconsidered when the notion of us having sex came into my mind, and I didn't want to be bloated. "I will have the branzino," I settled on something lighter. Then I leaned over the table toward Josh. "Do you want to get a bottle of wine?" He looked at me, surprised I guessed that I would be suggesting alcohol, then tightened his lips and exhaled deeply through his nose. He nodded slowly and bit on his thumbnail.

"Sure, can we see the wine list?" he asked the waiter.

"Certainly, let me get that for you," he answered as he walked away. Still silent, Josh looked down at his place setting and started uneasily playing with his silverware. The waiter returned with the wine list and handed it to him. "I'll give you a moment to look over it," he said as he stepped away from the table and watched from a distance. Josh read the menu to himself, and I was once again frustrated that I couldn't read his mind. Finally, he shifted his eyes up to me.

"I can't believe I don't know this, it's typically the first question I ask when I go out with a girl, but do you like red or white?"

"Red," I answered. He nodded and went back to the menu.

"I'm not a fan of Merlot. I find it to be dry. Do you like Cabernet? Pinot Noir?" he asked.

"Either, whichever you prefer," I said quietly. He ran his fingers over his lips as his eyes returned to the list. Watching him study the menu, I sensed his reluctance and felt bad that I had put him on the spot. It seemed like he didn't really want to get the wine, but he was doing it to appease me.

"Forget it, don't get the wine," I said softly. He looked up in surprise.

"You don't want it?" he asked.

"No, it's okay; I understand if you don't want to...." He rested the menu on the table and reached his hand over to signal for me to put my hand in his.

"No, I do want to," he assured me.

"Don't do it," I said, squeezing his hand gently. "We've gone this long without drinking; we've been so good. Let's not ruin that."

"Are you sure?" he asked. "I honestly don't mind getting a bottle of wine." I shook my head.

"No, don't. If we're being honest, I want to go back to your apartment after this and have amazing, mind-blowing sex with you. And I want to feel every part of it," I said. He finally smiled for the first time that night.

"Well, you do make a good argument," he said, calling the waiter back and giving him the menu. "We'll just stick with the Pellegrino." As the waiter walked away, he continued: "I'm not tying you up, either."

I let out a laugh. "You may get punched in the face," I warned.

"It's fine; the second round in the shower will cool it off. Plus, you can heal me, right?"

"Yes, I can heal you," I said, smiling.

"So, why weren't you going to take the role in *The Golden Train*?" he asked out of nowhere.

"What?"

"The day I met you at Haven and told you how great your performance was, you told me you almost didn't take the part. You didn't tell me why, though. You just said it was a story for another time. Maybe you should tell me now, considering..." his voice trailed off as he stopped himself from completing the sentence. I took a sip of my drink.

"It was nothing major. I didn't really like my co-star; we had worked together briefly before, and he is kind of a schmuck. Also, I wasn't overly impressed with the character I was playing, but I got to really make her my own, you know, incorporated myself into her. So, in the end, it worked out," I said. He smiled.

"Yeah, you did a fantastic job," he mentioned again. The waiter reappeared with our entrées as I watched Josh place his napkin on his lap. I could tell how anxious he was, thinking of things he should know or say, should he not have the chance to again. I knew he wanted to tell me he loved me, but he was debating whether he should. He knew I couldn't feel it back.

"Is there anything else you want to know? Or tell me?" I

pressed. He put his silverware back down and looked at me silently in thought.

"No," he finally said as he went back to his steak. "There's nothing you don't already know."

We didn't say much during dinner, and when we got back to his apartment, we did precisely what I had suggested earlier; we had amazing, mind-blowing sex. The first time was unrestrained, and my emotions toggled from passionate to violent to craving his touch to such an extent that I physically needed it. The second time, in the shower, where I could put my arms around him, I felt nothing but passion and lust for him. I woke up the next morning to him tightly gripping me. I backed out of his hold, looking at the massive black eye I had given him. We stared at each other in silence as he reached for the remote and turned on the TV. We both sat up, waiting for the anchorman to announce the doom that was happening in the world.

The news showed nothing like that, though. It was no different than any other day in New York City. Some street crime was reported, a cute animal segment, and the weather. Nothing too earth-shattering or apocalyptic. I climbed out of bed and went over to the window, perplexed, as he pressed the button for the shades to slide open; nothing but a typical busy day below. Taxis were driving like lunatics, people shuffling around hurriedly trying to get to where they needed to be, and the sounds of horns and sirens. I turned to Josh in shock, who stared back at me with the same look of uncertainty.

"Is it at the end of the 542nd day?" he asked, confused.

I went back over to the bed and crawled in. "Maybe? Or maybe the 542 days didn't actually start on that specific day?"

"So, when would it have started?" he asked. I shrugged my shoulders.

"I have no idea. Maybe when we met?" I guessed.

"So, part of me is obviously relieved, but now the other part is even more nervous that we have absolutely no idea when these 542 days actually start," he said. I laid my head on his chest as he ran his fingers through my hair. I slid my finger up to his eye.

"Well, now I really feel bad for decking you," I said sympathetically.

CHAPTER 33

For the next three months, Josh and I went back to our typical routines, silently waiting for the 542nd day from the time we met in Haven. Only, that day came and went also, making us extra suspicious as to what the message really meant, or more so, when it began. If it wasn't 542 days from the message in the mirror or our meeting, it was nearly impossible to determine when the clock started ticking. It created reticent anxiety that we both felt daily but didn't dare speak about. I began meditating twice a day, once in the morning to put myself and William in our bubbles and once at night, to detach from the day and release any negative entities or thoughts that no longer served me. It was in July when I had the dream that was about to change everything.

In all the time since my mother died, she had never come to me. I never dreamt about her; I never saw her in visions. Since childhood, she would go to Chrys often. We had suspected she never came to me because of my resentment towards her; Chrys would tell me you have to be willing to accept a spirit's presence. Which, in retrospect, didn't make much sense to me, considering I was basically being haunted by a teenage kid who hadn't been born yet, but whatever the case, she never came—until that night.

I was back in the purple field, standing by the lake, subconsciously waiting for Jacob. I couldn't explain the yearning I felt for him; it made no sense to me, other than he had to be a former version of Josh. I had no idea who he was but being around him made my entire body tingle. His mere presence made me ache to be able to love. I hadn't been in that place since the last time, but something about that specific location put me in a state of tranquility, unlike any other place I had visited on any other plane. I stood with the water to my waist, eyes closed, taking in the serenity when she approached me. I hadn't recognized her at first, looking into her emerald green eyes and long blonde hair, until she spoke.

"The Friday night before the full moon," she said. Her voice ran through me and sent chills down my entire body, bringing me back to being a child, taking for granted every time she spoke, having no idea at the time I may never hear her voice again. She extended her hand and handed me a rough, vibrant blue crystal with bright turquoise running through it. The stone was so brilliant that it almost appeared neon under the moon's glow. Along with it was an envelope with her handwriting detailing instructions.

"What is this?" I asked.

"It's an azurite and malachite; it will help you," she answered. I looked down at the envelope, her prominent handwriting listing items: lavender, rose, Epsom salt. Puzzled, I shifted my eyes from the note back up to her, but she had disappeared. I woke up frazzled, springing up and gasping for air.

"What happened?" Josh asked as he bolted from a sound sleep.

I placed my hand over my mouth and started rocking back and forth in bed.

"Was it Lucas?" he asked.

"No," I answered.

"Jacob?" he guessed again. I shook my head, unable to speak. He put his arm around me and pulled me into him as he lightly kissed my forehead.

"Who was it?" he quietly asked.

"My mother."

"Your mother? Has she ever come to you before?" he asked, shock in his voice.

I shook my head slowly. "No, but it was her; looked like her, smelled like her, sounded like her. She gave me instructions," I rattled out as I explained the dream in detail.

"Look, if your mom is suddenly showing up after all this time, something is happening. Maybe we should go to the metaphysical store and speak to Barbara," he suggested.

"You're right; Barbara has some part in this. She left the morganite with her. She may have some answers at least," I said, hopeful.

Later that day, we headed over to the shop. Barbara's face lit up as we walked in; she came over and took my hand in hers.

"What happened, sweetheart?" she asked warmly, obviously sensing I was coming to her for a reason.

"My mother came to me last night in my dream. The only other time she has appeared in any form was here, with you," I said.

She smiled and squeezed my hand gently. "What did she say?"

"She gave me instructions to buy this stone," I said, showing her a picture of the crystal I had googled on my phone. She walked us over to the aisle where the stones were laid out. "Pick one that calls to you," she reiterated. My attention immediately went to a rather large piece, coarse around the edges and shaped like a cluster. I handed it to Josh.

"What do you think?" He held the stone in his palm and rubbed the edges with his thumb.

"Rough around the edges, just like you," he joked.

"Now, this is a very powerful stone," Barbara continued. "It's nicknamed 'the stone of heaven'; it aids with insight, intuition, and creativity."

"She also gave me detailed guidelines for a bath; she said it needed to be done the Friday before a full moon. Does that make sense to you?"

"Yes, the Friday before a full moon would make a spiritual bath most effective; however, you need to make sure not to do it between six and twelve, a.m. or p.m.," she said.

"Why not those times?" Josh asked.

"They are the times we let our angels and spirit guides rest," she answered.

"Okay, so what do I do? Just take a bath?" I asked, feeling silly for even having this conversation.

"Exactly. Light a candle, close your eyes, and relax. Personally, I like using the Solfeggio Frequencies when I take a spiritual bath," she said.

"What are the Solfeggio Frequencies?" Josh asked. Barbara leaned into Josh, her eyes sparkling with excitement. She loved explaining these types of things to us; she felt the universe brought her into our lives to teach us. She was probably correct in that assumption.

"It's believed certain frequencies help in removing negative entities and assist in transitioning the human mind to a higher state of consciousness. Music and sound are said to help heal, such as a singing bowl can be used for cleansing as well," she said as she walked over to a different aisle, and we followed. She reached for a bronze bowl and, using the wooden mallet inside it, made a circular motion around the bowl, creating a high-pitched, peaceful tone.

"I'll take that too," I said without hesitation. She smiled and brought it over to the register.

"You know, the two of you together are an unbelievably powerful force," she said as she carefully wrapped my items in tissue paper and rang us up.

Josh gave me a flirtatious smile. I knew what he was thinking; he was picturing us in bed, having to tie me up. I gave him an authoritative smirk, *be serious for once*, I silently said, knowing full well he had read my mind. He lifted his hands in surrender position as Barbara swiped my credit card. "Remember that when you're apart," she warned without looking up from the register.

"Great, even Barbara knows about our imminent separation," Josh sarcastically said as we headed out.

Waiting for Friday felt like an eternity, but when it finally came, I decided to take the spiritual bath in my apartment alone. After filling the tub with warm water and adding the essential oils and salt, I carefully set up a candle and the stone on the edge of the tub. Then, with the Solfeggio Frequencies softly playing in the background, I closed my eyes and got comfortable. I was expecting to be greeted by anyone, whether it was Lucas, William, or even my mother, although I silently prayed it would be Jacob. That isn't what happened, though. Instead, I saw flashes of lights, illuminating and forming into a rainbow, and when I opened my eyes, I was on the roof of the barn I had been on with Lucas, looking over the miles of flowers alone.

"I shall make sure you have your own garden of flowers, every type of bud you could desire," I could hear Lucas whisper in my ear, as if he were behind me, although he was nowhere in sight. When I woke up from my trance, I had a clear message,

almost as if it had incepted itself into my brain. The last page of the book I had written, I needed to go back to it, and I needed to write the book.

I didn't tell anyone, even Josh, what happened during that bath. Instead, I spent the next three weeks writing the book backward based on the last page, from end to beginning. I felt like I was channeling someone using my body as a tool to write their story. When I completed the manuscript, I gave it a title: *The Broken Meadow*, and signed my new name; my now pen name, Jade Troy.

CHAPTER 34

The sound of scurrying through the corridor caught my attention, a woman in distress as it sounded like she was being dragged. The smell of flowers made me immediately realize I was in Lucas' house. I sat up straight on the couch and stretched my neck to hear what the commotion was about.

"Your Highness, we found her in your garden," I overheard a man say. I made my way to the parlor, where Lucas stood in front of three men, holding an attractive woman up with her hands tied behind her back. She was tall with dark hair, and I could sense fear emanating from her, but her hazel eyes stared at Lucas, stoned cold, with hatred.

"What are you doing here?" I asked Lucas in shock.

"Darling, I live here; have you forgotten?" he answered.

"You had duties today, did you not?" I asked.

"I did," he conceded. "But something told me I should stay home. Juliette," he said slowly, with a malicious smile, turning his attention back to the woman. I crept up behind him, as he held his arm out to keep me from going past him. "Have I not warned the two of you numerous times about playing with magick? Have you yet to learn that your magick won't work on me?"

"I take threats from no one, not even the king himself," she quipped back. He let out an inflated sigh and exaggeratedly rolled his eyes as he stalked toward her, coming right up to her face.

"Do you know what it means to be on my property?" he asked. She extended her neck forward to prove to him she was not reluctant to make eye contact with him, nor did she fear him as she probably should have. He tilted his head towards her and raised his eyebrows, awaiting an answer. When he didn't get one, he continued. "I own everything on this property, including you now, I suppose."

My heart dropped to the pit of my stomach as I felt genuine fear for this girl. As much as I admired the fact that she didn't give in to him, I was simultaneously terrified for her of what he might do. He stroked the side of her face with the back of his hand as she spat on him. Grinning, he wiped his face and pulled her closer to him by the small of her back.

"Bring her to the alcove," he commanded.

"No," I repeated, this time with certainty in my tone. I looked across the table into Debbie's eyes, pleading with me to reconsider. She silently looked down at the salad in front of her as I looked past her at the people walking down the street. With my hair tied up in a ponytail and wearing a hoodie and sunglasses, I was unrecognizable if anyone cared enough to look up anyway. I normally avoided eating outside, especially in a place as crowded as New York City, but when Debbie called me, she was desperate to get me to sit down with her. The weather was certainly nice enough to do so, so I agreed. A light breeze in the air made her blonde hair blow into her face, and even though I could tell she was bothered by it, she pretended not to notice as she pushed her lettuce around with her fork. I couldn't help but look around at the others eating their lunches, laughing with each other, on their phones, all probably living normal lives. Far from what I've ever had, especially now, which made me a bit envious.

"Please, Cali. I beg you to reconsider," she softened her voice just above a whisper, now looking into my eyes. As I shook my head, she continued, "It would be good for you, for your career. In the past year and a half, you've had a DUI, a mental breakdown on set...." I let out a scoff and rolled my eyes. A mental breakdown? Please, it wasn't a mental breakdown. I literally saw a vision of William for the first time, outside my house, outside my dreams, on the set as I was in the middle of reciting my lines. Okay, so maybe my exit was a bit dramatic as I stormed off the set smack in the middle of filming, but I wouldn't call it a mental breakdown.

"Just one commercial," she reiterated. "It will be good for your career, your *name.*"

"I'm done with that life, Debbie," I stated simply.

"You can't just be done! Look, I know you needed a break, and you had one; you need to come back and make up for your reputation. What are you so afraid of? Do you think you'll start doing drugs again?"

"What? No, I am happy now. I have a new career...."

"Writing is a nice hobby," she cut me off. "But it's far from a career, especially since you insist on writing under a different name. I bet people would be more inclined to buy a book Calista Reed wrote than whoever Jade Troy is."

"Good thing I'm rich, huh?" I retorted sarcastically. I sat back and stretched my neck, my eyes still scanning the other tables through my shades. I immediately regretted my decision to meet her. "I sent it to you. Did you even read it?"

"Yes, I did. It was good, amazing, in fact, you're a very talented writer. But Cali, you're an actress."

"Yes, Cali is an actress. Jade is an author," I remarked. She rested her forehead in her hand and shook her head, disappointed.

"Have I not done everything you have ever asked me to do?" she asked, agitated. "Down to changing my damn name!"

I rolled my eyes and let out a sigh. "Oh please, you didn't change your name. I am the only one that calls you Debbie; it's like a fun nickname," I defended.

"And did I complain?" she asked.

"Well, every time I said Alexa, the damn house would answer me! 'I'm listening,'" I said, mimicking the portable device's voice. "I like Debbie. It suits you better."

"Oh yes, Debbie sounds real Hollywood, coming from the girl who is up to her third name. I want to know what the hell happened to you in the past twelve years that the first thing you did when you left acting was to kill a guy on paper?" she asked.

Leaning over the table, I stared into her eyes to get as close as I could. "The answer is no. I am not doing a commercial, a TV show, a movie, or a damn social media ad. It's not happening. I've also told you this all on the phone. I love you, Debbie, I really do, but I didn't need to leave the house for this. Are we done here?"

She gestured for the bill by waving her fingers in the air as if she were signing a check and pushed her plate away from her. "For now. But please, Calista, I'm begging you to think about it."

She followed my lead as I stood up and hugged her. "Great seeing you as always; we need to do this more often," I said with a bit of mockery as I turned to head back to my apartment.

When I got into my apartment, I was annoyed, more than annoyed. I was *mad*. Debbie knew I wasn't interested in any gigs, and it occurred to me at that moment that she wasn't the friend she claimed to be, just another person using me for their own gain. Unfortunately, that happens way too often in Hollywood, and you never know who your real friends are until you hit rock bottom, and spoiler alert, you have no real friends. Debbie, however, had always been there for me, and I thought she was different. Evidently, I was wrong. She was simply biding her time to promote me again. She made quite the salary off my fame, and at the end of the day, I was nothing but a paycheck to her. Sad but true. And I was mad at myself for believing her.

Picking up my phone, I FaceTimed Josh, who must have still been at work, judging by his maroon button-down and black tie.

"Hey beautiful," he picked up enthusiastically.

"Can I come over?" I asked. He looked down at his watch.

"Yeah, let me have Brian cancel my meetings for the afternoon. Then, I'll be right over."

CHAPTER 35

*W*hen the copies of the books came, I studied the cover. The artist did a phenomenal job. It was on point how much it looked like the meadow of flowers from the top of the barn roof. I ran my fingers along the matte cover as the name Jade Troy appeared so boldly. I opened to the first page and signed my first autograph as Jade. I wrote it out to Barbara and stuffed it in my bag. I made my way to the metaphysical store. I didn't know exactly why I felt I needed to give her a copy, but a part of me knew she was a major piece of my awakening, and I wanted her to have one. In a weird way, even though I barely knew her, I had strong feelings toward her. She gave out a motherly vibe. Perhaps Dr. Michaels was onto something when he suggested I may have abandonment issues, but she made me feel something I had been lacking my entire life. She truly wanted to help me.

She didn't look up as the bell chimed at my entrance while she was busy helping another customer. I browsed the store, patiently waiting until she finished with the consumer.

Once she rang her up, I went over to the register. Her eyes lit up when she saw me.

"Cali! Where is Josh?"

"Oh, he's at work," I said.

She leaned over the counter. "How can I help you today, sweetheart."

"I didn't come to purchase anything. I came to give you something," I said excitedly. She rested her chin in the palm of her hands and reached over to peek inside my tote, curious about what I could have for her.

"I did a thing," I said as I reached into my bag, took out the book, and placed it on the counter. She pulled it closer to her, admired the cover, and flipped through the pages. She opened right to the signed page and read the words out loud.

Dear Barbara,

Thank you for your help in my journey. I believe you were brought into my life for a reason, and I am blessed to have met you.

Jade Troy

Her smile widened, and she looked up at me, her eyes getting watery.

"This is so sweet. I love it, and I cannot wait to read it," she said. "Did you choose the name Jade after the healing crystal?"

"How did you know I wrote the book? You didn't seem surprised at all," I asked.

"I suspected, and my gut feelings are usually dead on. Is that why you chose the name?" she asked again.

"Yes, I figured I would follow in my mother's suit of naming her children after stones," I admitted. "It's funny, actually. I didn't even know I could write; I had no intention or desire to ever to be an author."

"That's not funny; that's fate. We don't choose our destinies," she replied. "And most writers don't have a choice in the matter anyway."

"What do you mean?" I asked, leaning my elbows on the counter to get closer to her.

"In my experience, writers, the good ones anyway, can't control what they are born with. We are all born with natural abilities. We wouldn't be given gifts if we weren't meant to use them."

"So, you knew? You knew I was going to write a book?" she nodded. "Why didn't you tell me?"

"When we have visions, I feel it's important not to tell someone what their future can hold. It could alter someone's decision in doing it, which could be detrimental to fate. You wrote that book for a reason. What if my telling you about it made you apprehensive, and you didn't write it?"

"Of all the gifts I possess, I'm guessing this will be the least impactful," I laughed.

"Don't be so sure about that. That book will be around long after you're not. You're leaving behind a legacy."

"Can I tell you something crazy?" I asked hesitantly.

"Honey, nothing sounds crazy to me," she said.

"I feel like it's someone else's story. Like I was somehow just a channel when writing it," I explained. She came around the counter and took my hand in hers.

"An author isn't taught to write; the story derives from within," she said. Something about that statement sent tingles down my body. "I love it, and thank you so much for thinking of me."

I left the store with her words echoing in my mind. *An author isn't taught to write; the story derives from within.* It made me think back to when Josh asked if any story is truly fictional. I don't know why I wrote the book; I just knew I needed to. Things were accelerating at an abnormal rate, making me remember William's words that night in San Diego. He said things were going to happen very fast and that I shouldn't be afraid. That was an understatement. I went to sleep that night with all those memories fluttering through my mind, and when I awoke, I was in a new recollection.

∾

"Are you sure Lucas won't be back?" Juliette loudly whispered as we sat kneeling in my garden.

"Yes, it's his 'hosting' night," I said, resentment in my tone. She looked at the sky, the full moon shining brightly on us.

"We need to do this now; it's the only way to slow him down. One man alone should not hold the magnitude of his power. We need to bind him," she said as she prepared items for a ritual.

"He's going to know; he is very powerful," I warned.

"Perhaps, but not as powerful as you are. You need to do this, Claudia, and you need to do it tonight."

"Why shouldn't he have this power, but it's okay for me?" I asked.

"Because you don't have ill intent. A spell is only as good as the intentions behind it," she reasoned.

I lit a match and set the resins on fire as we both inhaled the potent scents of basil and myrrh. Together, we chanted a spell out loud.

"I will come back tomorrow while he is out and bury the ritual items," she said.

I woke up to Josh FaceTiming me. When I picked up, he had a look on his face I had never seen on him before. He looked like he had seen a ghost.

"Are you okay?" I asked, concerned.

"Can I come over? I need to tell you something," he said.

"Of course," I answered. Fifteen minutes later, he was sitting in my living room with me.

"I had a vision," he uttered.

"What kind of vision? Was it a dream?"

"No, my visions are different than yours. They happen when I am awake. Like, I get this visual and a message, but it's not like anyone is actually saying it, more like a 'knowing.' I guess it's because my third eye is open."

I moved closer to him on the couch and placed my hand on his thigh, anxiously awaiting what he would say.

"There was a piece of paper, clear as day, the name NaPalepso written on it. On top of the paper, there was a light pink stone, just like this," he said, reaching his hand out and holding my morganite charm in his hand. "The message was, 'her fight has not begun.'" He released the charm from his grip as I sat back and stared at him in panic.

"What the hell does that mean?" I finally asked.

"I have no idea but..." no sooner than the words left his lips, my phone rang. We both looked down to see the name Chrys flash on the screen.

"This is getting creepier by the minute," I said as I picked up the phone.

Chrys sounded rattled on the phone, speaking a mile a minute, which with her southern twang made it hard to understand her.

"Slow down; I can't understand you," I said calmly.

"I had a vision last night; Mom came to me," she said.

"Josh had a vision also, and I had another recollection. You were in it," I said.

"I know what we need to do to break the love spell! You guys ought to come here; I have the spell. We should all do it together." Josh and I looked at each other simultaneously.

"Okay," I agreed. "We'll get on a flight tomorrow."

CHAPTER 36

*S*itting back in Chrys' kitchen, the three of us drank coffee as she detailed her vision. Similar to me, her visions came in dreams as well.

"We need to use the elements; it's the only way to break the spell," she said.

"How do we do that?" Josh asked.

"Candle magick," she answered.

"The last spell you did must have worked. We're clearly all getting more powerful, although Lucas is showing up again," I said.

"And he will continue to; the spell from the last lifetime was a recollection spell. With the protection spell, and the bubbles you've been doing to yourself and William, I believe you are protected from him, but I'm not sure we can stop the memories from occurring," she said.

We followed her to her altar, where she laid out five tealights. "Each candle will represent an element. And now we ask for the aid of fire, water, earth, air, and spirit. Say this out loud," she said to me as she handed me a piece of paper with a spell written on it. "And when you're through, you will seal it with a kiss. You and Josh need to kiss, and once that happens, it should bring back the memories of you and Josh, theoretically Claudia and Jacob, and hopefully, Lucas' love spell will be reversed."

After she ran sage smoke around our bodies and her altar, I meticulously lit each candle as I named the elements out loud. Reading her spell as she instructed, I followed the directions to perfection.

"I'll leave the two of you alone," she said. "It may get emotional; it should be done in private. It will most likely bring you back to your first kiss ever."

As she left, I sat up straight, looking at Josh. "Are you ready?" I asked. He looked reluctant but took a deep breath.

"Let's do this," he answered. Cupping my face in his hands, he pulled me into him, and I felt his tongue gently slide into my mouth. I ran my fingers through his hair as he held me close and kissed me passionately. Nothing seemed to be happening, though, other than our mutual arousal. I don't know how long we were kissing, but long enough for Chrys to come back up and knock on the door. We pulled apart as she walked in.

"You guys having a make-out session or what? What is going on in here? It should have happened already; the memories should have come back."

"Well, then it clearly didn't work," I said, frustrated, as I stood up and went downstairs. I sat back at the kitchen table, resting my head in my hands, feeling defeated. Josh and Chrys followed.

"Are you okay?" Josh asked, taking my hand in his.

"Yep, great. So, I just won't be able to love, big deal. Love is overrated, anyway. And to think, you thought you were being punished for a past life," I said sarcastically. We sat in silence, not really sure what to say.

"So, Cali wrote a book," Josh said, trying to change the subject. Chrys looked up at me.

"You wrote a book?" she repeated.

"Yes," I said as I got up to get my pocketbook. "Here, I brought you one."

She took the book from me and studied it. "Jade Troy? Morgan, Cali, Jade, you really needed a third name?"

I rolled my eyes and got up to refill my now cold coffee.

"Hey, leave her alone. If she wants five names, she can have them," Josh said defensively. I returned to the table and sat down, pulling the book back to me. Then, after analyzing the cover, a sudden idea came to me.

"What stays around longer than we do?" I asked, remembering Barbara speaking of leaving a legacy behind.

"Let me guess, a book?" Chrys answered mockingly. Annoyed at our banter, Josh stood to refill his coffee now.

"Yes, a book! Same as the author did to write about us in our last life. If we write a book, same as whoever that author was, about the progress we made…." I stopped myself as a sudden revelation came to me. Chrys sprung up from her seat, staring at me, drawing the same conclusion that had just come into my head.

"You *are* the author! You wrote the book…. *Bounded by the Bond*, to remind us of how far we got last lifetime, this time around!"

I jumped up from my seat also. "I wrote the book!" I exclaimed. We grabbed each other's hands, as we bounced up and down in joy.

"I wrote the book!" I said repeatedly, and she kept reciting in sync, "You wrote the book!" Josh picked up his coffee mug and came over to the table.

"Guys," he said in a serious tone. We stopped jumping and, still holding hands, looked over at him.

"What?" Chrys asked.

"Look, I understand you're excited over the revelation that Cali wrote the book, and I hate to be the bearer of bad news, but if that is true, that doesn't help us; it hurts us." Chrys and I dropped our hands from each other's grasp as we looked at him, baffled.

"How does that hurt us?" I asked, confused.

"Because we were hoping that whoever wrote that book would have solutions. If *you* wrote it, you don't have the answers, and we have no hope of getting them."

"Shit," I said, disappointed that he was right, as I slumped back into my chair. Hopeless, Josh and I decided to spend the night and fly back to New York first thing in the morning.

I slowly walked into my bedroom, mine and Lucas' bedroom, and I was immediately startled by him sitting on the bed, obviously waiting for me.

"What are you doing home?" I asked.

"I live here, and this is *my* bedroom, remember? Or have you forgotten?" He stood abruptly and made his way over to me. "Where have you been?"

I tried to walk past him, but he blocked me from proceeding.

"I was at Juliette's," I lied. He let out a chuckle.

"You truly think I am a fool, don't you?" he asked. "I shall ask again, where were you?"

I looked down at the ground. "At Juliette's," I said again, under my breath. He grabbed me by the top of my dress so roughly that he tore it.

"Don't you dare lie to me or insult my intelligence," he said, angered as he grabbed me by the waist and pushed me onto the bed.

I turned my face as I felt a tear trickle down the side of my face.

"Look at me!" he commanded. Gradually, I rolled my head to face him as he stared deep into my eyes. "You look at me with such hatred, those same eyes that used to look at me with lust and admiration."

"I was young and foolish," I answered.

"Have I not given you anything a woman could desire?" he asked.

"All materialistic things," I rebutted.

"And suddenly, a woman doesn't desire materialistic things? Many women would be quite envious of what you have."

I lay in silence as he still rested on top of me, gazing into my eyes. "Such a shame, it truly is. Because I sincerely adore you," he said, as I cringed when his lips touched mine. He gently kissed my shoulder as he continued stroking my hair. "Now, go get cleaned up for supper," he said, lifting himself to get off me. Just as I thought he was about to leave, he came back to the bed and rested himself on me again. He put his face to my ear and whispered: "Oh, and if I catch you with Jacob again, I'm going to kill him."

I woke up terrified and sweating as the tears poured down my face. Josh awakened and immediately pulled me into him, rubbing my back.

"I can't do this anymore," I said through tears.

"What happened? Can't do what?" he asked.

"This," I said, waving my finger back and forth from me to him. "Any of it. He's coming, Josh; I can't handle any of this. I need a break from all of it."

He ran his fingers through my hair. "It's okay. We'll take a break. We won't look into any of this anymore...."

"I need a break from *everything*," I elaborated. "The more powerful we get, the more intense the recollections get, and I can't mentally deal with it anymore."

He pulled away from me and laid on his back, facing the ceiling, his hand on his forehead.

"You need a break from me, you mean," he said.

"All of it. Chrys, you, everything. Lucas is coming, I am sure of it; he's going to hurt you...."

"I can handle myself," he argued.

"I can't handle it if something were to happen to you!" He remained staring up at the ceiling in silence. "Say something," I pleaded.

He turned his head to look at me. "What do you want me to say? I can't ask you to stay with me because we aren't really together to begin with. What are you proposing? You want to stop having sex? That's fine. We don't have to...."

"I'm going to go back to California for a few months. I need a reset. I'll go to my Malibu house...." I trailed off as tears started forming in his eyes, but he was strong enough not to let them fall.

"So, you need a three-thousand-mile break," he said.

"We'll stay in touch," I pledged. He pulled me into him, his forehead resting on mine.

"If that's what you feel you need to do, I can't stop you. But, I promise you I will be here for you when you get back," he said softly.

CHAPTER 37

I needed to get away, that much I knew. Away from everything, away from Josh, away from Chrys, away from the recollections. The stronger we seemed to get collectively, the faster the past life memories were fluttering back, and I truly feared for Josh's safety. Along with my mental wellbeing. 542 days came and went, and we were no closer to finding answers than we were when we began this journey. Lucas was getting stronger too, and I could feel he was coming.

I promised Josh I would stay in touch, and I didn't exactly lie. I had fully intended to talk to him every single day, much like we did when he left Haven first, but when I got back to California, I just couldn't bring myself to talk to him. He must have called and texted me twenty times, and as messed up as it sounds, well, as it *is*, I ghosted him. I didn't know what to say. How to explain he was a big piece of what I needed to be away from. I knew he was in love with me, and knowing I couldn't love him back bothered me even more. It wasn't fair to him, although in retrospect, that was merely an excuse I told myself to feel better about the situation; I was being selfish. But here I was, back in my beautiful Malibu home, only now a different me, a new me, living a new life.

Things were not the same this time. I had changed my name once again. I wasn't at all excited about changing it, like there weren't enough versions of myself I was learning, but there was certainly enough garbage out there already with the Calista name. It seemed like I couldn't even open the news without seeing a story of who I was linked to romantically. Ironically, though, Josh had never come up. My old party days, and when I was expected to relapse after my trip to rehab were news fodder, though. It was as if the entire world was waiting for my demise, taking bets on how long I could stay sober as if that were suddenly entertainment. So, long story short, that's when I started reading.

I was never a reader. To say I hated it would be an understatement. Detest, and loathe, are probably both better synonyms. I never enjoyed picking up a book, smelling the pages, or getting "lost" in a story like so many others. I remember when I used to fly commercial, what seemed like lifetimes ago, until I learned the term "lifetimes" meant something different than I once thought; I would see so many others reading. Back when I was normal. Back when my name was Morgan. Calista just sounded better when I arrived in Hollywood decades earlier. Sexier, classier, I wanted to leave my entire past behind, including the uncomfortable seats in coach. But I do remember watching as people, older and young, men and women, held books in their hands while my headphones blazed through my ears, and how their facial expressions would change while reading. I remember thinking they looked stupid, smiling at a book, or even when they would get visibly upset. I just didn't get it. So many different times, I would want to say, "Dude, relax, it's a damn book!" but of course, I never brought myself to be that rude. Unprovoked, at least.

After writing my book, I joined all these author forums and social media groups with other writers, reading each other's books. No one knew that Jade was Calista, which was for the best, I had decided, although sometimes I did secretly wonder what someone's reaction may have been if they knew they were suddenly chatting with a celebrity.

That's how I found Star Thomas' book. I was in an online group, and it came up as an advertisement. The cover itself immediately drew my attention. Maybe it was the green eyes like my own. Perhaps the synopsis on the back engaged my interest: Spiritual awakening, astral projection, lucid dreams, the "illusion of reality." The answers I had been searching for the last few years, what exactly *am* I? Yeah, okay, apparently, I was a witch, but I knew there was more to that. Everything had happened so fast; my own awakening, and it was difficult to talk to anyone other than Chrys and Josh about it. People would certainly think I was crazy, especially given my already tarnished name for excessive drug use.

Suddenly, I had felt like one of my fans calling my name, trying desperately to get my attention. Star and I were in the same book clubs; maybe I'd just start a casual conversation with her through some sort of witty banter on a thread. I mean, it would be very odd to just message her out of nowhere and say something like, "so hey, how much of your fantasy, science fiction book was real?" She'd think I was insane, and rightfully so; I would have thought the same had someone said that to me years ago.

I picked up my phone and started drafting a message.

Hey, I loved your book; where did you get your inspiration?

No! Corny! I shook my head in disgust at myself and deleted the message. I felt like a teenager in school crushing over some cool kid I wanted to hang out with. It had been a month since I read Star's book, and I couldn't get this chick out of my mind. Not in a creepy, perverted way, but more so because I knew there was more to her. I knew there had to be a greater purpose for my writing; was this it? Was I meant to meet Star; would she have some solutions? Now, don't get me wrong, these thoughts didn't consume me constantly. It wasn't like I was obsessed with her or anything. I just somehow felt drawn to her.

I had just come back from a run on the beach, and I started chopping up fresh fruit to make a smoothie. While throwing out the fruit debris, and taking a sip of my smoothie, a notification of a message disturbed my Aero-smith trance. I let out a sigh and hesitantly looked down at my phone. This had better not be Debbie again; I was not ready to revisit that conversation. But the name displayed across the top of the screen didn't say, *Debbie;* instead, the name Star Thomas appeared on a banner. Slowly, I opened the message.

Hey, I hope you don't mind me reaching out to you. I saw the review you posted for my book; would you mind if I posted it as a free advertisement?

I went into the living room and sat on the couch, staring at the text, contemplating what to write back. There were so many things I wanted to say to start a conversation with her, but instead, I simply responded:

of course....your book was awesome!

Hurrying to the bathroom, I decided to take a relaxing bath. Candlelight illuminated the tile walls, and the scent of lavender and rose filled the room. As I let my body relax and continued the book that I was desperately trying to get into for one of the book clubs I was in, my phone vibrated. Almost relieved to take a break from the book, I looked at my phone. Star Thomas. I sat up, straightened myself out, and placed the Kindle on the tray in front of me.

I just finished reading your book and couldn't put it down. Truly amazing!

I read her words in shock. It was the first time a complete stranger recognized my book, such a different feeling than the attention I got as an actress.

Thanks, I am a big fan of your work too. I think your book is the best book I have ever read.

I waited for a response, but nothing. Finally, I closed my eyes and leaned back, trying to unwind.

When my eyes opened, I gazed ahead, trying to grasp my surroundings. I suddenly realized I was in Jacob's house. I felt a hand on my shoulder and could instantly tell it was his touch. I could feel his breath on the back of my neck as his hand slowly traced down my arm until his fingers were intertwined with mine. He moved his head towards my ear, and I could feel his goatee against my shoulder.

"Where have you been?" he whispered. I swirled around as his brown eyes stayed locked in my stare, and I instantly felt intoxicated by his presence. I placed my hand on his and, a little above a whisper, let out: "I have been looking for you."

He backed me up to the wall and tangled his fingers through mine. This man somehow made me powerless around him, at a loss for words, and nervous. I had to talk to him; I had questions I needed answered that I knew he could tell me, but I couldn't even begin to formulate the words as we uncontrollably began kissing. I grabbed him by the back of his neck and pulled him to me as I leaned against the wall. I felt his hands wander down my body as he passionately kissed me. His lips traveled up my neck to my ear as he whispered, "Stay with me."

All I needed at that moment was all of him; it felt as if he were the one puzzle piece I had been missing my entire life. Suddenly everything around me was blurring. I closed my eyes tight, "no, no, no," I said out loud, knowing my physical body lying in my bedroom was about to be awoken. He grabbed my hand tightly in his. "Hold on to me," he said in a pleading tone. I felt myself falling. "Hold it," I could still hear him beg as I felt myself lying in my bed. I tightened my eyes, trying my hardest to stay asleep, but once again, a failed attempt.

CHAPTER 38

*A*s my eyes slowly shuddered open, I gently slid my hand across the bed. Still in a slumbering state, I felt the cool, satin pillow next to me; as I quickly jolted my eyes open and was taken back for a minute, Josh wasn't there. It had been almost two months since I had seen him or had a recollection, and at that moment, I felt exactly how long two months actually was. I looked at the clock; 5:42 a.m. Of course it was, which meant it was 8:42 am in New York. I reached out for my phone to call him; I scrolled down to *Your Lifeline.* I smiled to myself at the memory of him putting his number in my phone and labeling it with that. But, as soon as I went to call him, I stopped. Two months is a long time! Long enough that maybe he was with a girl or so mad at me for not talking to him that he wouldn't pick up. Or perhaps he was at work. I had no idea what he was doing, which made me more upset with myself for blowing him off. It would drive me nuts having no idea why he didn't pick up, just as mad as he probably was when I ignored his calls. Instead, I scrolled up to Colleen.

"Wanna grab lunch today?"

She was already seated when I arrived. Colleen was beautiful. She was my age, tall and lean, with dark brown hair and brown eyes. She was naturally pretty and didn't need much make-up. We had met when I was in San Diego on a movie shoot a few years earlier, and we have kept in touch ever since. She was one of the real people in my life who didn't care that I was rich or famous and one of the few people who didn't fangirl out when she met me. She was a veterinarian and lived a very ordinary life compared to me. She was also the last person I saw, the one I partied so hard with the night of the DUI. Although we spoke occasionally, I hadn't seen her since. She smiled as I sat down.

"Weather is nice today," she commented, putting down the menu. I nodded in agreement as the waitress came over to take our orders. It was a nice restaurant, not too fancy, with tables spread out far enough that you weren't in on everyone else's conversation. It was trendy as far as food was concerned, with always something fresh and different on the menu.

"Can I get you a drink?" the waitress asked. I looked down, pretending to study my menu, but even after being sober for over two years, that question still made me hesitate. The first thought that came to mind was a vodka soda. What I wouldn't give to be one of those people who could drink just one at social gatherings without it leading to an entire day of drinking, typically ending with a night out and a nasty hangover in the morning. I could almost feel how the vodka would trickle through my veins, that feeling you get when you haven't had a drink in a while, and your body suddenly needed it. I looked up at the waitress and smiled slightly. "I'll just have a seltzer with lemon, please."

"I'll have an iced tea, and also, I am ready to order. I think

I will do the grilled chicken Caesar salad with extra croutons," Colleen ordered. Jotting it down in her pad, the waitress peeked over at me.

"I'll just have the avocado toast," I said, handing her back the menu.

"You know, we don't have to come to a place with a bar," Colleen said to me as the waitress walked away.

"It's fine," I said, matter-of-factly. "I can't avoid running into alcohol my entire life."

"Has it really been two years since I've seen you last?" she asked.

"Two years and two months, to be exact," I said, nodding.

"I read your book; it's really good," she commented.

"Thanks. I met a girl," I blurted out as the waitress miraculously appeared out of nowhere to drop off our drinks. She gave an embarrassed smile and quickly turned to leave us in privacy. Colleen leaned into the table.

"A girl," she said with a sly smile. "Now that's new... do tell."

I let out a chuckle as I took a sip of my seltzer. "Not that type of girl. An author, her name is Star. It's weird; I have some strange connection with her. I can't explain it. Not sexual. I don't even know what she looks like."

"And you talk to her?" she asked.

"We've chatted a bit, you know, on social media, she DMed me...."

"She slipped into your DMs?" she asked, laughing now. "You sure she doesn't like *you*?"

"No way, she doesn't even know what I look like or who I really am. Although after Josh, maybe it wouldn't hurt to trade teams for a bit," I joked.

"Speaking of Josh... what's going on with that?"

"Nothing. Absolutely nothing," I said as the waitress carefully inched over carrying our lunch, ensuring she wasn't walking into an awkward conversation. I looked down at my avocado toast but didn't touch it, now obsessing over what Josh could be doing as Colleen started drizzling her salad with dressing. "Wanna get tattoos?" I asked unexpectedly.

"Tattoos? Are you serious?"

"Yes," I said. "Dead serious. Let's go after lunch."

I'm not sure if she truly believed me until we were in the tattoo parlor an hour later. As she hunted through images on the walls, I went straight over to the artist. He had to be at least six-foot-two, with dirty blonde hair, green eyes, and a cleft in his chin. He was decked out in fresh ink, with full sleeves of tattoos down both arms.

"Hello, beautiful," he said. Josh called me "beautiful" all the time; that was like his pet name for me. I could almost hear the guy say it in his voice.

"You do that yourself?" I asked, motioning to the cobwebs inked on his neck.

"Sure did. You like?" he asked.

"Yes, I do," I answered flirtatiously, looking him up and down. Maybe this is what I needed. A new guy to take my mind off Josh.

"You know what you want?" he asked. I leaned in closer to him.

"I always know what I want. Are you willing to give it to me, is the question?" Yeah, I was *that* blunt. His smile widened as he sucked his lower lip and bowed to me.

"I meant as in a design, but yes, I'm willing to give you whatever you want. Over dinner, maybe?" he asked.

"That sounds like a plan. I'm Cali," I said, extending my hand to shake his.

"Cash," he said, taking my hand in his and leading me to the back room behind a curtain. I lifted my shirt to just below my breasts.

"Can you give me flames, Cash, right here?" I said, running my fingers down my rib cage.

"Painful spot," he stated. "You sure you want it there?"

"It's fine. I can take it," I said. What I really wanted to say was I deserved it for what I did to Josh, but in my mind, putting those flames on my body allowed me a way to have him with me all the time.

It took him about an hour to complete as Colleen sat in the chair next to me and got a little black cat tattooed on the inside of her wrist. It hurt like hell at first, but after the initial shock of the needle, everything got numb pretty fast, and I was more focused on flirting with Cash than the pain he was inflicting. When he finished, I stared at it in awe through the mirror that he held. I gave him my phone number, and we made plans to have dinner at eight.

CHAPTER 39

I chose a baby blue sundress for dinner. I studied myself in the mirror. I felt my armpits getting damp as my heart raced in anticipation. I hadn't been on an actual date in years, part of me was nervous about meeting someone else, and the other part felt guilty like I was somehow cheating on Josh. I knew that was ridiculous; we weren't even a couple, especially now that we hadn't spoken in so long. I looked down at my phone, and he was already ten minutes late. I looked through my messages to see if he had texted me, but nothing. Strike one already; rude for not letting me know he was going to be late. I sat down on the bed, annoyed.

Twenty minutes later, Cash texted me that he was outside without even apologizing. I grabbed my purse and went outside, where he sat on a Harley in ripped jeans and a Nirvana t-shirt. My mouth hung a bit as I stared at the motorcycle.

"What's wrong?" he asked.

"You're half an hour late," I said nastily.

"There was traffic," he said, unapologetically. I stood

motionless, looking at the bike. "What's wrong now?" he asked.

"I don't ride on motorcycles," I said.

"Oh, common, just get on the bike. I'm a good driver," he said. Motorcycles scared me to death, and I knew way too many people who got seriously hurt on them.

"Just tell me where the place is; I'll take an Uber and meet you there," I said, trying to make light of the situation. Irritated, he texted me the link to the place, and I called an Uber.

When I showed up at the spot, I realized it wasn't a restaurant at all. It was a bar, a dive bar, in fact. I was stunned at what atmosphere he chose for a date. I walked in, everyone in jeans and sneakers eating burgers and chicken fingers, loud music blaring. The furthest thing from romantic, I felt like I was overdressed. I made my way over to the high-top table he was seated at and carefully climbed on the seat. I went to rest my elbows on the table when I pulled back instantaneously as the top was sticky. I went into my purse, took out a bottle of Purell, and started wiping down my arms with a napkin. He stared at me as if I had three heads.

"Not fancy enough for you?" he asked sarcastically.

"It's fine," I said flatly, looking into his green eyes. At least he was hot, and I was not going to let this mess up my night. The waiter came over, wiped the table, and handed us paper menus.

"Hey guys, can I set you up with drinks?" the waiter asked.

"I'll have a Jameson, neat," Cash ordered, then looked at me. "Cali?"

The disbelief on my face must have shown as he leaned in and repeated, "Cali?"

"You're driving," I said, disgusted.

"So? I'll only have a few drinks. I'll be fine. What do you want?"

"I don't drink," I said. He rolled his eyes dramatically.

"Oh, please. Have a drink; it won't kill you. Maybe it will loosen you up a bit," he said.

"Loosen me up a bit?" I said defensively. "What the hell is that supposed to mean?"

"I'll give you two some time," the waiter said, sensing the tension, and walked away.

"One drink, it will take the edge off," he reiterated.

"I'm an alcoholic," I said, lowering my voice in embarrassment.

"Great, so you drink! I was getting nervous that you were gonna be like this all night," he answered.

"Like 'this'?" I said, using air quotations. "Let me rephrase. I am in recovery; I had a DUI; I am not cool with you drinking and driving." He let out a breath and started shaking his head.

"Typical actress, all judgy and shit," he said nastily. I stood up from my stool and grabbed my purse.

"Judgy? No, Cash, I am not judgy. You're just a dick. You showed up half an hour late, not even an apology. On a motorcycle to boot! Don't you think you should have told me you were on a motorcycle? I know a lot of women who wouldn't want to ride on a bike...."

"Okay, I'm sorry. I should have told you I was running late. Just have a drink and calm down. Maybe something light, a glass of wine, a beer?"

"And...." I continued on my rant, ignoring his statement, "you take me to some shithole dive bar and try to pressure me to drink? I got news for you, Cash; you missed out because, in truth, I just wanted an easy lay tonight. I'm leaving,"

"Go ahead, leave," he said, looking back down at the menu

without a care in the world. "I don't need some bougie-ass, has-been actress in my bed tonight anyway." My fist immediately clenched into a ball as my anger grew. I wanted to punch him in the face so badly, but instead, I just headed out and called an Uber, and made my way home.

～

I woke up in my purple field as I mechanically made my way over to the waterfall and walked into the water. This time, I felt a new female energy, and it wasn't my mother. Stepping out of the water, I searched around for a sign of life. In the distance, I could just make out the silhouette of a young girl sitting in the grass.

Slowly I made my way toward her until her shadow became visible. Sitting upright in the grass, she held her knees to her chest and stared at the stars. With long dark wavy hair and tiny freckles on her cheekbones that ran down to the bridge of her nose, her hazel eyes screamed sadness. She looked empty, defeated, and lonely. I carefully approached her so as not to startle her. Her eyes shifted to make contact with mine, but she wasn't the least bit fazed, as if she also knew I was there the whole time. I had never seen this girl before, but I knew I had looked into her eyes many times. She let out a hopeless sigh and laid back on the grass, resting her head in her hands. Reflexively, I did the same. She finally spoke as I lay down next to her, staring at the same vivid stars.

"Where have you been, Morgan?"

I abruptly sat up in shock. No one called me Morgan except Chrys.

"How do you know my name?" I asked, not looking at her. She slowly pushed herself up to face me, but I didn't look back at her. Silence. Finally, when I realized she wasn't going to answer my question, I turned my body around to face her and looked into her eyes.

"Who are you?" I asked. She reached out her hand to mine, and as I took it, I felt a shock run through us, some sort of static electricity feeling. Sitting on her knees now, she leaned in closer to me.

"You don't know who I am? You must be bound. Who would have bound you, Morgan? I need you to think. Who would have or *could* have done this?"

I stared at her, speechless. Finally, it must have hit her that I had no idea or remembrance of who she was. "It's me, Katie," she said. As I opened my mouth to speak, my surroundings started to blur, and once again, I felt myself falling, quicker this time. "No!" I woke up screaming as I bolted up from my bed, my heart racing and sweat pouring down my face. What the hell was that?!

A wave of emotions consumed me as my eyes slowly opened. I reached for my phone and went to my notes to document what had just occurred in my astral state. I started frantically typing everything I remembered, completely awake yet still in some sort of dream state. My mind raced with confusion. Okay, so there is this kid, if you can call him that because he's definitely not alive, following me around. Some dude I have sex with apparently in a place that I can only imagine is somewhere between our world and the after-life, and now, add in some random chick who shows up suddenly and is speaking to me as if she knows me. After reading my notes back to myself, there were things I knew for sure. For starters, it wasn't a dream. I was certain I was projecting; I could feel, see, and smell; all my senses were intact. I felt myself come out of my body and go back in, so that was real, well, if you can call any of this "real." Secondly, Katie. I recognized her, not so much by her appearance but by the look in her eyes. I've looked into those very eyes many times before. They were familiar, and even more so, somehow comforting. Her stare provided me a piece of security I had been missing for years; she was someone important, that was a given, but who?

She said I was bound. How did she know that? Never, not once, did another girl other than Juliette come up in any of my recollections. I had been away from everyone for months, and nothing had happened. Now, all of a sudden, I had recollections coming faster than ever before. Something was making me stronger. Maybe it was the separation from Josh? I so badly wanted to call him, to see if anything was happening with him, but I couldn't bring myself to do it. I was positive he hated me now. I clutched my pillow to my chest and closed my eyes to go back to sleep.

CHAPTER 40

I woke up on my mountain, mine and Josh's mountain, as I came face to face with him. He didn't look like his normal cheerful self; instead, he had a look on his face I had never seen. Anger, hurt, mostly disappointment. I approached him with caution.

"Is this real, or are we in a dream?" I asked.

"Neither of us is dreaming, although I wouldn't call any of this *real*," he answered simply.

"Are you expecting me to take my shirt off?" I asked, trying to lighten his mood. He stared at me steadily, and his facial expression didn't change.

"This isn't funny; I have been trying to get a hold of you," he said sternly.

"I wasn't trying to be comical; I'm not really going to take my shirt off. So, you can't get in touch with me, and you somehow think stalking me in an astral state was a good idea? Real mature," I said, turning my back to him and wrapping my arms around my chest. I had missed him so much, yet right then, I felt like he had invaded my privacy.

"What did I do so wrong, so horrible to you, that you just

exiled me from your life?" he asked, anger in his voice. I spun around to face him.

"I needed time," I spat out.

"I gave you time," he said, bringing his tone up an octave. "As a matter of fact, I gave you everything you asked for. You wanted distance? I gave it to you; three thousand miles of damn distance!"

"Did you? Then why are you here? How did you even get here? And more importantly, how did you get *me* here?"

"Practice, I guess, and obviously, you must have been thinking about me too since you're here," he said arrogantly. "Why do you hate me?"

"Leave," I said coldly.

"Not until you answer my question. Why do you despise me so much? After everything we've been through?"

"I don't hate you; I hate what's happening to me when I am around you," I answered.

"Oh, and that's suddenly my fault? What a lame attempt at an excuse," he quipped. He stalked closer to me until he was towering over me. He was in his usual joggers and hoodie and somehow looked so much more attractive when he was angry. It took all my self-control not to kiss him. But that was strictly my hormones talking. I was mad at him. Infuriated that he took it upon himself to beckon me to the mountain, invade my personal space, my private thoughts. I clenched my jaw as I could feel my fist tighten into a ball, and rain started pouring down violently, plummeting from the sky in enormous amounts. The wind picked up speed; it was like I was somehow creating a tornado. He looked at the sky and back down at me, pushing his wet hair out of his face.

At that moment, I wish I had better control over how and when I made it rain because he looked extra sexy drenched. He put his hand on my shoulder and opened his mouth to speak, but I cut him off.

"Don't get excited. This isn't foreplay. This is your only warning; stay out of my head, Josh! Next time, I am not going to ask so nicely!"

"Cali, just…" I closed my eyes tightly and tried to wake myself up; I could hear his voice trail off into the distance, "just talk to me."

I woke up just as furious as I was in the projection and reached for my phone to text Star. She and I had been chatting for two months already, and although I had never met her, I was closer to her at this point than anyone in my life. Turns out that her book was a mixture of real-life experiences and visions she was channeling throughout her lifetime. She was the first person outside of Josh that I admitted I was a witch too, and she was also. We had very similar stories, and there wasn't much I didn't feel comfortable talking to her about. We spoke of our own experiences of the awakening, all of it; the dreams, visions, Witchcraft, Jacob, Lucas—everything.

Star and I had a connection we couldn't explain, only to conclude that our paths must have crossed before, and maybe she, too, was someone I was supposed to meet. We often spoke of meeting up, and I sincerely hoped it wasn't just something we said as if it would be a cool thing to do but something we would never act on. Since getting the flames tattooed on my ribs gave me some closure with Josh, and although I didn't really date other men, I thought of him frequently. But not in that yearning, missing type of way, more that I hoped he was doing well. Until the night he showed up without warning.

But now, I was irritated that he came to me unannounced. Uninvited. Star let me vent to her for an hour, the entire story of Josh and my history flowing out of my mouth uncontrollably. She was a good listener and let me carry on, offering her opinion when necessary. But not some bullshit where she was telling me what I wanted to hear type of advice, more worldly and sound, rational thoughts.

After Star and I had been having late-night chats for almost six months, I had another dream of my mother. Back in the purple field, she didn't speak. Once again, she handed me a crystal, an amethyst this time. I had no idea what her obsession with amethysts was, but suddenly, I needed to find out. It shone so brightly under the moonlight that it appeared as if it was blending in with the purple misted water. I finally asked Star if she wanted to meet in real life, and she accepted the invitation. She lived in Canada, so we decided to meet somewhere neutral that we both loved, New Orleans. What better place to meet up and talk about Witch-craft than a place like New Orleans, where the streets were filled with metaphysical stores galore, and the vibe always made me feel comfortable and at home. We had decided to meet at a restaurant, so it wasn't too awkward. We often joked around that when we met each other in real life, we'd hate each other.

It was noon as I sat at a table, watching people stumbling in as if they were out all night. Decked out in beads, I could only imagine the nights they must have had, and I highly doubted it involved anything on a spiritual aspect. I had made the reservation under Jade; I still hadn't told Star my real identity. I didn't know her real name either. I kind of liked the idea we only knew each other under our pen names. It didn't take long before a very attractive brunette in her forties was escorted to my table. I stood to greet her as she stared at me in shock, realizing who I really was. I gaped at her in the same state of disbelief, staring into her hazel eyes.

"Do you recognize me?" I asked, still in astonishment. I stood dumbfounded, staring into the eyes I knew I had seen numerous times in my lifetimes, and most recently in the purple field, only now in a much older form of herself.

"Holy shit, are you Calista Reed?" she asked excitedly.

"Katie?" I said, just above a whisper. Her mouth dropped a little, and she squinted her eyes. She looked around her, then leaned into me.

"How do you know my real name?" she asked. I reached out and took her hand in mine, the same as she had on the field that night, and I felt the electric shocks run through my veins.

"Morgan," she uttered. Simultaneously, we both slumped down in our chairs and stared at each other. "I haven't seen you in years," she finally whispered. "We had to be kids. What eight, nine years old?"

"I don't remember any of it. I didn't even remember you until you showed up in an astral projection recently," I said. The waitress came over to our table to take our orders.

"I'll have the crab claws," I said, never taking my eyes off Katie.

"I'll have the same," she answered, also refusing to look up. I don't know if she even liked them or just wanted the waitress to leave and ordered in a hurry as I had.

"I'm sure it's because I am bound; I don't know when it happened. Maybe it goes back to when I was a kid, but I need to figure out how to get it off me. I think it's my only hope of breaking this spell," I said.

"We used to meet," she continued after the waitress left. "In an astral state. Then one day, you just never came again. I wrote it off as I got older, and convinced myself that you must have been an imaginary friend." She leaned in closer to me and spoke quietly but precisely. "I think I can help," she said. "We can do a spell that will help you 'see,' reveal who bound you. I think once we figure out who, and more impor- tantly, why, we will be able to get the hex off you. After this, we can go to a store, pick up some things, and maybe go back to one of our rooms and try to perform the ritual. You okay with that, or are you freaked out yet?"

I nodded. "Yes, I am more than okay with that, and trust me, *nothing* freaks me out at this point."

CHAPTER 41

fter lunch, we walked through the town, going in and out of multiple metaphysical stores on the way. The streets were filled with people partying, drinking on the curb, and hanging off balconies as the music boomed through the town. I had been approached about a dozen times by someone asking for an autograph before I stopped in a souvenir shop to pick up a baseball cap.

"Should have warned me I was going to be going out with someone who was such a big deal," Star chuckled. I rolled my eyes and slid the cap on my head.

"I kind of forgot who I was for a minute," I admitted as I adjusted the position of my sunglasses. "How does this look?"

"If you're trying to look like a tourist, you've succeeded," she joked.

"I am a tourist," I laughed. "Probably not the best place to come to, I mean, considering I'm a recovering addict."

Star pointed her finger to a group of belligerent guys stumbling down the street, being loud and obnoxious. "Ah, yes, you too can act like that," she laughed. My stare followed her finger to focus on the men, walking around shirtless flaunting their beads while holding large plastic cups of alcohol and hollering at girls.

"I didn't get like that; I didn't yell or fight. I flirted. I saved the fighting for when I was sober and could remember it!" I justified. After paying for the hat, we continued shopping for products. We must have gone into ten metaphysical stores within a mile radius. When we returned to my hotel room, I was excited to open up all my new goodies as I poured the contents onto the bed: crystals, incense, resins, and some beaded bracelets. Star had also picked up quite a few things as we looked over each other's trinkets.

"Here," she said, handing me a small bag containing a resin. I examined the pieces of brown crumbled fragments in my hand as I turned the bag around and smelled the vanilla-ish aroma.

"What is this?" I asked.

"A gift for you. It's benzoin. It can be used for numerous things, cleansing an area, clearing and balancing energy, but it also helps with anger. Hence, why I got it for you," she said. I smiled gratefully as I put it in with my other things.

"I should be insulted; however, you're not entirely wrong, so I will just say thank you," I said. "If we're going to be burning things, we should probably go on the balcony, so we don't set off the fire alarm."

I watched as she mixed up some herbs, placed them on top of a steaming charcoal, and put it in a small black metal cauldron she had purchased. I watched in awe; she seemed like a pro at it. She had so much more insight and experience in all this stuff than I did. I followed her lead as she slid open the balcony door and stepped out.

"Let's try to be discreet. I don't need paparazzi snapping pics of me playing with magick," I warned. We turned to face the room, with our back to the street. "What's in there?" I asked, peeking my head down to get a glimpse inside the smoking pot.

"Myrrh, which is used in clearing negative entities in the way of seeing the truth. Lavender, and rose, because I resonate with the element Earth, same as you do with water," she explained. "Now close your eyes and concentrate as I say this chant, and hopefully, we can see who did this to you."

"So, am I just going to see a name? Or am I going to be taken to the place it happened, like the other recollections?" I asked. She shrugged and clamped her teeth together.

"I have no idea. Everyone sees things differently, but don't get scared with whatever you see. Hold your position wherever you end up. I'm here with you," she reassured me. I closed my eyes and inhaled the smoke emanating from the cauldron as I drifted into a different plane.

Apprehensive at first to open my eyes, for fear of not knowing where I'd be, I slowly pushed them open and scanned the room. Bewildered, I recognized exactly where I was. I must have been ten years old, in the second foster house we had lived in. I was in my bed after waking up, startled by a dream. As if I was that same ten-year-old girl sitting on the bed, I recalled the exact dream I had. I was in my cabin, *our* cabin, mine, and William's special place. The second I laid eyes on him, I told him to leave, remembering how upset my mother had gotten over my dreams of him. He watched me with disappointment in his stare but didn't say a word. He didn't move or leave; he just looked at me with tortured eyes. Suddenly, I was lost in the memory of what happened when I had woken up frazzled, my heart accelerating at a speed that scared me half to death.

I carefully climbed over Chrys, who was sleeping soundly, and crept through the hallway towards the attic. I tried to reach the pull-down ladder, but I was way too short to reach it. I slowly tiptoed back into the room and dragged a chair toward the ladder, determined to get it down. I steadied myself on the chair and yanked at it. As the steps dropped, I climbed up to the attic on a mission, with the purpose to find my mother's belongings.

I scurried through the dust in the dark, trying to read the labels on the boxes. Finally, after what seemed like hours, I came across one labeled "Olivia NaPalepso." It was small; she didn't have much in there besides some old photographs and an assortment of healing crystals. I pushed aside the crystals and reached down for what I had really been looking for, what I was there to retrieve, her spell book. I tucked the book under my arm and carefully stepped back down the ladder. Trying my hardest to remain as quiet as possible, I made my way to the backyard and laid the book open in the garden, surrounded by flowers and grass, drunken in the moonlight. The dazzling full moon illuminated the pages of the book as I turned each one looking for a spell, one I could use to make me forget. To make my powers go away—to bind me. Settling on a particular spell I found, I recited the words repeatedly until I was uncontrollably crying and convinced myself nothing else could be done. It had either worked or didn't, and I would know shortly thereafter, I had assumed.

That's the thing about forgetting; if all is lost, you don't know it ever existed. I hadn't realized the spell worked because I had no reminiscence of doing it. For years, nothing, not William nor the memories, haunted me anymore. I erased my own past.

My eyes opened to see Star, anxiously awaiting my findings. I described to her in detail what I had seen and done. She thought this was the best news that I could have found because if I was, in fact, the one who put a spell on myself, I'd be able to break it. It also explained why someone was powerful enough to bind me. The next thing we needed to do was an unbinding spell to release me from the hex I inflicted on myself and let my full potential break free.

"There's something I need to tell you too," she said, hesitancy in her tone. I tilted my head and looked at her. "I had a vision also."

"Was it about me?" I asked.

"Yes, I saw your sister, and it wasn't a good feeling."

"Chrys?" I asked in shock. Chrys would never do something intentionally to hurt me. We may have had our differences in the past, but she was the furthest thing from malicious or vindictive. "What did she look like?" I asked. Star shook her head.

"Look, I don't know what it means; it's just what I saw. And I didn't see her clearly. It was just feminine energy that I somehow *knew* was your sister, and it was dark. Maybe you need to have a heart-to-heart with her; she may know more than she's letting on. Now let's get this curse off you." She disappeared back into the room and returned with a new bundle in her hand and a plastic baggie holding some crushed leaves.

"Now, typically, when you do an unbinding ritual, you ask for the hex to be sent back to the sender. Considering in this circumstance, you *are* the sender, and you can't say that. You need to ask for it to be returned to the universe in a ball of protective light, unable to harm anyone or anything. Get it?"

"Yes," I conceded as she took some leaves off the sage bundle and handed them to me.

"This is blue sage, which is very different from white, it's a lot stronger. It's also known as Grandmother Sage. In magick, it is used to rid negative energy and remove malevolent spirits, and in ancient times also used in exorcisms. Also, here are some crushed blackberry leaves," she handed me the bag. "This is also used to remove evil entities and keep you safe from intruders or enemies in psychic attacks. If Jacob is an illusion of Lucas...."

"He's not," I cut her off. "He's real; I know he is."

"Well, if he isn't, you'll know soon enough. Take the leaves from the sage and the blackberry and mix them together with the charcoal in the cauldron. I'm going to go back inside. You should do this yourself, smudge yourself and say your prayer."

I placed my hand on my right wrist, feeling the energy of the fluorite and the labradorite bracelets I was wearing shudder through my body.

"You can do this, Jade," she smiled. "Cali, Morgan, all of you can do it," she continued, laughing.

"Very funny," I said.

"Now, once we finish this, we'll just have to work on getting the love spell off you," she reminded me. "Your recollection spell brought William here this lifetime, and then you went and bound yourself."

"Okay, one curse at a time," I said, teasing and shooing her away with my hands.

As I waved the smoke around my body, I swayed into it and inhaled deeply, feeling as if a dark piece of me had left my body and restored my soul.

CHAPTER 42

"*H*ow do I look?" I asked Debbie as I emerged from my room to the living room, where she sat on my couch waiting. Sporting a tight, short red dress that perfectly matched the bottom of my Louboutins and a diamond necklace that sparkled so brightly, you could probably see it from a mile away.

"You can take the girl out of Hollywood, but you can't take Hollywood out of the girl," she exclaimed, springing to her feet. "You look hot as hell!" I had been back in New York City for a week, and Debbie had convinced me to go to a charity event on the Upper East Side. Even though she claimed she understood that I now considered myself retired from acting and was focusing on my writing career, I took her recommendation to get out and at least show an appearance. Especially given the event was so close to my house.

As we got into the car, I couldn't help but glance down at my phone. I'll admit it, I was hoping for a response from Josh. I had texted him a week ago to tell him I was coming back, but he never answered. I wrestled with the idea of texting him again, but I understood why he was mad. I stopped talking to him for no reason, knowing it was wrong. I wanted to tell him what happened in New Orleans, everything that occurred between Katie and me. I was hoping he'd at least give me a chance to apologize or explain myself, if nothing else, and not in some creepy astral attack like he had done to me. But no such luck. Cameras snapped a mile a minute as we arose from the car, people screaming my name. I smiled and waved as I kept walking into the venue. Debbie shot me a playful sneer.

"Don't ask; I don't miss it," I muttered under my breath. My attention went straight to an older, balding man, surrounded by a crowd laughing at some bullshit joke he told. "When did Larry Ackner get out of jail?" I asked Debbie as she reached over and took a cracker covered in caviar.

"Caviar?" she asked, pointing at the server holding the tray. I stuck out my tongue and made a wincing face.

"Hell no, that shit is nasty," I said, making a face of disgust. She took a bite of her cracker and jerked her head towards a couple standing, looking at a piece of artwork.

"It's delicious. You clearly have no taste," she joked. "Around the same time, Lea Marson and Tony LaDonna became an item. Have you not kept up on any Hollywood gossip?" she asked, now grabbing a glass of champagne off another server's tray.

"No, I have been actively avoiding it," I stated.

"Incoming," she whispered, swallowing her cracker with a swig of champagne as I watched a gorgeous brunette with golden eyes head in my direction. She must have been five-foot-eleven without heels and a body to die for. Her long wavy dark hair hung down her back, and her diamond accent black dress matched perfectly with the five-inch stilettos she was wearing. She was so stunning; I was almost girl crushing on her. She smiled widely at me as she headed in my direction, waving at me while the ushers were trying to get everyone shuffled to the back terrace for the auction to begin.

"That's Emma Dawn, the supermodel. She was just on the cover of Sports United last month," Debbie filled me in quietly.

"Calista Reed!" Emma exclaimed, extending her hand out to mine.

"Emma!" I boasted as if I was supposed to know who she was.

"It's so lovely to meet you!" she said. "I am a huge fan of yours. *The Golden Train* was absolutely wonderful! It's my all-time favorite movie!"

"Thank you," I said bashfully, holding her hand in mine. I felt inferior to her as she towered over me, silently praying she did not bring up the incident at my last filming.

"Can I take a picture with you?" she asked.

"Of course," I said as I stood next to her, and Debbie took her phone to snap a picture of us together.

"Thank you so much!" she said, as she leaned down towards me and softened her voice. "Okay, this is going to sound crazy, but my boyfriend has a thing for you. Not like in a creepy way; I can just tell when you come on TV. I think you're like his celebrity crush; he's in the bathroom. Do you mind waiting a second before we go out to the terrace? He'll kill me if he sees that I met you and he didn't; he's very competitive," she laughed. I looked over at Debbie, who was clearly very pleased with herself that I was "back in the game," as she would put it.

"Sure," I said. After a few minutes, Emma started waving her hand in the air, signaling for her boyfriend from across the room.

"Babe, over here!" She called out.

"Hope he's tall," I joked with Debbie quietly, as I didn't

pay attention immediately to the suited man walking over until his fingers were intertwined with hers.

"Look, babe, it's Calista Reed!" she excitedly said as I looked up and came face to face with Josh. He was tall, alright. My heart fell into my stomach, and I suddenly felt like the room was spinning as his face lost color, and he stared at me blankly. "It's Calista Reed," Emma said again, running her hand down his arm. It took all the self-control I had not to rip her hand off of him, as I put a fake smile on and looked at him while he stood there, still frozen, staring at me. Not only did he have a gorgeous, supermodel girlfriend, but he also didn't even tell her about us! Oh, I was livid! She introduced me as if she had no idea that he knew me. He cleared his throat.

"Cali," he said softly, extending his hand to shake mine as if he were just meeting me for the first time.

"Calista," I corrected him. "Only my friends call me Cali." He raised his eyebrows and let out a slight chuckle like I had just slapped him across the face with my words, which, truth be told, I wish I could have, with my actual hand. He looked absolutely gorgeous in the charcoal gray suit, the light blue shirt accentuating his eyes, and his facial hair groomed to a perfect five o'clock shadow. I could smell his musky cologne and all I could picture was his face buried in my neck.

"My apologies," he said politely. "It is nice to meet you, *Calista*," he ground out as he took my hand. The warmth immediately raced through my blood, calming me down instantaneously. Except I didn't want to be calm, I wanted to be mad. I was mad, and he had no right to take that from me.

"Can I get a picture of the two of you?" Emma asked, pushing Josh in my direction. I felt his hand on the small of my back as I leaned in for them to snap the photograph. Everything around us seemed to be moving extremely fast, except the four of us. I felt like we were all somehow standing still in time as Emma put her arms around Josh, and I wanted to scream: take your hands off him! I remembered being in Tennessee, and Josh asking me: *"How would you feel if you wanted something so bad, then someone came out of nowhere and took it from you? 'Accidentally' at that."*

"It was so nice meeting you, Calista. Thank you so much!" Emma very nicely said to me. Too nicely, if you asked me. At that second, I hated her. She was gorgeous, classy, polite, everything he deserved. Everything I *should* have been to him. Instead, I ran away, left him, and let her take him from me. *"I don't know; no one has ever taken what I wanted,"* I had answered him that day. Now I knew, I hated her with every ounce of feeling I had left in my body. And they made an amazing couple, which burnt even more. The ushers came over to tell us once again we needed to go outside, and I watched him walk away with his hand intertwined in hers. I could taste the vomit in my throat as I made my way to the terrace with Debbie.

"Are you okay?" she asked me, obviously having no idea that was Josh.

"No, I don't feel good," I managed to get out.

"You need something?" she asked. Yeah, self-control, I thought to myself as I watched the first drop of water fall from the sky. No, no, no, not now, don't make it rain; he's going to know you're upset. Don't show him it bothers you! I coached myself. It didn't matter what I told myself. Nothing could hold it. The rain started pouring from the sky as people hurried back inside to avoid getting wet. I stood paralyzed in the rain; my eyes fixated on Josh and Emma. He didn't even turn around to look at me. Instead, he took his suit jacket off and held it over her head as he escorted her inside. Debbie grabbed me by the arm.

"Come on, let's go inside. You're getting soaked," she said.

"I'm going home," I managed to let out.

CHAPTER 43

J couldn't get out of bed for three days, nor could I stop the thunderstorm I started that night that wouldn't subside. The vision of Josh and Emma anguished me. Don't get me wrong, part of me was happy he found someone who adored him, and rightfully so, but the other part of me was enraged with jealousy, an emotion I had never felt in my life.

I lay in bed, almost paralyzed with depression. I never found out what significance amethyst played with my mother; Chrys evidently had no idea what Star could have possibly meant when she had seen her, and Josh. Oh Josh. A perfect man that I ruined for myself. A man who loved me like no other person ever did in my life, and I just walked away. I had convinced myself it was for him that I left, but the truth was.... it was me. I couldn't deal with the recollections anymore. And now, I couldn't deal with reality. I felt like I was losing my shit; I barely ate, and I shut my phone off. I shut myself off from the world.

"Ms. Reed," Logan's voice came through the intercom. "Mr. Knight is here to see you." I sat up in bed, stunned. He was here? Now? He had better not be reading my mind again!

"Let him up," I said, trying not to sound angry. I got up and made my way to the door. As I opened it, he walked right in without waiting. He looked me up and down, then shifted his eyes to the ceiling when he saw I was wearing a nightgown.

"What the hell do you think you're doing?" he growled irritably. Wearing black joggers and a light gray t-shirt, he looked sexy as hell.

"I didn't know you were coming; it's almost midnight. I was in bed," I defended myself.

"I don't mean the nightgown!" I headed toward the kitchen to get a water bottle as he trailed behind. I held a bottle out towards him.

"Water?" I asked nonchalantly. He shook his head in disgust.

"What do you think? I didn't get your text that you were coming back to New York? I got it, and I didn't answer it. I purposely didn't answer it! You know why I didn't answer it?" he started rattling out questions. I stayed silent, assuming he wasn't really expecting an answer. "You left!" he continued. "Not just left, ran. Stopped talking to me, disappeared like I was just a piece of garbage in the street you threw away when you were done with it! Nine months to be exact. Nine months you were gone for! Not a call, not a text; you told me to leave when I found you on the mountain...."

"Found me on the mountain? You mean beckoned me to the mountain? When you invaded my personal headspace?" I interrupted. He started pacing back and forth in the kitchen.

"You refused to talk to me; at least, you could have been a woman and told me leave you alone. Instead, you were just a coward. You left me no choice!"

"And you think the sane thing to do was mentally stalk me?" I rebutted.

"Well, I would have sent you flowers if that didn't send you off the edge like a damn lunatic," he quipped back sarcastically.

"Look, Josh, I am sorry, I really am, I...."

"I relapsed. Did you know that? No, how could you know that; you weren't here!" he barked. I could feel the tears welling in my eyes when he said he had relapsed. I was not expecting that from him; he was so tough, stronger than I could ever be. He was apprehensive about drinking, even when he thought the world was ending the next day.

"How long?" I quietly asked, looking down at the ground. I couldn't even bring myself to look at him. He was right, I was a coward, and I betrayed him.

"A month and a half, but that's not the point; I don't need your pity. The moral of the story is, who helped me out of it," he said.

"Emma," I simply whispered.

"That's right, Emma. Because she's not a selfish bitch. She's caring and nice and loving...."

"Please stop," I begged as I felt a tear trickle down my cheek. He turned his attention to the island in the middle of the kitchen. I guess he couldn't bring himself to look at me, either.

"And now what? You're back; you've decided to grace me with your presence. What am I supposed to do, Cali? Jump for joy? Stop my life? Break up with my girlfriend?" he roared, now inching closer to me, gaping at me with anger-filled eyes. I just shook my head.

"No, I don't expect you to do that." He ran his hand through his hair in distress.

"Well, I did," he said, stopping dead in his tracks and

staring down at me. I looked up at him and finally made eye contact.

"What? Why?" I asked.

"Because when it comes to you, I have no self-control," he said as he lifted me onto the kitchen counter and ravished my lips. I ran my hands aggressively through his hair, pulling him into me harder while he held my thighs around his waist. His lips wandered from mine down to my neck, and he held me tightly into him. "I missed you so much," he mumbled. He reached across to the removable faucet, turned it on, and held the head above us; water tumbling down both our bodies.

My fingers clenched onto his t-shirt as he doused me in water. "I want your arms around me," he commanded as I released my grip on his shirt and wrapped my arms around his shoulders. It was the most emotional experience I had ever had with him; we had done this over and over for life-times, but this time it felt as if it were our first. I ached for his touch as I became intoxicated by his cologne. His lips never left mine as he kissed me fervently the entire time.

After, he grabbed a dish towel and started wiping me down, drying my body that he had just soaked. When he had me as dry as he could, he lifted my nightgown above my head, threw it to the floor, and carried me into my bedroom. He carefully laid me down as he lay next to me, kissing me softly. He pushed me back slightly as he ran his fingers up and down the side of my body, where he stayed focused on the flames on my ribs. He stared at it in awe as he traced the lines of the tattoo with his thumb. Then, he shifted his gaze from my ribs to my eyes.

"It's stupid, I know," I began, embarrassed. "I guess I kinda felt like you were always with me." Without moving his stare, he reached over to his t-shirt and lifted the sleeve to show me his ink. He added water around his flames, making them appear like it was hugging the fire. I delicately rubbed his tattoo with my pointer finger and lightly kissed it. He pulled me into him, gripping me tighter than he ever had, and buried his face in my shoulder.

"Did she take it badly?" I asked.

"Yes," He nodded his head into me. "Did you find what you were looking for?"

"Yes."

He slept peacefully wrapped around me as I lay awake, deep in thought. I loved being with him, but I had remorse. I felt guilty that he broke up with Emma for me. She could give him the one thing I couldn't—love. I was tormented all night, thinking of how I could potentially hurt him all over again. The next morning, the pecking of his lips on my shoulder alerted me that he had woken up. I felt his kiss run through my entire body as his fingers gently ran down my back, and his lips finally met mine. I hesitantly kissed him back. Sensing something wasn't right, he pulled his lips off mine.

"What's wrong?" he asked. I looked down at his chest. He backed up, rolled over onto his back, and sighed. I stayed quiet. "Just say it."

"I don't think you should break up with Emma," I finally said. He shot up from the bed, shaking his head fiercely as he scoured the floor for his joggers. I sat in bed as I watched him angrily pull his pants up.

"Josh," I began. He held his hand up to stop me from speaking.

"Don't," he abruptly said as he pulled his t-shirt over his head. I climbed off the bed and moved toward him as he backed away from me. "I don't want to hear it," he said firmly.

"I just don't want to hurt you," I argued.

"Really? Because you seem to be making a habit out of it,"

he said before storming out of my apartment and slamming the door behind him.

Tiptoeing through the garden, I slowly opened the back door and carefully made my way into the pale-yellow kitchen. The potent smell of fresh flowers filled my senses as my heart raced to try to sneak past the kitchen to make my way to the bedroom. Just as I thought I had succeeded in creeping in, a very angry Lucas stood still in the archway.

"Where have you been?" he roared furiously.

"At the market," I lied. He came closer to me, grabbed me by my arm, and pulled me aggressively towards him. I felt his lips sink into mine as I tried my hardest to act casually and kiss him back. He pulled his lips away from me and stared at me steadily.

"You were with him!" he yelled. He leaned in to get to eye level with me as I brought my arm up to cover my face and flinched. Bringing his face closer to mine, a look of rage distorted his appearance. "Don't you dare lie to me," he said through clenched teeth.

CHAPTER 44

I woke up scared and alone. Josh was gone, Lucas was back, and I was losing my mind. Once again, I had chased Josh away. At this point, I was convinced I was a glutton for punishment. It had been a week since the kitchen incident with Josh, and I couldn't get it out of my head. I argued with myself profusely over whether or not I should call him. I finally brought myself to get out of bed and take a shower. I needed to see him, and now I was feeling brazen. I pulled a pair of jeans up and finished it off with a black thermal shirt, a camo army jacket, and a baseball cap. It was fall already, and despite the rain, the weather was nice enough to wear only a light jacket. I threw my sunglasses on and had Logan call me a car.

I walked through the front door of his office, a large lobby with tile floors, and pictures of beautiful models hung along the walls. Beautiful women were sitting in the waiting area with hopeful looks on their faces as they anxiously awaited their big shot in Hollywood. I wanted to warn them; tell them all to run. I immediately noticed the picture of Emma; I shook it off and made my way to the reception area.

A good-looking guy wearing trendy clothes and tattoos up his arm greeted me. "Hi, I am Brian. Can I help you?"

"I'm here to see Joshua Knight," I said. He looked down at his computer screen.

"Do you have an appointment?" he asked.

"No," I said quietly. He tilted his head and scrunched his nose, apparently shocked I would just walk straight into a modeling company and request a meeting with the CEO. "I'm a friend of his," I said.

"Your name?" he asked.

"Just tell him a good friend," I answered. He smiled politely and asked me to have a seat as he got up from the desk and made his way to the back. Appearing again a few minutes later, he came over to me.

"I'm sorry, Mr. Knight is tied up all day. If you'd like to make an appointment, I will gladly help you...." Standing with urgency, I took off my sunglasses and hat as Brian looked at me in shock, immediately recognizing who I was.

"Oh my, are you...."

I nodded. "Yes, please tell him I am here," I said. He came back shortly later.

"Follow me," he said as he led me through the hallway. He led me to the last office, more pictures of gorgeous models from photo shoots draped along the walls. He knocked lightly and opened the door to let me in. His walls were decorated like the rest of the office, with leather sofas on either side, each with coffee tables and magazines. His large glass desk with two computer screens sat in front of a large window, viewing New York City. The raindrops seemed to be implanted on the glass. He looked up from his screen, wearing a navy-blue suit with his jacket off, a light pink button-down, and a blue and gray tie. He folded his hands and pulled them up toward his lips as he watched me slowly walk to the middle of the room.

"Can I get you beverages?" Brian offered.

"I'm good," Josh said dismissively.

"No, thank you," I said. I watched him slowly shut the door, and Josh just stayed in place, waiting for me to talk. I walked around the office, looking at every picture of every girl hanging, silently wondering how many he had slept with. When I came to the picture of Emma, hypnotized by her golden eyes, I said out loud, "I like your office," not being able to take my attention off the picture.

He dropped his hands and swiveled his seat around to face me. "Is that why you came all the way here? To check out my office?"

"No," I said, turning my body around to face him. "I was going to call you, but I wasn't sure if you were with your girlfriend."

"I don't have a girlfriend," he said, matter-of-factly.

"You didn't get back with Emma?" I asked, surprised. He ran his hands down his thighs and leaned towards me.

"No, believe it or not, not everyone listens to your orders. I didn't think it would be fair to her, knowing how she feels about me. You know, to continue a relationship with someone who is so nice, and you know you're only going to hurt," he answered. He pulled his elbows back on his chair and leaned back. "But you get that, right? Isn't that your excuse?"

"Josh, it's not like that," I argued.

"What do you want from me?" he asked, visibly annoyed.

"Nothing, I don't want anything from you," I whispered. He stood up finally and made his way over to me, towering over me.

"Then why are you here?" he asked angrily.

"Because, like you, when it comes to you, I have no self-control," I said as I stood on my tippy-toes and tugged him by the back of his neck to kiss me. He pulled me back as he leaned against the desk, dragging me between his legs and kissing me aggressively. We kissed for what seemed like an hour until he finally peeled his lips off mine and held me in his arms, resting his chin on my head as I rested mine on his chest. I felt so safe in his arms. I didn't want to move.

"Holy shit," he muttered in amazement, moving me slightly away and turning my body around to look out the window. A beautiful double rainbow appeared outside his office, stretched out across New York City. The most vibrant rainbow I had ever witnessed in my life formed a dome over the skyscrapers. "I guess that's what happens when you mix fire and water," he said.

We spent the next week at his place. After I had filled him in on everything that had happened while I was away, he convinced me to go away for the weekend, to get away from everyone, and spend some time together, alone. He booked a room in St. Marten, so we wouldn't have to worry about having a nozzle handy to soak me with. The hotel was a beachfront paradise, elegant and classy, with crystal chandeliers hanging in the lobby and marble floors.

We both had doubts about going to an island, worried that memories of Haven would come fluttering back, but once we arrived, we were both immediately put at ease. Walking in, hand in hand, anyone who had seen us would have assumed we were a couple.

The room was breathtaking, a three thousand square foot space with everything from a kitchen to a separate bedroom with a king-size bed, a hot tub, a full indoor pool, and a fireplace. The balcony wrapped around the corner room, overlooking the ocean. Truth be told, I didn't care if we stayed in a shack as long as I was with him. This time was different; we had been through so much together in the last two years; I think we both needed an escape, and not from each other as I had initially thought.

We had an early dinner at an outdoor restaurant nearby, our candlelit table overlooking the ocean. "When I was away, I learned how to shut my mind, like you do. How to put it in a state of subconsciousness," I said as I took a bite of my sea bass.

"I really freaked you out, huh? Showing up like that?" he asked.

"A little bit," I admitted. "Not so much you, per se, but I got nervous that if you could do it, someone else may be able to also."

We watched in admiration as the sun dipped into the water, making the water illuminate purple and red.

"There's this place I end up a lot in my projections," I told him, taking a sip of my seltzer. "It's a beautiful field, all illuminated in purple. There's this gorgeous waterfall. I could stare at it all day."

"Where you saw your mother?" he asked.

"Yes, and Katie. Outside that barn roof, it's the most serene place I have ever been. I am in such an unexplainable state of comfort when I am there; I wish I could take you with me. Maybe we can practice. You seemed to be able to master astral projection when you found me that night. Maybe I can take you there."

He leaned across the table and took my hand in his. "I think you've created your place, the safe place to reach your higher level of consciousness. You originally mentioned a waterfall, remember? You have been so inundated with recollections from the second we tried the Reiki healing on you, you never actually made it there," he surmised.

"But that was different. What I had initially envisioned was more…." I racked my brain for the right word. "Real. Bright, daytime, cool breeze," I said, closing my eyes and picturing my original creation. "This is calming, don't get me wrong, like I am in a complete state of nirvana, but it's always night. And how do you explain the purple? I don't even like the color purple!"

"That I don't know," he said, shaking his head. "But think about it, you've only seen your mother and Katie, no one negative."

"Jacob," I said, just above a whisper.

He tried not to look jealous as he moved his neck from side to side.

"Ah, yeah, Jacob. Well, I guess he's never done anything bad really; I mean, assuming he's not Lucas messing with your mind." I looked down at the plate in front of me, at a loss for words.

"If you think about it, Lucas has never shown up in an astral state, only Jacob. Anytime I have seen Lucas, it was a recollection," I rationalized. He looked over at the ocean, processing what I said, then turned his gaze back to me.

"The waterfall, it sounds beautiful," he said, changing the subject. "But right now, I am not interested in going with you to any world other than where we are now. Let's just enjoy this, not think of the past or the future. Just now, just me and you." He smiled, squeezing my hand gently, his dimple appearing. His blue eyes sparkled in the sunset as a hint of his new water-submerged flames peeked out of his black polo shirt.

"Where do you want to take me?" I asked flirtatiously. He gave me a mischievous grin.

"Everywhere on this island, but first our pool," he said, lightly biting his lower lip.

"Check, please," I said, as I motioned my hand in the air in a signing motion to the waiter.

CHAPTER 45

*A*s soon as we got back to the room, he was eagerly sliding the spaghetti straps of my dress down as he kissed my neck, backing me towards the pool. He stripped off his clothes and got in, pulling me down to him. Being in the pool was a genius idea on his part. I felt so comfortable, so at ease, with my arms draped around him. Afterward, we were sprawled out completely naked in front of the fireplace, the flames' heat drying our wet bodies. He held me from behind in a spoon position as I watched the fire, mesmerized.

"Make it dance," I muttered as my head lay on his bicep. He raised his hand towards the flames as I watched the sparks move to his rhythm. I let out a giggle and rolled over to face him.

"I could watch you play with fire for lifetimes," I said as he gazed into my eyes.

"And I could hear you laugh for lifetimes," he said.

"Really? My laugh?" I asked.

"*Really*, your laugh. It's one of my favorite things about you."

"I wish you could see my memories, every time we've laid

in front of a fireplace together," I said somberly. He swept my hair out of my face and leaned his forehead closer to me.

"I do too."

"Do you miss Emma?" I don't know why I decided to ask that at that moment, but I needed to know.

"Yeah, a little. She was a really nice girl; we spent a lot of time together," he answered honestly.

"How long were you with her for?"

"Six months," he said.

"Was she in love with you?" I asked.

He slowly nodded.

"Yes."

"Did you love her?" Why was I doing this to myself?

"Probably not," he said, with remorse in his voice.

"What did you guys do together?"

"What do you mean?" he asked.

"Well, I am sure she didn't like going to metaphysical stores," I said. He laughed and shook his head.

"No, those weren't the types of rocks she was into. We went to restaurants, movies, shows; she liked Broadway a lot," he said.

"It must have been nice to have normal sex with someone without having to restrain them or douse them in water," I said quietly, shifting my gaze from his eyes to his chest.

"Normal is in the eye of the beholder," he said nonchalantly.

"I don't think that's the correct saying," I laughed.

He placed his hand under my chin and lifted my head to look at him as he stared into my eyes but didn't say anything. He didn't need to; I knew what he was thinking. He was so in love with me that things like that didn't matter to him.

"What are you thinking?" I finally asked.

"You know what I'm thinking," he whispered.

"Tell me." He let out a nervous laugh and looked past me.

"Please," I asked, almost begging. He took a deep breath and bit the inside of his cheek. He pulled me into him and closed his eyes. I could tell he was about to communicate with me telepathically. I ran my hand gently down his face, feeling his scruff under my finger beds.

"No, *tell* me," I said firmly, sliding my thumb gradually over his bottom lip. He let out a sigh and swallowed hard.

"Okay," he said. He inched his face closer to me, so he could gaze directly into my eyes. "I am hopelessly, utterly, and uncontrollably in love with you. There is nothing in this world you can ask me to do that I would say no to, well, with the exception of the genocide of roosters, maybe," he let out a chuckle as I smiled at him. Then he got serious again. "I would sacrifice anything and everything, in this lifetime or any lifetime, to be with you." Despite trying to fight back any emotion, I felt a tear trickle down my cheek, and he wiped it away with his thumb. "Why are you crying?" He asked.

"I promise we are going to fix me, Josh. We are going to break this spell. Just please, please, don't stop loving me," I asked, never in my life feeling as vulnerable as I did at that moment. He kissed me sensually.

"I couldn't if I tried, and trust me, I have."

It was an amazing four days, to say the least, and it was exactly what we needed for what we thought was our reunion. When we got back home, what had originally been weekends spent together, turned into every day. We stayed either at my house or his; we were rarely apart. About a week later, we stopped at a bodega for a pack of cigarettes when a magazine cover caught my eye.

"You've got to be shitting me," I grumbled as I reached out and grabbed the magazine. On the cover, Josh and I stood, holding hands on the beach in St. Marten. He looked down to see what I was looking at.

"Calista Reed Swept Away by a Knight in Shining Armor," I read the headline aloud, disgust in my voice.

"I see what they did there. Very witty," he said, sarcastically.

"Is *this* what you want, Josh?" I asked, throwing the magazine back down. "To be in the spotlight with a hot mess?"

"Hot, yes, mess, not quite. And yes, I want to be anywhere you are, whether it's in a rehab facility, an exotic island, or the spotlight," he very sweetly answered.

"This isn't going to look good on you, going from Emma to me," I warned. He let out a laugh.

"Are you kidding? I went from a supermodel to an Oscar-winning actress; I look like the man," he joked. I picked up the phone, texted Debbie, and reluctantly took her advice of doing a tell-all interview on a popular late-night show that had been trying to book me for the last year. And a week later, the three of us arrived on set.

Debbie pulled Josh over toward her to stand behind the cameraman as the host's personal assistant helped me with my microphone.

"You got this," Debbie mouthed to me, holding her thumb up. I meticulously walked toward the stage, trying my hardest to walk carefully despite the five-inch heels I was wearing against the tile floor. I held my dress down as I slowly sat down on the chair.

"And five, four, three…."

"Hi, and welcome back to The Speak Easy. I am your host, Valerie Erin, and I am here today with Oscar-winning actress Calista Reed!" Valerie announced. The crowd erupted into applause, and I could feel Josh's stare pierce me. Dressed in a royal blue dress suit that made her blue eyes pop, Valerie was in her forties but looked like she was in her thirties. A well-known talk show host with years of experience making celebrities break down on stage. Debbie was right when she coached me before the interview. The questions weren't so terrible at first. Starting out with easy softball questions, they progressively got more brutal and more personal, and she questioned the most intimate parts of my life. Debbie had forewarned me she'd try to break me. She asked about my time in Haven; where I really was, to which I had a blanket answer already down perfectly to that question. Then she went into my "breakdown" on set while filming a movie. I still hated that it was referred to like that and then she moved straight to Josh.

"So, you have been seen spending a lot of time with Joshua Knight," she remarked inquisitively. "It's been said that you two were spotted numerous times in St. Marten only a few weeks after his breakup with supermodel Emma Dawn." I stayed quiet as I felt the audience hush to hear my reply. "Who is Mr. Knight to you?" she asked.

I should have been mentally prepared to answer that question, but something in my mind just spaced out. I peered ahead, squinting through the spotlight shining in my eyes to try to see past his shadow and into his eyes, but the light prevented me from seeing him. I looked back over to Valerie as little white orbits floated around in front of me, the after-effect of the glare.

"He's my," I froze. He's my what? We weren't exactly in a relationship, but he was clearly more than my friend. "He's my Significant…" my voice trailed off. No, I couldn't say he was my significant other; that wasn't even true. I could feel my underarms dampen and my hands clammy as I swallowed hard.

"He's your significant…"

The lights dimmed just enough to see Josh staring at me intently, with a questionable look on his face as to what I was going to say.

"Nobody," I muttered, trying desperately to erase the word significant I had just spurted out of my mouth.

"He's your 'Significant Nobody'?" she asked mockingly. Josh creased his forehead and shook his head a little bit.

"No," I said, letting out a nervous chuckle. "He's not my significant *nobody*; that doesn't make sense. He's my...." I watched him as he closed his eyes and telepathically said, *boyfriend*. He opened his eyes, and I saw him smile slightly across the room.

"He's my boyfriend," I uttered uncontrollably.

CHAPTER 46

"*E*lijah!" I yelled through the hollow woods, my heart racing at an alarming rate. "Elijah!" I screamed again, only to hear the echoing of my own voice. I could feel my breathing become heavier as I circled in and out of every tree, every type of area a five-year-old could possibly be hiding. "This isn't funny!" I bellowed, choked up as tears started pouring down my face. Finally, after what seemed like hours of looking for him, I crouched down against a tree and pulled my legs up my chin as I cried, left feeling defeated and heartbroken and wet from the rain pouring down.

"Excuse me, does this belong to you?" I heard a deep voice ask. I looked up to see Jacob holding my baby in his arms.

"Elijah!" I exclaimed as I sprung up and grabbed him from Jacob's arms. I held him tightly in my embrace, cradling him back and forth. "My poor baby, I thought you were gone! Don't ever do that to your mother again!" He buried his face in my shoulder and cried.

"He fell," Jacob explained. "Banged up his knee pretty rotten. I took him to clean him up. My apologies: I didn't mean to scare you. He said he couldn't find his mother."

Tracing my hand down Elijah's leg, he held out his knee to show me, which was nicely bandaged. "We were playing hide and seek. I don't know how he got away so fast. I am a terrible mother," I cried. He put his hand on my shoulder.

"No, I am sure that isn't true. Boys will always find a way to be mischievous, even if not intentional," he reassured me.

"Thank you for fixing him up," I whimpered. "Do you have a boy?"

"No, ma'am, no children. I'm Jacob Oliver," he said as he bowed his head to me.

"I'm Claudia Wellington. This is my son, Elijah," I said quietly.

"Yes, we've met. Wellington? You aren't Queen Wellington, by chance?" he asked, astonished. I looked down at Elijah as I ran my hand over his hair.

"I am the wife of King Wellington; however, I am no queen," I answered.

The phone rang, waking me from my dream. I looked down to see Chrys's name displayed on the screen. It was two a.m.; she would never call this late; something must be wrong. Josh sat up and watched me nervously as I picked up the phone. Chrys was rambling so fast that I told her to slow down. She called to tell me she had done the research after hearing about the vision Star had seen. I put her on speaker.

"I knew it, *we* knew it; we knew Laura was hiding something. Mom, she had another kid before me, and Laura took her in. That must have been what she meant when she got tired of cleaning up Mom's messes. She has Laura's last name, which is why I never found her. Her name is Amy Everhart. Laura took her in as her own. We need to go back to Santa Monica. We need to find our sister!"

"Okay," Josh interjected. "It's the year 2019. Anyone want to take a quick 23 & Me test and assure no more secret siblings are running around we don't know about?"

"Josh, this is serious. We need to go," I said as I shot him a look to shut up. "Chrys, we can be there tomorrow; I will call to have a jet take you there. We will meet you in Santa Monica," I said as I hung up the phone.

We barely packed anything, just a few changes of clothes and toothbrushes. We finally had a glimmer of hope in finding answers as we boarded the jet.

"Maybe this is when the 542 days begin. Maybe this is the piece we've been missing," I said, hopeful. Josh put his arm around me.

"I hope so because this 542 days thing is really starting to creep me out. I mean, how are we even supposed to know when it begins? Or, for that matter, who even wrote it in the mirror."

"It was William. I am sure of that. It had to be; he knew he couldn't get through because I had bound myself. It was his only way of sending me a message for help. This chick, Amy, is a big piece. Mark my words; we are going to find a lot out," I said. He put his hand in mine.

"Let's just make sure whatever we find out now helps the issue and doesn't further complicate it. As much as I love playing detective with you, I would really like to just move on with our lives and our future. I mean, after all, I am your *boyfriend* now," he said, winking.

"Oh please, I was put on the spot!" I argued playfully.

"Well, you said it. On TV, in front of millions of viewers. Should I pull up the YouTube video?"

"No, that's quite alright. I remember it," I laughed.

"And to think, all those years practicing smoke rings to become famous. All I had to do was take you away on vacation," he joked.

"Didn't make you a Gen-Zer," I said.

"No, it made me something better. Calista Reed's *boyfriend*," he exaggeratingly said the word boyfriend.

"You always gonna say boyfriend like that? Because that could get old, real fast!"

"Go to sleep, beautiful," he said, pulling me into him. "I have a feeling we have a long few days ahead of us."

The next day, the three of us stood outside Laura's house, mentally preparing to go back in.

"Don't lose your temper this time," Chrys warned as we made our way to the steps and rang the doorbell. As soon as Laura saw us standing outside, she went to push the door closed. Josh held it open with his hand.

"Not so fast," I said, walking straight in. "You have a lot of explaining to do. Who the hell is Amy?"

She let out a deep breath and sunk into her couch as Chrys and Josh followed me into the living room.

"I told you your mother had a lot of secrets," she said.

"Well, time to start telling them," Chrys said sternly.

"Your mother got pregnant at sixteen; our father was rigorous, wouldn't let her keep the baby. I took her to take care of her until she was old enough to take her back. But then she met your father and didn't want him to know. I raised Amy as if she was my own."

"Where is she now?" I asked.

"Last I heard, New York. Brooklyn, I think. We haven't spoken in ten years. She's not a good person, mixed up with the wrong crowd. An addict, she practices that shit you all talk about."

"Magick?" Chrys asked.

"Yes, but it's dark, nothing like your mother used to do. It's almost as if she has a dark cloud around her at all times," she said, tears forming in her eyes. "I tried so hard; I really did. But there's only so much I could do. Amethyst had her own way of doing things; she's stubborn, proud....."

"Amethyst?" I asked in shock.

"Yes, Amy is short for Amethyst. I told you your mother named you all after healing crystals." Chrys and I looked at each other; that was what my mother had been trying to tell us this whole time: the significance of the stones.

"Does Amethyst, by chance, have a son?" Chrys asked. Laura nodded.

"Yes, and he's a bad seed also," she answered.

"Or a product of his environment," Josh said defensively. "What is his name?"

"Mason," she answered. She went into the kitchen and came back with a piece of paper she had jotted an address on. "This is where she lived most recently. Maybe she's still there; I don't know. But I swear, this is all the information I have," she said.

"Thank you," I finally said as we headed out.

"So, we must have really screwed up the last lifetime, now he's both of our nephew, and we somehow created an evil sister," Chrys said, defeated.

"Well then, we need to make sure we fix it this time! We'll get a room and stay overnight; tomorrow, we'll head to Brooklyn. This Mason, he's William, Jayden, Andrew, Elijah, and he needs our help," I said.

CHAPTER 47

*C*arrying my injured Elijah up the steps into my house, I carefully brought him to his bedroom and lay him in his bed.

"I'm sorry I got away, Mommy," he forced the words out through tears.

"It's okay, darling, as long as you promise me you will always find your way back."

"I promise," he said. I kissed his forehead.

"Go to sleep, my prince. You've had a long day," I said as I turned to leave his room. I couldn't get the meeting with Jacob from my mind. He was such a nice man to help Elijah as he did, something so inviting in his warm brown eyes. Lost in thought, I jumped in shock when I came face to face with a woman in my kitchen.

"Claudia, what are you doing home?" she asked.

"Elijah injured himself; his knees are bloodied. Why are you here, Diana?" She looked around the room nervously. She stared at me expectantly as if she were scared of me.

"I brought some fresh berries," she finally answered.

"Can I get you a cup of tea?" I offered. She shook her head rapidly.

"No, thank you. I must get home. I will see you soon," she said as she hurried out the door. Lucas appeared almost immediately; he sat down at the kitchen table, reading a letter, and I made myself a cup of tea.

"Diana was here. Did you know that?" I asked him, not looking up from the kettle.

"Was she?" he asked, engaged in the note.

"She was a bit off, she seemed frightened of me," I mentioned. He let out a chuckle.

"My beloved, you are the most powerful witch in the village. Many women ought to be frightened of you." I poured the boiling water into a mug.

"Where are the berries?" I asked. He looked up at me.

"What berries?" he asked. It was written all over his face. He had just slept with her; that was why she was so afraid of me. Sure, I was the most powerful witch, but Diana would know I was harmless unless provoked. She knew she pushed the button.

"*This* is Amethyst's house?" Chrys asked, disgusted, as I rolled the window down of the passenger's seat. We had just driven through a terrible neighborhood of Brooklyn. Covered with graffiti all over the buildings, people in the street drinking alcohol out of brown paper bags, the smell of marijuana lingered in the air, and loud music shrieked through the streets. I stared at the poorly maintained house, with iron bars on the windows. I took a deep breath and opened the door.

"Let's go," I said. Josh, Chrys, and I walked up to the door and rang the doorbell. No answer. We waited a few minutes and rang it again. Still, no answer. As I tried to get a glimpse through the window, Josh started banging hard on the door. Finally, a teenage boy holding a baseball bat opened it. He was in black basketball shorts, a white t-shirt, thick dirty blonde hair, and grayish-blue eyes. I stood paralyzed in shock as he resembled William more than Elijah. Stunned, I couldn't bring myself to speak.

"Is this Amethyst Everhart's house?" Josh said.

"Are you child services?" the boy asked.

"What? No," Josh answered. He went to close the door, but much like he did at Laura's house, Josh held it firmly with his hand.

"We need to come in," I finally managed to let out. The three of us walked in as the boy clenched the bat tightly in his hands. The place was a mess, with a pull-out couch that was opened to a bed with a folding snack tray next to it, packages of TV dinners, candy bar wrappers, and potato chip bags all over the floor. There was a cloth loveseat with cigarette holes, and an old beat-up armchair opposite. The beige carpet was filthy, brown with unidentifiable stains, and clothes were thrown everywhere. A horrid stench of stale food and smoke filled the air.

"When was the last time your mother was home?" Josh asked.

"Are you going to tell me you're my new mother?" he asked, looking at me.

"No," I replied.

"Are you cops?" the boy asked, sitting on the armchair.

"No," Josh said as he searched the room. I stayed close behind him as he examined everything.

Chrys put her arms around her stomach as she leaned against the wall.

"Are you okay?" I asked.

"No, there's so much bad energy in here; it is sticking to

me," she said. I looked at my hand as I formed a ball of light and threw it over her. I touched her arm and closed my eyes, taking in all her negative feelings and healing her. It felt like poison running through my veins as I released my grip, and she gave me a thankful smile.

"You know, if you are the police, you're not allowed to say no; you have to admit it," the boy said. Ignoring him and walking into the kitchen, Josh stopped at the table, where there were remnants of white powder. He dipped his finger and put it on his tongue.

"It's cocaine," he said. We both looked at each other and then back at the cocaine, like we both had the same idea at the same time, how it would feel just to take a line. Chrys immediately came over and wiped the table off.

"Thank goodness someone here has self-control around drugs," she remarked as she went into the bathroom to flush it down the toilet. She suddenly bolted back out, screeching, "roach!"

"Where's your mother?" Josh asked.

"Dunno."

"When is she coming home?"

"Dunno."

"When did she leave?" Josh was getting more and more irritated by the minute, interrogating the boy.

"Dunno."

"If you say 'dunno' on more damn time, I am going to lose my shit on you," Josh growled. "What *do* you know?"

The kid pulled out a small jar from the side of the armchair and stood up. "I know you're a dick; that's apparent," he said arrogantly. "I think everyone needs to calm the down and take a gummy," popping one in his mouth and holding the bottle out in our direction.

"How old are you?" I asked in shock.

"Sixteen," he said.

"Are you Mason?" Chrys asked.

"How do you know my name?" We went back into the living room, where Mason slumped back into the armchair, and Chrys and I sat on the loveseat. Josh sat on the foot of the pull-out bed.

"We spoke to your grandmother Laura, now will we wait here for your mother," Josh said calmly. I was relieved he was doing the talking. I was still in a state of shock, seeing Mason's eyes for the first time in person. Mason started tapping the base of the baseball bat in his hand as he stared at Josh with anger in his eyes.

"I'm not afraid to use this," he threatened. Josh sprung up and walked over to Mason.

"Stand," he barked. Mason stayed still, pretending not to be terrified of Josh.

"Josh," I said, trying to calm him down.

"I said *stand!*" he ordered again, this time with authority in his tone. Mason stood. He looked like a peanut in comparison to Josh.

"Now look at me and look at you. Do you really think that bat is going to help you?" Josh asked, through gritted teeth, in a gruff voice. He reached out and snagged the bat from Mason's hands.

"Are you going to kill me?" Mason asked, growing fearful.

"Yes, but first, I want to hear every smarmy remark you can possibly come up with," Josh answered sarcastically, shaking his head. "Sit the hell down."

Mason sat back down in the chair. "If your plan is to wait for my mother, it may be a while. I don't know when she's coming back. I would offer you something, but there's no food in the house."

"You don't have any food?" I asked. He shook his head in embarrassment.

"Did she leave you money?" Chrys asked. He shifted his eyes to the ground in humiliation, making my heart sink..

"When was the last time you ate real food?" Josh asked, pointing to the garbage on the floor. Mason just shrugged his shoulders. Josh looked at me.

"Why don't you google a restaurant near us? We'll order some food," Josh said as he mellowed his tone. He shifted his attention to Mason. "Are you hungry? Do you want to eat?"

"Okay," he said meekly.

"I found a diner!" I said, excited. "What would you like, Mason?"

"Chocolate chip pancakes," he said. I couldn't help but smile at his request. He was still a little boy at heart for such a tough kid.

CHAPTER 48

After we all ate, Mason took me up to the roof. Thankful I was wearing sneakers, I followed him through the tar-covered cement until he got to a tiny shed and retrieved a filthy blanket. I helped him as we laid it across the floor and rested down on it, staring up at the stars.

"I love this place; it's mad peaceful," he stated, staring up at the sky. "It's a full moon." I nodded.

"Beautiful, isn't it?"

"Are you a witch?" he asked me bluntly.

"Yes," I suddenly found myself admitting.

"My mother is a witch," he said. "But I think her spells backfire a lot. I feel like there's always a dark cloud around me."

"What kind of spells does she do?" I asked.

"Protection and stuff, mostly money, though," he answered.

"How's that working for her?" I asked sarcastically.

"Did you see my house?" he asked, laughing. For a sixteen-year-old boy, he seemed way older and mature beyond his years. "Your husband is kind of an asshole." I let out a laugh.

"He's not my husband, and he really isn't an asshole. He's harmless, and he is just trying to help me."

"Help you with what? Why do you want to see my mother so bad?" he asked. I looked from the sky into his eyes as my whole life story flew out of my mouth. I told him everything, about the 542 days, about my abilities, meeting Josh in rehab, retiring from acting, and becoming an author, everything but the boy. He sat silently, enthralled in my story.

"So, you're famous?" he finally asked.

"Yes," I conceded.

"Do I call you Cali, Morgan, or Jade?" he asked, rolling his body over to face me. I thought about his question for a minute.

"You can call me Morgan," I answered. "What grade are you in?"

"I stopped going to school two years ago," he said. I looked over at him, astonished.

"You just stopped going?" I asked. He looked up at the moon as he nodded. "What does your mom say about that?"

"Not much; she prefers I work anyway. She doesn't think school is important," he shrugged it off.

"What do you do?" I asked, racking my brain for what a sixteen-year-old could possibly do for work. His gaze shifted to the ground.

"I sell weed," he said quietly. "Sometimes pills, but mostly weed." I could feel my mouth hang open in shock as I tried not to come off as too judgmental.

"And your mother knows this?" I asked.

"Yeah, I sell it for her boyfriend."

"Who were you expecting at the door today? I mean, you opened it holding a baseball bat," I asked.

"Him," he admitted. "My mom's boyfriend. I owe him a lot

of money; he threatened to kill me if I didn't have it this week."

"How much?"

"A thousand dollars," he answered.

"Do you have it?" I asked. He shook his head.

"No."

"You really have no idea when your mother is coming home?" I asked, at this point wanting to kill her for this poor kid's life.

"No, I just know she's with some dude; she's been gone over a week," he said.

"Come on, let's go downstairs," I said, trying to process what he had just told me. I could give him the money to help him, but that really wasn't an answer. He was going down the wrong path and fast. As Josh and Chrys were emptying bags of food into the refrigerator and cabinets, we made our way back downstairs.

"What are you doing?" Mason asked.

"Stocking your house with food," Chrys said as she touched Mason's cheek gently. "We also cleaned the place." I grabbed Josh's hand.

"Come, I want to show you something," I whispered. I led him up to the roof; he looked up at the moon shining down as I sat on the blanket.

"You wanted to show me the full moon?" he asked, confused.

"No, I wanted to get you alone," I admitted as I patted the space next to me. He sat down and took my hand in his. "Thank you, Josh, for everything. I know you hate Mason," I said, lying down. He followed my lead and laid down next to me, resting his hand in mine.

"I don't hate him; he's just a teenager. Opinionated and stubborn, reminds me of myself as a kid," he said. I smiled at the thought of Josh as a kid.

"Is this foreshadowing of what our son would be like?" I asked, giggling.

"Our son?" he asked as he lifted his eyebrows in surprise. "You want kids?"

"I think I do," I said, nodding. "You?"

"I never pictured myself with kids, to be honest, but the thought of making one with you is definitely enticing," he said, smiling. "Can you imagine a mixture of you and me? He'd be farting rainbows."

"Mason is in a lot of trouble," I said as I explained the story to him.

"So, you want to give him the money?" he asked when I finished filling him in. I stayed quiet. "Oh no," he said. "I see wheels spinning in your head...."

"I'm thinking of asking him to move in with me," I blurted out.

"What? I mean, Cali, that's very sweet of you, but you don't even know this kid. He's sixteen years old and used to a certain lifestyle...."

"You said it yourself; he's a product of his environment. What if he had the opportunity to have a normal life? A chance at being just a kid? He sells drugs to eat. That's *surviving.* What if he didn't need to worry about money; he could go back to school and have the same opportunity as other kids. He's related to me, Josh, even if I didn't know he existed."

"You're at my house half the week," he said. "What is he going to do, go back and forth between our houses? That makes no sense."

I pushed my hair behind my ears and looked down at my lap. I could feel the tears well in my eyes that threatened to drop at any moment. He reached his hand out and took mine in his.

"Or you can just move in with me. I mean, that way, he has one steady room that he can call his own," he said.

"Really?" I said as I sat up straight, a glimmer of hope in my voice.

"Really. I mean, I am your *boyfriend* now," he said, enunciating on boyfriend. I was so blown away by his offer that I didn't even mind how he said it. I leaned over and kissed him. His soft lips meshed into mine so naturally as I kissed him in a trance, his touch sending heat down my entire body. It was at that moment I prayed for the first time, *really* prayed for someone to allow me to love him, to break the spell. Suddenly, it occurred to me; it had become so obvious. I quickly opened my eyes and pulled my lips from his.

"What wrong?" he asked, sitting up.

"We did it wrong!" I exclaimed in revelation. "The spell! My mother informed Chrys to use the elements; we used candles as a surrogate for each, but Josh, we *are* the elements!" He tilted his head and stared at me, waiting for me to continue. "You're fire. I am water, Chrys is air, and William spirit. Katie was the missing piece; she told me she resonates with earth! That's why I was meant to write the book; it was to meet Katie! I knew she was important from the minute I met her. We need to tell Chrys; I think we can break this spell!"

CHAPTER 49

We jumped up to run downstairs to let Chrys know what I had just discovered. The four of us sat at the kitchen table, with Katie on Facetime as Chrys relayed the instructions. We all had our own chant to say, as we all would light a candle in honor of our element.

"This is so cool; you guys are really going to break a spell?" Mason asked, excitement in his voice.

"I hope so," I said. "Josh and I will do our thing on the roof. The timing is perfect, and the moon is full. As long as we all do our parts at exactly the same time, it should work."

Mason ran into his mother's room and returned with candles. "See, everything happens for a reason!" he said.

"Should we really be using these candles? She practices dark magick," Josh said, worried.

"It's not the candles that make her magick dark. It's her intentions," Chrys reminded him, taking the candles from Mason and handing us each one. "Now go, and remember, seal it with a kiss."

Josh and I walked back up to the roof, sitting once again on the blanket as we waited to get the texts from Katie and

Chrys that they were ready to begin their part. I responded we were as well, while Josh carefully lit our candles. Excitement rushed through my body as the thought of kissing Josh and feeling love for him thrilled me more than I could ever imagine. I had been waiting for this moment for what felt like an eternity. I closed my eyes, and we chanted our prayer in unison. I slowly leaned in to kiss him, but just as my lips almost touched his, he suddenly backed away. I sat up straight, opening my eyes, as I watched his face form into a state of distress. He took my hand in his.

"What if you don't love me?" he asked apprehensively. I studied my thumb as I ran it in tiny circles on his palm. He was right. Ignorance was bliss, after all. I realized if we did, in fact, break the spell and I didn't love him, it could potentially tear him apart more in the end. He said he knew when he saw me for the first time, that I was the girl he was meant to be with and that I was going to break him.

"You're right; let's not do it," I whispered. He squeezed my hand tightly.

"You would sacrifice being able to love for me?" he asked.

"We have a great relationship; I want to be with you. Like you told me, I am the happiest when I am around you. *You* make me happy. So, yes, I would sacrifice feeling love just to have you in my life," I answered. "I am honestly completely addicted to you; that should be enough."

"Except it's not," he said, and without warning, he planted his lips on mine, tightly and with urgency. The world seemed to start rapidly spinning as I clutched onto him for support, and I felt like we were falling. Keeping my eyes closed and concentrating on his kiss, I immediately knew we were back in the past by the scent of flowers.

I felt his kiss run through my body, realizing we were brought back to the first time we had kissed. Butterflies grew in my stomach as my heart raced at the touch of his hands on my face, and my chest grew heavy. "I love you so much," he muttered in my ear as he rested his head on my shoulder.

Running my hands through his hair, I looked up at the brilliant full moon shining down on us; as I grasped, we were on the barn roof, looking out at miles of flowers.

"I love you too," I said, caressing the back of his neck. "Promise me you won't change?"

"What could possibly change my love for you?" he asked, not lifting his head from my shoulder.

"When you become king," I answered as he lifted his head, and I looked into the piercing blue eyes of Lucas staring back at me. "Money and power change a man."

"Perhaps, but so does love," he answered. "I knew two things the minute I saw you; you were the girl I was supposed to be with, and you were going to be the mother of my child," his lips instinctively reattached to mine. Everything clicked at that moment as I realized Josh was right the entire time that he wasn't Jacob. He was Lucas. It all made so much sense suddenly. Lucas only appeared in my visions when I was with Josh. That first time Josh had ever touched me, when performing the Reiki healing, Lucas came hurling into my life.

All the recollections came scampering back quickly. The day I lost my virginity to him, all the times we made love, our wedding vows, the birth of Elijah, the beautiful moments we had, and the love we shared, scattering across my brain like a montage. The memories started quickly spiraling into a downward collision, though, and the recollections became horrific. Lucas getting corrupted by power, his affairs, his abuse, leading me right into the arms of another man. The spell he put on me. Every recollection I had seen through the years, only they were in order. I realized that every memory that came to me throughout the last few years came in backwards, the same as *The Broken Meadow* was written, from end to beginning. Then finally, we stood at the podium, in front of the town, as he roared: "Stand!"

"I said stand," he snarled again. I stayed frozen in place, terrified. "Fine, so be it. You won't stand? Perhaps he'll make you stand," he gestured behind me to call someone in. I looked to my side to watch a man being hauled in before me, his arms also tied behind his back, bloody and beaten, with a hood covering his face. I instantly knew it was Jacob, as I quickly sprung to my feet. One of his men removed the hood from Jacob's head as I stared at his bloodied face. Lucas approached me, his face so close to mine I could feel his breath on me. Jacob grimaced at the sight of Lucas kissing my cheek.

"Did you tell him, Claudia? Did you tell him what I would do to him if I found the two of you together again?"

I looked into Jacob's eyes as he tried to look strong for me. "Say it, my beloved. Tell him his fate; it sounds so much better coming from you. Let the last words he hears be said from your sweet voice," Lucas continued, tauntingly, as he ran his thumb across my bottom lip. "From your beautiful lips." A tear trickled down my cheek as he shoved me towards Jacob. "Tell him!" he howled.

"Get your hands off my mother!" I heard from behind me. Lucas' men steadied themselves in attention form as we both turned around to watch Elijah inching towards us, a pistol in his hand. Lucas' men started towards Elijah as Lucas threw his hand up to halt them.

"Stay away from my boy," he ordered. "Elijah, go home. This does not concern you."

"Get your hands off my mother!" Elijah said again, firmly, pointing the gun directly at Lucas as he stared at him with anger-filled eyes. Lucas released me from his grip as he stalked toward Elijah, fearless.

"Now, son, you wouldn't hurt your father; surely you

know you'd be cursed with a karmic debt. Put the gun down," he said, very calmly. Elijah's hand trembled as he tried to hold it in place.

"Elijah, please, put the gun down," I begged, crying hysterically. Elijah looked from me to Lucas, then back at me, but stood in place holding the gun. "Please!" I pleaded.

Lucas rolled his eyes and pointed at Jacob. "Fine then, if you won't say it, I will," he said to me and signaled to his men. "Kill him," he said casually. I fell to my knees in what seemed to be slow motion, as I watched the sword penetrate directly into Jacob's stomach and at the same time, heard the loud bang of a gun. I watched in horror as both the men I loved fell to their deaths. I threw my hand over my mouth, while tears uncontrollably streamed down my face. "Elijah!" I screamed out, as Lucas's men closed in on him.

CHAPTER 50

*J*osh pulled himself off me and fell to the floor, tears in his eyes, as he rested his forehead in his hands. He saw it all, every memory that came back. He rocked back and forth in shock, refusing to meet my stare, recognizing he was Lucas.

"Josh," I said, behind tears. Still, he wouldn't look up at me. I ran over to him and dropped down next to him, throwing my arms around his shoulders as he buried his head in my neck and sobbed.

"I always knew I was being punished; I am so sorry, Cali," he cried.

I ran my hands through his hair until they rested on his neck.

"Look at me," I begged. He lifted his head slowly, his watery blue eyes fixated on mine. "It was never that I couldn't love; it was only *you* I couldn't love…."

"Because love spells backfire," he finished my sentence. I held him tightly.

"You were my first love, and you'll be my last love," I

whispered as I kissed him tenderly and felt nothing but love for him. I could taste the mixture of both of our tears blended in with our saliva. Suddenly he pulled his lips off mine.

"They're coming!"

"What? Who?" I asked.

"Amethyst's boyfriend, and he's not alone. I feel it; I *know* it. He's with someone, and it's going to get bad. Get him out of here!" he warned. I stood up to make my way to the rooftop door to go get Mason when I heard "Cali, wait," in the most solemn tone I had ever heard come out of Josh. I slowly turned around to face him as he stood paralyzed, staring at me with his mouth hanging slightly open, and tears in his eyes. I gradually made my way back to him as he grabbed me in his embrace and held me tighter than he ever had before. He kissed me passionately as if it were going to be the last time he would ever kiss me. "I love you so, so much," he said, choked up.

"I love you too," I said. "I'll call you later." He nodded as I ran downstairs and grabbed the car keys. "Mason, come with me, no questions," I ordered.

Mason followed me out to the car.

"Didn't you lose your license?" he asked.

"Not the time for that. Get in the car," I said as I got in and started the engine. I didn't know exactly where I was driving. I only knew I needed to just drive. Something awful was coming, and I needed to get Mason far away from it. As I raced down the streets, my mind rattled with all the recollections that had just occurred.

"Where are we going?" Mason asked. I turned my head to look into his eyes when my mother's words came flickering back to me. *I hope that when you look into the eyes of your son, you realize the unconditional love I have for you, and you find it in your heart to forgive me.* Unconditional love. Suddenly, every-thing clicked, and all the dots connected. This was my moth-er's vision, the same one that haunted her, the same one that Josh had before I left the roof. Josh thought he was being punished for his past, but he wasn't. He redeemed himself; he became everything Lucas wasn't, humble, modest, unselfish. Lucas and Jacob both died because of my affair, not Lucas'. And at the hand of my own son, my firstborn. In the end, we all need to pay for our sins. Jacob was the one haunting me, tormenting me for my mistakes. I closed my eyes and silently tried to reach Josh telepathically, praying his mind was open.

"Josh?"

"I'm here," he said.

"We did it. We broke the spell."

"Yes, we did."

"I love you, Josh. I truly love you with all my heart," I said. He didn't say anything at first.

"I know you do," he finally said.

"We will never have to fight to be together again in any life-time. This is just our separation; I look forward to our reunion." I closed my mind before he could say anything else.

"Put your seatbelt on," I said to Mason, urgency in my voice. He clasped his seatbelt in place.

It was never Elijah with the karmic debt; it was me. Every single lifetime Elijah would die, and I would be tormented with trying to save him. Not this time. Mason, along with any future version of himself, would never be cursed with my punishment again. This was the lifetime my karmic debt would be paid.

"Close your eyes," I said.

"What? Why?" he asked, petrified.

"Close your eyes!" I ordered as I watched a ball of light form in my hand, and I threw a protective bubble around him. I could see what was coming for the first time in my life, and there was nothing I could do to stop it.

This is the part my mother couldn't watch one more day. Josh was correct; I was about to break him. I made the same light of protection and threw it in the direction of the car heading toward us at full speed that just blew the red light— the part my mother couldn't watch, the part that would torture Josh, the part where I die. I tried to turn the steering wheel as I stomped on the brakes, and the car skidded out of control. I closed my eyes and saw my mother. "I forgive you, and I love you," I whispered before the world went black.

"Flatline!" I hear as I bolt up from the bed, IVs plunged in my arms. Doctors are scurrying to the bed next to me. I can't see beyond the curtain, but I can hear them desperately trying to revive her. Finally, a sigh of defeat as a doctor says, "Time of death, 3:05 p.m."

I watch three doctors emerge from behind the curtain, heads buried in sorrow. As they walk out, I catch eye contact with one of the doctors, who stares at me in shock.

"Oh my God, she's awake," he says in disbelief as he hurries over to me. He holds up two fingers in front of my face. "How many fingers am I holding up?"

"Two," I say.

"Do you know your name?" he asks.

"Britney Johnson," I answer.

"Britney, this is going to be hard to hear, but you were in a terrible accident."

"My brakes failed," I say, horrified.

"You've been in a coma."

"Is that Calista Reed?" I ask, pointing over at the curtain.

"I'm sorry, patient confidentially, I am not at liberty to say," he answers, but I can see in his eyes that the answer is yes. I can feel her in my veins, like I had some crazy connection to her. Lying back down, staring at the curtain next to me, I remember the last thing I saw when I was wheeled in here.

The faint sound of beeping woke me. As I tried to open my eyes, I suddenly felt as if each eyelid weighed ten pounds. Struggling to push them open, I felt dizzy and nauseous as the room seemed to spin. I heard my breath against a plastic mask covering my face that appeared to be in sync with my heartbeat. I was panic-stricken as I overheard a police officer on the phone in the near distance: "Mrs. Johnson, this is officer Russo of the NYPD. We have your daughter..." he is immediately cut off by the intercom, "Doctor Chin, Ext 102." I managed to open my eyes just enough to see the IV in my arm. I was in a hospital, I knew that much, and I was moving fast.

I could barely move my head as I tried to focus my eyes on my surroundings. A nurse was at the foot of my stretcher, pulling me with urgency. She was head to toe in blue scrubs, a paper mask, and plastic goggles, but for a quick second, we made eye contact, and her eyes screamed fear. "Relax," I barely heard the nurse behind me, who must have been pushing the stretcher, say to me just above a whisper.

Another nurse rushed to open the door to a room as a team pushed a different stretcher in and mine followed behind. I should have been in pain; however, I suspected whatever they had been feeding through the IV was exceptionally strong, which was most likely adding to my state of sedation. They placed the first stretcher under the window and laid mine parallel to it. I managed to tilt my head to the left as the patient next to me, in a similar state, tilted hers to the right. The last thing I saw was her emerald green eyes staring back at me with sympathy, before everything faded to black.

The day we were transported into a private room. It must have been done intentionally, so she could keep me in her trance, so she could tell me her story.

"How long have I been in a coma for?" I ask.

"A year and a half." I look back over to the curtain.

"How many days?" He looks at me with confusion on his face.

"What?"

"How many *days* was I in a coma for?" I repeat, desperately. He pulls my chart and looks down at it, searching for the date I came to this place.

"542 days," he states.

She saved my life when she threw that bubble of light over me, the same as she saved Mason's. She knew in the end when she died before he did this time around, it was the only way of preventing history from repeating itself. I wasn't in a coma; I never was. It was always her holding me under.

"Let me call your mother. She has been here every single day waiting for you to wake up," the doctor says as he hurries out, and I stay in bed motionless, trying to process what just happened.

Josh and Cali spent years trying to find out the significance of 542 days. They had thought it would start at a certain point and lead to an event. Nothing happened, though. Nothing was ever going to happen. 542 days was the exact amount of time Cali needed to tell me her story. Like she told Colleen in San Diego that night, she was just an actress portraying a role in a world the writers created. If there was one thing I learned from Cali's story, it is that everything happens for a reason. It wasn't chance I was in the car that hit her; it had to be *me*. She needed me to build her world. She needed me to tell her story. Because like Barbara had told her when she wrote *The Broken Meadow,* an author isn't taught to write. The story derives from within.

CONTINUE THE SERIES WITH:

The Broken Meadow (Book 2)

ACKNOWLEDGMENTS

It's amazing how so much can change in just one year. Although every book I've written has some significant meaning to it, this one was by far my favorite to write. This edition was made specifically for the awesome teenagers in my life:

To Johnny, Matthew and Brianna…. love you guys.

And thank you to every reader that picks up my books. Life is crazy and can change in a minute. We've all heard the saying, don't live to be the person you think you want to be in that moment; live to be the person you want to be remembered for. Life is too short; choose your time wisely.

www.steviedparker.com

ABOUT THE AUTHOR

Born and raised in New York City as a "nineties teenager," Stevie D. Parker grew up studying journalism. When life took her in a different direction, she spent the past two decades as a Public Relations Executive. A position that involved traveling throughout the US and dealing with many different types of people. A self-proclaimed "realist" with an astute sense of people and situations. She is fun loving, and spontaneous but believes that everything happens for a reason. Passionate about everything she does, Stevie now spends her time writing fictional stories based on real life experiences.